NORAH
OF BILLABONG

By

MARY GRANT BRUCE

ILLUSTRATED BY J. MACFARLANE

CHAPTER I
BREAKING UP

When Sheelah in the morning

Comes down the way,

It needs no more adorning

To make it gay.

—Victor J. Daley.

AVERY tall boy came up the gravel path of Beresford House. It was "breaking up" day, and an unwonted air of festivity and smartness was evident, even to the eye of a stranger. The garden looked as though no leaf had ever been out of place, no sacrilegious footmark ever imprinted on the soft mould of its beds, where masses of flowers still bade defiance to the heat of an Australian December. The paths were newly raked; the freshly mown lawns were carpets of emerald, soft underfoot and smooth as bowling greens. Aloft, on the square grey tower, fluttered the school flag—a blue banner, with a device laboriously woven by the fingers of the sewing class, and indirectly responsible for many impositions, since it was beyond the power of the sewing class to work with its several heads so close together as the task demanded, and yet refrain from talking. It was a banner of great magnificence, and the school was justly proud of it. Only the sewing class regarded it with what might be termed a mingled eye.

It was early afternoon—too early for guests to be seriously thinking of arriving. A couple of motors were drawn up in the shade of a big Moreton Bay fig; but they belonged to parents who lived at a distance, and had come earlier in the day, to talk solemnly to the head mistress, and then to whisk emancipated daughters away to an hotel for lunch—which necessitated a speedy whisking back, so that the daughters might be apparelled in white, in readiness for the afternoon's ceremonials. In the garden, little groups of girls might be seen already clad in festive raiment and walking with a seemliness that in itself showed that this day was different from all other days. They turned interested glances upon the newcomer, who, resenting the gaze deeply, stalked on up the path, his straw hat tilted over his brown face. Girls in general had not come much in his way. It was distinctly embarrassing to run the gauntlet of so many frankly curious eyes.

"There's some, one's brother," said a red-haired damsel, surveying the stranger across a bush of New Zealand flax. "Yours, Laura?"

"Mine?" said Laura, regretfully. "Not much—mine is fat. He's a dear, of course, but his figure's something awful! I'd be frightfully proud if he looked like that!"

"I wonder who he belongs to," said the red-haired girl, with a cheerful lack of grammar. "Doesn't he look miserable—he knows we're talking about him!" She giggled with wicked enjoyment. The giggle turned to a whistle. "Gracious! Just look at young Norah Linton!"

Two younger girls, with arms linked and heads close together, had come into view in a distant corner of the garden, walking decorously, as befitted their white dresses. It was the taller of the two, a brown-faced girl of fifteen, with dark curls and extremely long slim legs, who had caught sight of the boy walking towards the house, and had promptly acted as though electrified. She relinquished her companion's arms, uttered an incoherent exclamation, and dashed wildly across the lawn, taking the flower bed that bordered it with a flying leap. The sound of the racing feet made the boy swing round quickly. Then a smile broadened on his face, and his eyes twinkled. They pumped each other's hands enthusiastically.

"Oh, Wally!" said Norah, breathlessly. "Oh, you old brick!"

Wally Meadows laughed outright.

"You don't know what a blue funk I've been in," he said. "This is a horribly scary place to come to alone—and I've been picturing you made as prim and proper as all these girls seem to be. But you're not!"

"Indeed, I'm not," Norah answered. "And no more are they!"

"Aren't they, really?" asked Wally, much interested. "Well, they look it; there's a girl over there with red hair who looks nearly too good to be true"—wherein Mr. Meadows showed as much penetration as is usually given to man. "You don't mean to say that they're all accustomed to getting across a flower bed in your fashion, Norah?"

"Oh, I'll get into a dreadful row if Miss Winter happened to see me, I expect!" Norah said. "It's against the rules, of course—but I had to run or to yell, or I'd have missed you—and it's riskier to yell. Oh, Wally, I am glad to see you!"

"So am I," said Wally, heartily—"to see you, I mean. You've grown immense, too, Norah."

"Yes, haven't I? All my frocks are too short, and I know Dad will say I've put my feet too far through them. Oh, Wally, have you seen Dad—and Jim?"

"Saw them yesterday. They ought to be here pretty soon—but my brother motored me down, so I didn't come with them. Norah—there's a girl looking at me, and if you don't take her away I shall scream!"

"Why, that's Jean Yorke," said Norah, wheeling. "She's my chum, and you've got to be extra nice to her, 'cause she is coming home with me for the holidays."

"Then she deserves any one's kind sympathy," said Wally, solemnly. He advanced upon Jean with outstretched hand and a smile that went far to put that somewhat shy individual at her ease, while Norah murmured a haphazard introduction.

Jean was a short and rather thickset person, with blue eyes and a freckled nose, and a square, honest face. Neither chum could have been regarded as pretty. They were wholesome-looking girls—alike in the trim neatness that is characteristic of the Australian schoolgirl; and alike also in the quality of sturdy honesty that looked straight at the world from blue eyes and grey. Jean was fair, her thick masses of hair gathered in more tightly than Norah's curly brown mop ever permitted—whereat Norah was frankly envious. She was also wont to be apologetic, because, although a year the younger, she towered over Jean by half a head. The unfulfilled ambition of Jean's dreams was to be tall and slender, and Norah bore a lasting grudge against Fate for denying so moderate a longing on her friend's part. She watched her anxiously for signs of growth, and at frequent intervals measured her height, while tactfully ignoring what she herself would have called her girth.

Across the introduction came a cold voice.

"Your brother, I presume, Norah?"

Both girls jumped.

"No—only it's all the same, Miss Winter," Norah explained, lucidly. "It's Wally Meadows—my brother's chum." At which Wally removed his hat and said: "How do you do?" with such fervour that it seemed that his peace of mind hung upon Miss Winter's answer. That severe person's coldness was a trifle modified as she answered, but it was Arctic again when she turned back to Norah.

"I saw you crossing the grass—and the flower bed!" she remarked. "Such conduct is inexcusable, Norah—I am amazed at you. The garden is not the hockey field, nor is the arrival of any friend to be the signal for such conduct!"

Norah was scarlet.

"I'm awfully—I mean I am very—sorry, truly, Miss Winter!" she said. "I forgot all about everything when I saw Wally. You see, he's nearly the same as Jim, and I hadn't seen him for ten months! I won't do it again. And Jean never did it at all!"

"I could see that for myself," said Miss Winter, drily—whereat Jean became even more scarlet than Norah. "However, it is too late in the term for impositions—which is fortunate for you!" There came into the culprit's eye an irrepressible twinkle, and the teacher relaxed a little. "Ah, well—it's nearly holiday time," she said, smiling. "But, Norah, dear—do remember that you are over fifteen!"

"I will, Miss Winter—I truly will," said the criminal. "I'll behave beautifully—see if I don't!——"

The iron gate clanged, and she glanced round with the quick instinctiveness that never leaves the bush-bred. A tall man and a lad almost as tall came into view, and at sight of them Norah's "behaviour" suddenly fell away from her, and with a little cry that was half a sob, she fled to meet them. The gravel scattered under her trim-shod feet; her long legs twinkled with amazing swiftness. Then the big man put out his arms to her, and she flung herself into them.

"Oh, Daddy—Daddy!" said Norah. "Oh, Jim! Oh-h!" Words failed her.

"My girl!" said David Linton. Over her head he looked at the teacher, and found that she was human. He smiled at her in friendly fashion.

"We try to teach Norah deportment," she said, greeting him, and laughing, while big Jim hugged his sister frankly, totally unabashed by the amused glances from various parts of the garden. "But I am afraid the effect isn't very evident on breaking up day!"

"I'm quite certain we're demoralizing influences," he told her. "But what can you expect, from the Back of Beyond? We'll try to make her remember the deportment when we get her back to the station, Miss Winter. At present, you must make allowances."

Miss Winter thawed amazingly under the influence of the quiet voice, deep and courteous, and the Linton smile, which was a wonderfully pleasant one. It was very frequent upon the face of her pupil, and had at all times a tendency to upset discipline; and now the same smile appeared, if more rarely, on the bronzed giants, father and son, who confronted her upon the path. They were very alike—over six feet—Mr. Linton had yet a couple of inches to the good, but Jim was overhauling him fast—lean and broad-shouldered, with the same well-cut features and keen eyes. Norah said that they had absorbed the good looks of the family, leaving her none; which was partly true, although the remark would have moved her father and brother to wrath. In their grey suits and Panama hats, they were excellent specimens of long-limbed Australia, and Norah gazed at them as though she could not take away the eyes that had been hungry for so many long months.

It was evident that neither Jim nor his father found it easy to talk polite nothings to Miss Winter. Their eyes kept straying to the slim figure that was the main thing in their world—Norah, who jigged irrepressibly on one foot and broke into sudden smiles, and forgot altogether the discipline and deportment that had been instilled into her during three terms at Beresford House. To put her there at all had been a proceeding much like caging a bush bird, for, until she was fourteen, Norah had known only home and its teachings. And home was Billabong Station, where, apart from lessons that had been a little patchy, she had lived her father's life—a life of open-air, of horses and cattle, and all the station interests. Jim had been sent to the Grammar School in Melbourne comparatively early, and Norah's city relatives, particularly a number of assorted aunts, were wont to deplore that the little girl had not had the same opportunity of polish. But the bond between David Linton and his motherless child had been too strong to break, and the silent man had snatched at every pretext for delaying the pang of parting.

After all, as he told himself, half in excuse, Norah was no discredit to home teaching. In books she might be below the average; but of the unvoiced learning that lies beyond the world of books she had, perhaps, rather more than falls to the ordinary schoolgirl. A big station is a little world in itself, and the Bush teaching makes for self-control and self-reliance, and a simple, straight outlook on the world that is not a bad foundation of character. Lessons in deportment and manners are not part of its curriculum: but there are a good many ideas in thought and practice that it cultivates half unconsciously. Norah had an almost superstitious regard for doing what Jim termed "the decent thing."

Moreover, her father had given her an ideal to follow. The mother who had gone away from them so soon had never been far from his thoughts or his slow speech: and "Brownie," the old woman who had taken the little dark-haired baby from her weak arms, had helped to make the picture of "Mother" that was so real that Norah had always known and loved it. Vaguely she knew that there was a lack in her father's life which she must try to fill. It had tended to make her gentle—to bring out something that was almost protective in her nature. There is a trace of motherliness in every girl-heart; Norah always felt that, while Dad and Jim were very large and strong and dependable, yet it rested with her to "look after them." Had she put her thoughts into words it is quite likely that the objects of her care might have felt a shade of amusement; but as she did not, they appreciated her attentions mightily. To them, the heart of Billabong had dropped out when Norah went away to school.

And school had been something of a trial. Norah's bringing-up had been along lines where rules of conduct are understood rather than expressed; although she was a well-behaved damsel, in her own setting, it had not been easy to find herself suddenly hedged in to such an extent that she lived and breathed and ate and slept by regulation and timetable. She realized that it was necessary to conform; but practice was a harder matter, and the time at school had seen many "scrapes" and many impositions. Common sense and good temper helped her through, and the appearance of Jean Yorke upon a somewhat lonely horizon had helped in a different way. But only Norah herself knew just how bad had been the homesickness and the silent longing for her own old life. She knew that Dad and Jim would be hurt by knowing, therefore she kept these matters to herself, and diligently cultivated Jim's prescription of "a stiff upper lip."

Now it was over. There would be other years; but no year could ever be quite like the first, especially since there was now Jean to help—Jean being a comprehending person, whose heart had gone out to Norah since the day of her arrival at Beresford House, three months ago. Jean came from New Zealand, and she, too, was lonely, with the desperate loneliness born of the fact that she would not see home or the home people for two years. When Norah contemplated Jean's woeful plight she was ashamed to admit that she had been homesick on her own account. So they "twin-souled" immediately, and made life very much easier for each other.

How this last week had crawled! Each night Norah had crossed out the finished day upon her calendar with thick, red strokes that were some relief to her pent-up feelings; always doing it just at the last moment before turning out the light and jumping into bed, so that she might have the friendly darkness to cover her as she buried her face in the pillow, wriggling, with sheer physical inability to keep still as she realized how near were home and Dad and Jim. Near—but how slow the days! Examinations and matches were over, and the work of the school slackening. She flung herself headlong into games and "break up" preparations to make the slow hours pass, dividing each day into hours and half hours—she even reduced them to minutes, but the sum total looked too enormous! Her school work was characteristic of her turmoil of mind. Once she rattled over the provisions of Magna Charta for the Latin master with a fluency that paralyzed the unfortunate man, who had merely asked her to decline an inoffensive noun; while Miss Winter gave her up as hopeless on being informed that Thomas a'Becket Archbishop of Canterbury, lost his life by drowning in a butt of malmsey! Norah saw nothing incongruous in the prelate's alleged death, and spent much of the hour's detention that followed in drawing a spirited picture of it—representing a large barrel, from the yawning mouth of which protruded two corpulent legs, clad in gaiters, and immaculately shod. The charm of the picture was in the portion of it that was not visible. It was unfortunate that it fell into the hands of Miss Winter, who was handicapped by a literal mind. Altogether, the last week had been more or less exciting and painful, and it was quite as well that it was over.

The great bell of the school rang out sharply, and a kind of white flicker came over the garden as the girls moved quickly in answer. It was the signal to assemble in hall. Norah exchanged looks of longing with Jim and Wally. Then she and Jean moved off towards the house, endeavouring to calm spasmodic footsteps.

A little later saw the three visitors making a gallant attempt to dispose their long legs among the crowded rows of chairs reserved for parents and "belongings," while the boys sent rapid telegraphic signals to Norah, by this time a mere speck amid the white-clad girls massed upon the platform. The big hall was packed with visitors—proud parents, each supremely confident that "our girl" was something quite beyond the average; big sisters, anxious to create the impression of being far removed from matters so juvenile as school; brothers, wearing the colours of different schools, and assuming great boredom. Then came Miss Winter, followed by church dignitaries and other notable people, including two members of Parliament, who behaved as though engrossed with affairs of State; whereat the infant classes arose and sang a roundelay with much gusto, and the business of the day began.

The Billabong contingent was not happy. It was uncomfortably crowded; its view was obstructed by immense erections of millinery on the heads of ladies immediately in front; frequently it was tickled on the back of the neck by similar erections belonging to ladies who leaned forward, from the rear, manœuvring for a better vision of the proceedings. It was much embarrassed by the French play, acted by the senior class—the embarrassment being chiefly due to fear of laughing in the wrong place. Nor did lengthy recitations from Shakespeare appeal to it greatly, or a song by the red-haired girl, the said song being of the type known as an "aria," and ungallantly condemned by Jim as "screamy enough to scare cockatoos with!" It brightened at a physical culture display, and applauded vigorously when a curly-haired mite essayed a recitation, broke down in the middle, and finished, not knowing whether or not to cry, until much cheered by the friendly clapping. The moment of the programme—for Billabong—came when Norah, very pale and unhappy, played a Chopin nocturne. Wally joined wildly in the succeeding applause, but Jim and his father sat up straight, endeavouring to appear unconcerned, but radiating pride. Norah did not dare to look at them until she was safely back in her place. Then she shot a glance at the two tall heads; and what she saw in their faces suddenly sent the blood leaping to her own.

Afterwards came the distribution of prizes—a matter which did not greatly concern Norah, whose scholastic achievements could scarcely be classed as other than ordinary. However, she had carried off the music prize in her class—music being born within her, and, even in lessons, only a joy. She was still flushed with excitement when the long ceremony was at an end, and she was able to slip from the platform and find her way to the waiting trio—standing tall and stiff against the wall, while the crowd seethed in the body of the hall, and other book-laden daughters were reunited to parents as proud as David Linton.

"I'll look after that," Jim said, with a masterful little gesture, possessing himself of Norah's prize. "Well done, old chap!" He patted her head with brotherly emphasis.

"Proud to know you, ma'am," said Wally, humbly. "Norah, I was nearly asleep until you came on to play!"

"And quite asleep afterwards," grinned Jim. "Snored, Norah—I give you my word!"

"That's one I owe you!" said the maligned Mr. Meadows, vengefully. "I clapped until my horny hands were sore, Norah. Made a hideous noise!"

"Then there were two of us," said Norah, laughing. "I never knew old Chopin sound so funny—catch me playing before a lot of people again! I was scared to look at old Herr Wendt. Probably he pulled out most of his remaining locks—I know I made at least three mistakes."

"It sounded all right," said her father, and smiled at her. "Now, young woman, this is very nice, but one can have enough of it." A wheat-trimmed hat brushed across his face, and he emerged in some confusion. "How soon will you two girls be ready?"

"Must we change?"

"I sincerely trust not," said Mr. Linton, appalled at the thought of awaiting two feminine toilettes of a greater magnificence than was familiar to him with his daughter. "Not if you have big coats—I've a motor outside. Your heavy luggage has gone, I believe."

"Yes, it went by carrier," said Norah, happily. "All right, Daddy, we'll be back in five minutes. Come on, Jean!" They disappeared, to re-emerge presently, muffled in heavy blue coats and wearing sailor hats. Farewells hurtled through the air.

"Good-bye, Miss Winter. Merry Christmas!"

"Good-bye, Carrots, dear!" This to the red-haired singer, who accepted the greeting and the appellation cheerfully.

"Good-bye, young Norah. Behave yourself, if you can. But you can't!"

"Good-bye, Jean!"

"Good-bye, every one. Mind you all come back!"

"Good-bye!"

"Merry Christmas!"

"Good-bye, school!" The note of utter thankfulness in Norah's voice brought a twinkle to Jim's eyes.

The motor chug-chugged on the path. Norah did not like motors—horses were infinitely better, in her opinion. But this one seemed a chariot of joy. They bundled in, pell-mell.

"Are you all right?" queried Mr. Linton.

"I never was so all right in my life!" said Norah, fervently. The car slid away into the dusty haze of the white road.

CHAPTER II
NIGHT IN THE CITY
Oh, the world is wondrous fair

 When the tide of life's at flood!

There is music in the air,

 There is music in the blood.

And a glamour draws us on,

 To the distance, rainbow-spanned.

And the road we tread upon

Is the track to Fairyland.

—V. J. Daley.

JEAN, can you button me up?"

"Half a minute till I get this ribbon tied," said the lady addressed, wrestling urgently with an obstinate bow. "There—that's got to do! Turn round, old girl—I can't see. There you are."

"Thanks," said Norah, shaking out her skirt. "Is my hair decent?"

"Yes, it's all right. Curly-haired people like you always look right."

"Wish I thought so," said the owner of the curls. "Dreadful mop, I think. Will I do, Jean?"

"Do?" said Jean, in some bewilderment. "Why, of course—you look all right. Why are you worrying?"

Norah reddened slightly.

"Well—I never had dinner in a big hotel like this before," she said. "Melbourne hotels are a bit different to the Cunjee one, I guess. And I don't want Dad and Jim to be ashamed of me."

"I don't think you need bother your head," said the more travelled Jean. "You look nice, truly. And I shouldn't think your father and Jim were very hard to please."

"Oh, they never would say anything. But they might think—and be disappointed if I weren't all right. You see, it never seemed to matter when I was only at Billabong. But after all this time at school they'll naturally expect me to be different."

"And do you think you are?" queried Jean, anxiously.

"I don't think I am, a bit!" Norah answered. "That's what's worrying me. It won't bother me when I get home, I expect, but this big place seems different." She glanced round the hotel bedroom with a quaint air of anxiety. "I feel just exactly the same as if I'd never been at school at all."

"Well, I believe that's how your father'll like you," said Jean, sapiently.

"And——" Norah flushed more redly, and paused.

"What?"

"Will dinner be—difficult? You know I haven't been anywhere like this," said poor Norah. "Will there be lots of knives and forks and glasses I don't know anything about? I don't want to make an ass of myself, you know!"

Jean nodded comprehendingly.

"Don't you worry," she said. "It's all quite easy. I stayed here with father when he brought me over from Christchurch, you know. He helped me a bit over ordering when the waiter came round—the menu is rather mixed until you get used to it. You tell your father to do the same. And I really won't know a bit more than you, so if we make mistakes we'll make them together, and it won't matter!"

"You're a dear," said Norah, gratefully. "I say, would you mind if I go and find Dad now, and have a little talk to him? His room is quite near."

"Of course I won't," said her friend. "Hurry up—it's nearly dinner time."

"I'll come back for you," Norah called, disappearing into the corridor. She hesitated a moment in the unfamiliar place—all the doors looked so exactly alike. Then from behind one came a line of a song, in Jim's deep voice, and Wally joined in:—

"So we went strolling, down by the rolling—

Down by the rolling sea!"

It made the corridor seem suddenly homelike, and Norah broke into smiles. Beyond, her father's number caught her eye, and she tapped at the door.

"May I come in, Daddy?"

"Certainly you may!" said David Linton, with somewhat startling emphasis, mingled with relief. "And tie this blessed evening tie!" He submitted meekly to his daughter's ministrations. "Ridiculous!—I'm far too old to get into these clothes!"

"You look beautiful," said his daughter, fervently. "Daddy, will I do?"

"Do? I should say so. That white thing looks very fine as far as I'm a judge."

"Then that's all right. And, Dad——"

"Yes, my girl?"

"I'm awfully scared of dinner!" Norah confessed. "Will you keep fierce waiters off me, Daddy? And tell me what to say I'll have?"

David Linton looked at her and smiled with something like relief. He sat down and drew her towards him.

"Do you know," he said, "you've looked so fine a young lady to-day that I almost feared I'd lost my little Bush mate. I suppose it's the clothes!"

"Daddy!"

"But I fancy I haven't," said her father twinkling. "Don't bother your little head about dinner—we'll see you through. I don't quite know how I'd have liked it if you had been self-possessed about it."

"Self-possessed!" uttered Norah. "Why, I'm scared to my bones! And as for the clothes—if you'll wait until to-morrow and let me get into a linen collar again——!"

"I'll know you thoroughly when I have you back at Billabong in your riding habit," said her father. "But these clothes are nice, too. I'm not quarrelling with them. You're not sorry to come back to your old Dad?" He paused, watching her.

"Sorry!" said Norah. "Sorry!" And then her tongue suddenly refused to do its duty. She put her head down on his shoulder, and drew a deep breath. His arms tightened round her. They were silent for a minute.

"Jim is a good mate," said David Linton, "none better. But my little mate's place has always been empty. It's been a long time, my girl."

"Long—to you, Daddy?"

"One of the longest I remember. You see, I never bargained for your spending midwinter having measles."

"Neither did I," said Norah, ruefully. The memory of that inconsiderate ailment was still a sore thing; at the time it had been almost too sore to be borne. "It seems just ages since I saw home. Is it just the same, Dad?"

"I don't think there's any difference. Everyone has been busy putting on a bit of extra polish for the last week; and Brownie says she's half a stone lighter—but she doesn't look it; and there's a new inmate in the little paddock near the house calling for your immediate inspection!"

"A new inmate?" Norah echoed.

Jim had come in, unnoticed. He grinned down at her from the hearthrug.

"A rather swagger inmate," he said, nodding. "Seeing how out of form you must be, I don't think it will be wise to let you try him—we'll put you up on an old stock horse for a week or so!"

"Will you, indeed?" said Norah, with some heat, yet laughing. "You're going to lend me Garryowen—you said so!"

"Garryowen!" said the owner of that proud steed mournfully. "Poor old Garryowen's tail will be hopelessly out of joint. One thing, I'll be able to ride him myself—being of a meek disposition!" His eyes twinkled.

Two red spots suddenly flamed into Norah's face.

"Dad! You don't mean——" She stopped, looking at him uncertainly.

"There's something of a pony there," said Mr. Linton, his keen eyes watching her through his smile. "An ownerless one—wi' a long pedigree! I looked eight months before I found him. His name's Bosun, Norah, and he wants an owner."

There was a mist before Norah's eyes. She tried to speak, but her head went down again upon the broad shoulder near her. A muffled word escaped her, which sounded like, "Bricks!" Norah was least eloquent when most moved.

Jim patted her shoulder hard, and said, "Buck up, old chap!" being also a person of few words. For there had been another pony of Norah's—a most dear pony, who now slept very quietly under a cairn of stones on a rough hillside. Not one of those three, who were mates, could forget.

From the corridor Wally's voice came, gently consolatory.

"I think they've all been kidnapped," he was explaining. "Many a little hungry kidnapper would think Jim quite a treat! You and I seem left alone in this pathless forest, and probably the birds will find us, and cover us with leaves. Don't let it worry you—I believe the leaves are quite comfortable!"

"Come in, Wally, you ass!" said Jim, laughing. "He may come in, Dad——?"

"Apparently he's in," said Mr. Linton, resignedly, getting up. "Come on, Wally—and Jean, too."

"We've been lost—at least, we were until we found each other," said Wally. "We came to the conclusion that none of you Billabong people were left in this little inn. Jean would probably have cried if I hadn't been crying—as it was, she felt she couldn't, which was very rough on her. Mr. Linton, do I know you well enough——"

"For most things," said the squatter, laughing!

"——To mention that I am hungry?" finished Wally, unmoved. "My last nourishment was at twelve o'clock, and it's nearly seven now; and theatres in this benighted district begin before eight when they're pantomimes!"

Mr. Linton uttered an exclamation.

"I declare, I'd forgotten all about either dinner or pantomime!" he said. "Thank you, Wally—I'm obliged to you. Where's my coat? I hope all the rest of you are ready."

"Are we going to the pantomime, Dad?" Norah's eyes were dancing.

"Jim says so," said her father, laughing. "I'm in his hands." He caught up his coat, while Jean and Norah hugged each other in silent ecstasy. "Now, hurry up, all of you!"

Downstairs, the big dining-room brought back Norah's shyness anew. She felt suddenly very young—infinitely younger than Jim and Wally, tall and immaculate in their evening clothes, although, as a rule, they seemed no older than herself. She kept close to her father's wing, greatly envying Jean's apparent calm.

The huge room was crowded. It was full of tables of varying sizes, not one of which seemed unoccupied—until a waiter, catching Mr. Linton's eye, hurried up and led them to a corner, where a round table was reserved for them. It commanded an excellent view of the room, and the sight was a little bewildering to the two schoolgirls.

Every one seemed in evening dress—and even Norah knew she had seen no dresses like those the women wore—rich, clinging things, in soft and delicate colours like the inner side of flower petals. The masses of electric light took up the leaping light of jewels on their necks and in their hair; all up and down the room the eye caught the many-coloured gleam, twinkling and sparkling like rainbow stars. Everywhere was laughter and chatter and the chink of plates and glasses; and somewhere, unseen, a string band was playing softly a waltz tune with a lilt in it like a bird's note. Norah forgot all about being nervous. Indeed, she remembered nothing, being deeply occupied with gazing, until she found a deft waiter putting soup before her.

"That's my order," said her father, and smiled. "You and Jean have had an exciting day, and you're to eat just what I tell you."

By these wily means any difficulties the menu might have suggested disappeared. Moreover, the waiter was a man of tact, and seemed to regard it as only ordinary if his clients kept him waiting while they put their heads together over the merits of various items with very fine French names.

"Experience in these things is everything," said Jim, surveying a peculiar substance on his plate. "I ordered something that read like a poem, and it turns out a sort of half-bred hash! Thanks, I'll have beef!" So they all had beef, and finished up rather hurriedly with jelly, which, as Wally said, could be demolished quickly; for the hands of the clock were slipping round, and a pantomime was not a thing to be kept waiting—especially as there was no likelihood that it would wait!—a reflection that made the situation far more serious. Jim raced up for coats for the girls, and they all hastened out.

In the street the lights of Melbourne lit the sky. Far as the eye could reach the yellow glow shone against the star-gemmed blackness. Here and there a point of special brilliance twinkled—it was hard to tell whether it was a tall arc light reaching up into the very heavens, or a lonely star that had leaned down towards the friendly earth. Up and down the Bourke Street hills the lamps formed a linked chain of diamonds on either side, while in their midst the low gliding tram-lights were rubies and sapphires. The big head-lights of motors made gleaming flashes as they turned, or shot straight up the wide street, twin eyes of a dazzling radiance—so bright that when they flashed past darkness seemed to fall doubly dark behind them. And there were creeping bicycle lights, and streaks of white fire, that were the lamps of motor cycles; and red and white lights that went by in silent rubber-tyred hansoms, noiseless save for the jingling bit and the "klop-klop" of the horse's hoofs upon the wooden blocks. Advertisement signs in huge electric letters flickered into sight and disappeared again—one moment dazzling, the next velvet black; and over picture theatres and other places of amusement were gleaming signs of fire. And up from the city below came the deep hum of the people that only ceases for a little when the lights go out—that wakes again even before the pencils of Dawn come to streak the eastern sky.

Then a tram came by, took them on board, and in a moment they were slipping down the hill towards a busy intersection where the post office stood, a mighty block of buildings, with its tall clock just chiming the quarter-hour above them. On again, through the wide, busy street, full of hurrying theatre crowds. Barefooted newsboys ran beside the car whenever it stopped, calling out harrowing details from the evening papers. They passed cabs, climbing the further hill; and swift motors slipped by them—in each Norah and Jean caught glimpses of women in evening dress, with scarfs like trails of coloured mist. Everywhere the shop windows were brilliantly lighted, although it was long after closing time; and scores of people were staring through the glass at the gorgeous displays within.

Norah gasped at it all. It was her first experience of the City by night, and she found it rather bewildering.

"Does Melbourne ever stop being busy?" she uttered.

Mr. Linton laughed.

"Not often," he said—"and not for long. Personally, I prefer old Billabong. But this is all very well for a little while."

The car stopped at a point where an electric theatre sign blazed right across the footpath; and they hurried down a side-street. A string of motors and cabs had drawn up by the kerb and passengers were hastily disembarking before a glittering theatre, with uniformed commissionaires holding the doors open. Norah and Jean had no time to look about them; they were hurried up a wide flight of marble stairs, and in a moment were following Mr. Linton into darkness, for already the lights had been turned off in the theatre, and only a dun green ray filtered from the stage, where an old man of the sea was engaged in making unpleasant remarks to a fairy. The orchestra was playing softly—weird music which, Wally whispered, gave you chills up the backbone. They stumbled down some steps to seats in the front row, and as they thankfully subsided into them, the green sea-caves and the fierce old man suddenly vanished in a whirl of light and a blare of joyful music; and Norah was whisked straight into fairyland.

In these advanced days of ours, pantomimes come very early into the scheme of our existence. Most of us have seen one by the time we are six; at nine we have become critical, and at twelve, bored. After that, the pantomime may consider itself lucky if we do not term it a "pretty rotten show." This painful phase lasts until we are quite old—perhaps eight and twenty. Then we begin to see fresh joys in it, and if we are lucky, to work up quite a comforting degree of enthusiasm. At this stage the companion we like to select must not number more years than six. Then we feel sure of a comprehending fellow-spectator—one who will not wither us with a bland stare when we are consumed with helpless laughter at Harlequin, or rent with anxiety by the perils of the "principal boy."

But it happened that none of our party had ever been spoilt by over-much pantomime. It was, indeed, Norah's first experience of a theatre. Jean had seen but little more, and Jim and Wally, big fellows as they were, had worked and played far too hard at school to be much concerned with going out. None of them was at all brilliant; theirs were the cheerful, simple hearts that take work and pleasure as they come, and do not trouble to develop either the critical or the grumbling faculty—which are, in truth, closely related. If the boys had not the ecstatic anticipation that seethed in Jean and Norah, at least they were prepared to enjoy themselves very solidly.

To Norah, it was all absolutely real, and therefore wonderful past belief. The evening to her was, as she remarked afterwards, "one gasp." The hero puzzled her, since it was evident that he was not a "truly" boy; but the heroine claimed her heart from the first, and the funny men were droll beyond compare. Indeed, from Mr. Linton downwards, the Billabong party succumbed to the funny men, and laughed until they ached at their antics. The fairies were certainly a trifle buxom, compared to the sprites of Norah's dreams; but the Old Man of the Sea was fascinatingly lifelike and evil, and caused delightful thrills of horror to run up and down one's spine. And then, the gorgeousness of the whole—the flower and bird ballets, the mysterious dances, the marches, splendid and stately, the glitter and colour and light! And through all, over all, the music!—swaying, rippling; low and soft one moment, with the violins wailing and the harp strings plucked in a chord of poignant sweetness—the next, swelling out triumphantly, wind instruments in a blare of vivid sound, and drums and cymbals clashing wild and stately measures. Afterwards the wonder of the night merged in Norah's brain to a kind of kaleidoscopic picture, swiftly changing in colour and magnificence; but always clear was the memory of the orchestra, weaving magic spells of music that caught her heart in their meshes.

She was a little breathless when the curtain fell on the first act, and the lights flashed out over the body of the theatre. Instinctively her hand sought her father's.

"Is it all over, Dad?"

"Not much!" said Mr. Linton. "This is half-time. What do you think of it?"

"Oh—it's lovely!" breathed his daughter. "Isn't it, Jean?"

"I should just think so!" Jean said. "Will there be more like it?"

"Very much the same, I expect," said the squatter, laughing. "And what do you think of this part of the house?"

It was not the least interesting part. The closing of the city schools had set free hosts of pilgrims on the ways of knowledge, debarred, as a rule, by stern necessity from such relaxations as pantomimes. Now it seemed that parents in general had risen to a sense of their duty, for it was clearly a "young" night. There were girls and boys in every part of the theatre—in big parties, in twos and threes, or even singly, accompanied by a cheery father and mother, in many cases keener to enjoy than their charges. Everywhere were fresh young faces—girls with bright hair and glowing cheeks, and sunburnt boys with shining collars: and everywhere was a babel and buzz of talk and laughter as the young voices broke loose. A procession—chiefly men—left their seats and filed out; a proceeding which puzzled and pained Norah, who was heard to regret audibly that they were making the mistake of thinking the theatre was over. Wally laid a big box of chocolates on her knee, remarking that she looked hungry—an insult received by the maligned one with fitting scorn. At the moment Norah could scarcely have noticed the difference between chocolates and corned beef!

"Won't do," grinned Jim, watching her dancing eyes. "She's getting too excited, Dad—we'd better take her home to bed!"

"I'd like to see you!" said Norah, belligerently. "Oh, my goodness, Jean, it's going up again!"

"It"—which was the curtain—flashed up suddenly, as the lights went out, and straightway Norah forgot everything but the wonderland on the stage. She leaned forward breathlessly, half afraid of losing even a glimpse of the marvels that were unfolded with such apparent calm. "As if," said Norah later, "it was as ordinary as washing-day!"

Ever since she could remember, she had danced. But the dancing on the stage was a new thing altogether. It was music put into motion; it was as though the fairies had caught the spirits of joy and poetry and youth, and turned them all into a rhythmic harmony. There was gladness in every swaying movement; gladness and grace and beauty. "They all look so awfully happy!" breathed Norah. But then—who would not be happy, dancing in Fairyland?

Only, near the end, come one thing that Norah did not like. A children's ballet, dressed as flowers, had just danced its way off the stage, leaving at one side a tall tiger lily; and from the other corner a tiny thing toddled out to meet it. A wee baby form, almost ridiculous in the quaint tights of green that made it an orchid—a little face, peeping out of the green peaked cap. Very daintily, a little hesitatingly, it began to dance; the orchestra's music softened and slackened, as if to help the little half-afraid feet. The theatre rang with applause and laughter.

"They shouldn't let it—it's a shame!" she uttered very low. "It's just a baby—and it ought to be in bed! Jim do they make it do this every night?"

"I expect so," Jim answered. "Bless you, old girl, I suppose they pay the kid!"

"Then they haven't any business to—I don't know what its mother's thinking about!" whispered Norah. "I'm perfectly certain it's as scared as ever it can be! It's only a frightened little baby—I think it's mean to dress it up in those silly clothes and make it come out here in front of all these people!"

"For all you know, old chap, it likes the game," Jim said, practically.

"I'm sure it doesn't—look at its eyes! I never saw anything so—so anxious. Makes you want to pick it up and nurse it," said his sister, a straight young monument of indignation. "Thank goodness, it's gone!" as the little orchid danced off with the tiger lily. She subsided, somewhat to Jim's relief. He was not sure that he had liked the baby orchid himself.

Then came the final scene, a vision of Aladdin's Cave, massed with every gem known of man, and a great number more known only of the stage; and all gorgeous and glittering beyond any mortal dreams. Rubies as big as turkeys' eggs, and emeralds the size of barrels; and walls and ceiling a flashing, scintillating mass of diamonds. "Worth while having a vacuum cleaner there," Wally commented—"you'd only get diamond dust!" And in this wondrous setting, a shifting panorama of moving figures, almost as vivid as the gems themselves; fairies and sprites and marvellous flowers, and tall, slender soldiers in gleaming coats of silver mail. And always the music that made the magic by which everything grew real.

Then, suddenly the curtain; and Norah came out of her trance, blinking a little.

"Is that the end?"

"Quite the end," said her father. "Come on, my girl; it's high time you were in bed." He put a protecting hand on her shoulder, and piloted her through the crowd, while Jim and Wally performed a like kind office for the similarly dazed Jean.

Out in Bourke Street, the cooler air blew gratefully upon Norah's hot face. But she was very silent as the tram took them back to the hotel; and when she said good-night, her father scanned her face keenly.

"Sure you're not over-tired, Norah?"

"Not me!" said Norah, absent-mindedly and inelegantly. "I'm all right, Daddy."

"Then you're half in the theatre yet," said he, laughing. "Go to bed."

Norah went, obediently. Just as Jean was falling asleep, a voice came from the bed across the room—

"Wonder if any one's tucked up that poor little orchid!" said Norah. From Jean's corner came a sound that might have been termed either a grunt or a snore, according as the hearer might be more or less kindly disposed. Norah was pondering the problem when she followed her through the gate of sleep.

"I almost feared I'd lost my little Bush mate."

CHAPTER III
THE CRY OF THE CHILDREN
Yet long ago it was promised by Someone,

Who lovingly help for the children implored,

That if only you gave one a cup of cold water,

You surely in no wise should lose your reward!

—John Sandes.

I'VE an idea," Mr. Linton said, putting down his morning paper.

Four faces gave him instant attention. It was breakfast time, and plans for the day were being discussed, a trifle lazily, as befitted people unused to over-night dissipation.

"We—ell," said the squatter, and hesitated.

"You have lovely ideas, always, Dad," Norah told him, kindly. "Tell us."

"I don't know that you'll regard this one as lovely," said her father. "Still, I'd like to do it."

"Well, then, it'll be done," said Jim, with finality. "What is it, Dad?"

"If you keep up this mystery any longer, I won't be able to bear it, Mr. Linton," said Wally, much moved. "Prithee, sir——"

David Linton smiled.

"The mystery's a tame one, you'll think," he said. "I thought of my plan before I left home—old Brownie has been knitting a big bundle for the Children's Hospital, and she gave me the things to bring down. Then there's a letter in this paper about the hospital. It's getting near Christmas, you see; and I don't suppose those little sick youngsters have much of a good time. Would you all think it a very slow sort of entertainment if we went to see them?" He looked round the four young faces—a little afraid of seeing their eagerness die out.

But Wally smiled broadly, leaning forward.

"I think it's a ripping idea, sir," he said. "I guess we all like kids, don't we, chaps?"

The "chaps," who evidently included the ladies of the party, assented with enthusiasm.

"Tell us more, Dad," Norah said, "I know you've more plan."

"Well—I'm open to suggestions," her father answered. "We won't go empty-handed; we can take up toys and books and things. It isn't visiting day at the hospital. In any case, I think it would be better not to go at a crowded time. If I telephone to the Matron, I fancy she will let us come; and she can tell me something about the number of children. I—I'm a shocking bad hand at preaching, you know"—he hesitated, gaining encouragement from their friendly faces—"but—well, we're looking out for a pretty good time ourselves, and it wouldn't hurt us to share some of it."

"But I think it will be tremendous fun, won't it, Jean?" Norah said. To which Jean nodded vigorous acquiescence.

"Then we'll get it done at once," said Mr. Linton. "You can put your four wise heads together, and consult as to what we're to take up—I don't know what sick youngsters like."

"That's half the fun," said Norah, happily. "Isn't it, Jean?" And Jean nodded.

"Then I'll go and telephone," said the squatter; "by which time you hungry people may have finished breakfast—unless you mean to make this meal run into lunch, as doesn't seem unlikely!" He made his escape, Norah regretting deeply that hotel etiquette prevented her from reprisals.

He joined them, a little later, in the lounge, where big leather-covered chairs and tall palms made a cool retreat in the hottest days.

"If there's a more exasperating institution than the Melbourne telephone, I have yet to find it out," said he. "I've been standing in that small Black Hole of Calcutta that they call a telephone box until I nearly died of asphyxiation, and all the response I could elicit was from a frenzied person who sounded like a dressmaker, and wanted to know desperately if I would have tucks on the bodice! However, I got the hospital at last, and we can go up when we like. So that means a busy morning. How soon can you girls be ready?"

"Three minutes, Dad!"

"Amazing women!" said Mr. Linton, regarding them with much respect. "I suppose, in a year or two, Norah, you'll keep me waiting while you put on your hat; but at present you're certainly an ornament to your sex in that respect. The car will be here in a few moments, so hurry up!"

The motor hummed up to the gate of the hospital a little later—a heavy gate, set in a high stone wall, behind which towered grim buildings. A neat maid admitted them to a wide corridor, with white walls and shining floor, where the Matron, white-gowned and gentle, welcomed them.

"No sweets, of course?" she queried, glancing at their parcels.

"No; we were afraid to bring them."

The Matron nodded approval.

"Some children can have them," she said. "But very many cannot, and there is no use in causing disappointments by making any difference. If you only knew how hard it is to make the mothers understand!"

"Poor souls!" said Mr. Linton. "I suppose they are keen to bring them something of a treat."

"Yes—and one is sorry for them. But the risk to the children is very great—only they won't believe it, and many of them think we are hard-hearted monsters. We always question the mothers as to what they are bringing the children, and watch them carefully; but even so, they manage to smuggle things past us. We had a dear little boy here in the winter—a typhoid patient, just pulling round after a very bad time. Of course he was on strict liquid diet, and equally, of course, he was very hungry."

"Poor kid!" said Jim, sympathetically.

"That's what his mother thought. So she smuggled him in two large jam tarts in her muff, and bent over him so as to hide him while he ate them."

"And did they hurt him?"

"They would have killed him. Luckily Nurse became suspicious, and caught him, as she said, 'on the first bite.' She rescued every crumb from his mouth, and nearly choked him in the process. But if she had not we couldn't have saved him."

"And what did the mother say?"

"The mother? Oh, she said that Nurse was 'an in'uman brute,' and nearly fell on her, tooth and nail. You can't teach them. Many of them are terribly poor—but they will spend a few pence on some cheap and dreadful sweetmeat, or a cake that looks—and often is—absolutely poisonous, and expect to be allowed to watch a sick baby eat it. Visiting day has many anxieties!"

Something called the busy Matron away as they reached the first ward, and they hesitated in the doorway. It was a long, bright room, cheery with sunlight and gay with flowers and plants, while the red bed jackets made bright notes of colour against the white quilts. Many of the boys were sitting up, working or playing at boards that fitted across their cots to serve as tables. Others were lying quietly, and very often could be seen the structure beneath the bedclothes that speaks mutely of hip disease. There were framed placards over many cots, stating whose gift they had been; perhaps raised by the efforts of children, or given by some sad mother in memory of a little child. Looking down the long rows of bright faces it was hard to realize that they were all sick boys—that Pain lived in the ward night and day.

In one cot a little lad was crying softly—a tired cry, as if afraid of disturbing others. The nurse bending over him straightened up, patted his shoulder, said, "Be a good boy, now, Tommy!" and came to greet the visitors.

"You mustn't mind the little chap who cries," she told them. "His leg is hurting, poor man. He won't speak to any one."

The eyes that were buried deep in the pillow were the only pair that were not turned upon the group in the doorway. The hospital children knew nothing about the Billabong invasion; only the nurses had been told of the unusual offer that had come over the telephone that morning. It seemed to the Matron a little uncertain, peculiar; better, perhaps, not to excite the children by anticipation.

But the first glimpse of the newcomers was sufficient—the children of the very poor are not slow brained. Something like a thrill of delight ran through the ward. There was no mistaking these people—happy-faced and well-dressed, and laden with fascinating parcels that could only mean one kind of thing. The eyes were very bright, watching from the cots.

It was a surgical ward, and most of the inmates looked happy. Life is not at all unbearable when you are a surgical case. To be a "medical" means headaches, and fevers, and soaring temperatures, and other unpleasant things. You are not allowed to eat anything interesting, and you frequently desire only to keep extremely quiet. But the "surgicals" know fairly well what to expect. Pain comes, of course—plenty of it; and the daily visits of the doctors are apt to leave you a bit short of self-control, even if you bite the pillow extremely hard in your efforts to show that there is decent pluck in you. But after a time you forget that. The ache in your leg, or your back, or your hip, or perhaps all over you, becomes part of the programme, and you learn to put up with it; and there is much of interest with other "cases" to talk to, songs to sing, and games that the sick can play—and nurses who are often very jolly and delightful. The nurse in this ward was little and dark and merry, and the boys called her "Brown Eyes." She had a knack of helping you through almost any pain.

She welcomed the newcomers cheerily now, though her eyes were a little tired. Behind her the faces were alight with silent eagerness.

"Can we talk to them?" Norah asked, shyly.

"Why, of course!" said the nurse. "You'll find most of them great chatterboxes—except little Tommy there. His pain is bad to-day."

The boys were quite ready to talk. They told all about themselves glibly, with a full appreciating of their value as "cases."

"I had a daisy of a temp'rature, I had!" said a cheerful soul of nine. "Doctor he came three times a day. Better now."

"Mine's a leg," volunteered another. "Broke—a cart runned over me. They brought me up from South Gippsland—sledge first, and then in the guard's van." He shivered—a reminiscent shudder. "Sledge was a fair cow!—bumped till I went an' fainted with the pain." He gave other details that set Jean and Norah shuddering, too. "But the guard's van wasn't half bad fun—y'see, I hadn't never been in a train before. My word, that guard was a kind man! Went an' bought me oranges with his own money!"

"Oh, I'm near right again," a merry-faced little Jewish lad told them. "Had me stitches taken out this morning—an' I never howled!"

"Well, I did then," said his neighbour, sturdily, "I don't think getting unpicked is any fun. But it don't take long, that's one thing." The other boy grinned at him in an understanding fashion. "Y'see, he's two years younger'n me," he told Norah. "He's only a bit of a nipper!"

Tommy alone declined to make friends. He burrowed into his pillow when they came to him, and refused to show so much as the tip of his nose. The sound of his sorry little wail followed them over the ward.

"Don't mind him," the nurse told the girls, as they turned away from the cot, with downcast faces. "He'll be better after a while, and then he'll be delighted with his presents. He's homesick, poor mite." They went on down the ward.

Jim turned back presently. He sat down near Tommy's cot and took out a toy watch that had beautiful qualities in the way of winding. But he did not offer it to Tommy. Instead he sat still, dangling it from his fingers.

"Had a sick leg myself, once," he remarked casually, apparently to the watch. As might have been expected, the watch made no response; neither did the black head burrowed in the pillow turn at all.

"Hurt it falling off a horse," Jim went on. "At least, the horse fell too. Tried to jump a log on him—and he shied at a snake lying on the top of the log."

The boy in the next cot was listening with all his ears. Tommy's low crying had stopped.

"Big black snake," said Jim. "Must have scared him a bit when he saw the horse rising. At any rate he slid off like fun—and my old horse shied badly, and went over the log in a somersault. Landed on his head, and pitched me about fifteen yards away!"

"Was you much hurt?" The boy in the next cot shot out an irrepressible question.

Jim was not in a hurry to answer. The black head was turning ever so little towards him, but he did not seem to see. He played with the watch in an absent-minded fashion.

"Hurt my leg," he said at length. "I managed to catch the old horse, because he put his foot through the bridle, and hobbled himself; and I got on by a log and rode home. Didn't jump any more fences though. And when I got home I couldn't stand on that leg. Had to be lifted off. Makes you feel an ass, doesn't it?"

The question was for the now visible Tommy, but Jim did not wait for an answer.

"Then I had to lie still for days," he said. "My word, I did hate it! I feel sorry for any chap with a sick leg. It's so jolly hard to keep still when you don't feel like it."

Something in the low, deep voice helped the little lad in the cot, with sore mind and body. This very large brown person understood exceedingly well.

"But legs get better," said Jim. "After a while you forget all about them, and play cricket again, and go in for no end of larks."

He shifted his position, still fingering the watch.

"The man that sold me this said it would go," he said. "It's got works all right, and I know it can tick, because he made it. But I'm blessed if I can get the hang of it!" For the first time he looked squarely at Tommy. "I suppose you couldn't give me a hand with it?" he asked, casually. He held out the watch.

A small finger advanced about an inch, and the watch came nearer until it was within touching distance.

"Thanks, awfully," Jim said. "I ought to be able to get it going now." He fumbled with the stem Tommy had indicated. "No—I can't! I don't know what's the matter with the silly thing."

"Me!" said Tommy, with a great effort. It was hard to speak; but harder to lie silent, knowing quite well that you could extricate this other fellow from his difficulties. And so well Tommy knew where that watch ought to be wound.

"Well, perhaps you'd better," said Jim, with relief. He handed over the offending watch. "I suppose it's because mine's a different make," he said, drawing out his own. "See—mine winds so-fashion. I wouldn't mind betting you can't get a tick out of that one of yours."

"Mine?" said an infinitesimal voice.

"Yes—it's yours, of course. A pity you can't make it go. Oh, by Jove, you have!" He bent over the cot, his brown face alight with interest. "However did you do it?"

Five minutes later, when the Billabong party were ready to leave the ward, Jim and his patient were deep in a discussion of watches. Once a weak little laugh rang out from the cot, and the nurse looked round quickly.

"That's the first time that poor little chap has laughed," she said.

Jim stood up, at last, and held out his hand.

"They're waiting for me," he said. "Well, so long, old chap. Buck up!"

Tommy shook the big hand solemnly.

"So long," he said. He made a great effort to speak. "Is—is you' leg quite well?"

"Quite well, old man. So will yours be if you keep your pecker up. Promise!"

Tommy nodded. His eyes followed the tall lad out of the room. Then he slipped his hand under his pillow for his watch, and lo, there was a pocket knife as well. And the boy in the next cot had one, too—so that presently they were friends. And something had taken the worst of the ache away from his leg.

It was Wally's voice that guided Jim to the next ward.

Wally had been entrusted with a number of toy balloons, and in detaching one for an enthusiastic person of three with a broken ankle, he had let it slip through his fingers. A draught of wind took it down the ward—and Wally, hastily thrusting the others upon Mr. Linton, had pursued it frantically, his feet sliding on the smooth boards. The ward broke into a sudden shout of laughter.

Luckily, the string was long. It kept the balloon from rising quite to the ceiling; and just at the end of the room, Wally gave a wild leap into the air and caught the dangling end, uttering a school war cry as he did so. He brought it back in triumph, laughing; and the patients, evidently considering him a kind of circus let loose for their especial entertainment, shrieked with joy. The nurses were laughing as well, with an eye on the door lest an inquiring matron should appear. Hospital decorum was at a low ebb.

"I really don't think you're the kind of visitor to bring to a place like this," laughed Mr. Linton. "Will you ever have sense, Wally?"

"Don't know," said the culprit, sadly. "It doesn't look very like it, does it? But aren't they a jolly set of kids!" He broke into smiles again. "Takes such a little to make 'em happy, doesn't it?"

It did not seem to take much. All the watching faces were smiling and eager; if some were white and lined with suffering they hid it bravely with smiles. These were girls, short cropped, occasionally, and looking just like the boys; or with long hair carefully braided to be out of the way. There were little touches of adornment here and there—a bright ribbon in the hair, a flower pinned to the red bed jacket; and dolls were visible on many beds.

But when she talked to them, Norah found that these small people were not as care-free as the boys. They brought their worries with them to the hospital.

"I simply got to get home soon," one little girl told her. She was ten, with an old, worn face. "Daddy was here yes'day, an' he says me mother's sick—an' there's only me to look after the kids!"

"How many?" asked Norah.

"Four. The youngest's not a year old yet, an' he's a reg'lar handful."

"But you can't look after them!" Jean protested.

The child stared.

"Well, I done it nearly all me life," she said. "Mother, she goes out washin', an' I run the house—y'see, I got a doctor's c'tificate that I needn't go to school, 'cause of me hip, so that leaves me plenty of time. An' then me jolly old hip must go an' get worse on me! An' now Mum's sick." Her lip quivered. "I don't see how on earth they're goin' to get on if I don't go home!" she said anxiously. "Do you think you could say somethin' to Matron? An' then, perhaps, she could put in a word for me with Doctor!"

Norah promised; it was hard to deny the pleading of the great brown eyes. But when, later on, she found her opportunity, the Matron shook her head.

"Poor little soul!" she said, sadly. "She does not know that she will never go out."

"Not go out?" Norah stared.

"No; she has been here five months, and it is quite hopeless. And it is better so—she could never be strong." The Matron patted Norah's shoulder, looking gently at her aghast face. "You don't know how many there are for whose sake we are glad when the end comes," she said.

Out on the broad balconies many children were lying—there seemed no corner in all the great building that was not full of patients. One verandah had babies' cradles only—such weary, old-looking babies that Norah could scarcely bear to look at them; it was so altogether extraordinary and terrible to her, that a baby could possibly look as did these mites from the slums. That was the saddest part of all the hospital.

Then there were medical wards, into some of which they could not go; they left their parcels with the nurses, since David Linton had planned that every child in the hospital should have a gift from his children. Some of these small patients were too ill to be disturbed. There were one or two beds round which a screen was drawn significantly, and the children near the screens were very quiet. But even where sickness or pain was hardest, there was but little complaining, and very seldom did a child cry. The children of the poor soon learn to suffer in silence.

"But they don't all suffer," said the nurse the boys called "Brown Eyes." "Most of them are happy—and it hurts, sometimes, to see how many hate to go home. You see, many of the homes are so poor and comfortless—not even a decent bed. They dread going back, after having been cared for here—they know their mothers haven't time or money to look after them properly. But there are always more waiting to come in—we have to send them out as soon as possible."

The Billabong children were very silent as the motor whirred through the busy streets, and back to the hotel. Even Wally was quiet; he stared before him, whistling under his breath, in an absent-minded fashion. And Norah looked at Jim's long legs, thinking of the crippled limbs that were so ordinary in the hospital day's work.

But back in the hospital the tongues wagged freely. It would be very long before the Billabong visit was forgotten.

"Weren't they jolly—just!"

"Didn't they speak nice!"

"That long feller with the thin face—wasn't he a hard case?"

"Them little girls wasn't dressed a bit swell—they was only in print frocks. My best dress ain't print—it's Jap. silk!"

"They lef' us lovely things. An' the man said they was our very own. I'm goin' to take my doll home to Myrtle when I go out!"

"They left brightness wherever they went," said little "Brown Eyes"—who was not usually poetical. "I'm not even tired to-night!"

In the boys' surgical ward, after the lights were out, there was still talking—it had been a great day, and excitement yet seethed. Little Tommy was silent. He had fallen asleep, one hand thrust beneath his pillow, where the watch had gone to sleep, too. The other hand held his new knife in a tight, hot clasp. There was the shadow of a smile on his thin little face. One might fancy that he had found his way to a Dream Country, where there were no crippled boys any more.

CHAPTER IV
GOING HOME

A land of open spaces,

Gaunt forest, treeless plain;

And if we once have loved it.

We must go back again.

—Dorothea Mackellar.

"WE haven't too much time," said Mr. Linton, looking at his watch.

The motor was standing before the door of the hotel. Norah and Jean were tucked into the back seat, knitting their brows over a lengthy shopping list. It was their last day in the city. Already, visions of Billabong and its welcome were making Norah seethe with an excitement that promised ill for the success of her purchases.

A clatter of feet upon the steps of the hotel, announced the arrival of Jim and Wally. They swung themselves on board; the chauffeur did mysterious things to the car, and in a moment they were gliding down Bourke Street. They crossed the Yarra over Princes Bridge, where, looking westward, the river seemed full of ships, and the wharves hummed like a hive of bees. A big inter-State liner was nosing her way gently up the centre of the stream, as if looking for an anchorage; they could see the passengers clustering on her decks, glad of the end of the journey. Something of the romance that never fails to cling about ships made the dingy old river beautiful.

"I remember," said Wally, dreamily, "many a time——"

"In your long-dead youth?" asked Jim.

"In the early Forties, he means," put in Mr. Linton. "Don't disturb his eloquence."

"My inborn respect for your father prevents my saying what I would like to both of you," said the victim. "Anyhow, I remember——"

"Full well," said Norah, with emotion.

"Oh, get out, you Linton tribe!" ejaculated the harassed one. "I'm talking to Jean."

"Why?" queried Jean, unexpectedly. Mirth ensued at the expense of Wally.

"Never mind, Wally, old man," said his host. "Mention what you remember."

"I've nearly forgotten it now," Wally answered, much aggrieved. "I believe I was pretty close to being poetical—that blessed old river always sets me thinking. Ever so many times I've landed there on a Monday morning, coming down from Brisbane; and I used to be such a homesick little shrimp. It was always a struggle to get off the old Bombala. I was great chums with the captain, and he made the old boat seem like a bit of home. Also, I never was sea-sick in her!"

"No wonder you loved her," said Jean, fervently. She shuddered, with painful recollections of the voyage from New Zealand.

"Oh, she's an old beauty—she can't roll, I believe," Wally answered. "Or if she can, she isn't let—so it's all the same. Anyway, I never liked leaving her and wending my lonely way down to school. There's the old shop now!"

They had swung round across St. Kilda Road, and were running up Alexandra Avenue—on one side the river, and on the other trim gardens leading towards the trees of the Domain and the massed green of the Botanical Gardens. Beyond— Wally had spoken more by faith than by sight—the grey stone of the Grammar School, mantled in ivy, stood lonely, bereft of its usual cheerful hordes. Nearer, Government House loomed up, its square tower crowned with a fluttering flag, silhouetted against the summer sky; and the Queen's Statue looked calmly towards the city. All the rocky slopes towards the gardens were clothed with creeping plants, now a sheet of vivid colour. A boy in a skiff was lazily pulling up-stream, his pale blue sweater a bright spot on the brown river; and motor boats were chugging gently down towards Melbourne, to lie off Princes Bridge. Across the stream a woman had come down to the water's edge and raised an imperious hail of "Ferry!" and in answer, a battered old boat was putting off from a little landing, sculled by a very ancient mariner. It was all very peaceful and leisurely—a sharp contrast to the other side of the bridge, where the crowded wharves and shipping made the river a busy place either by day or night.

They turned south presently, and were soon slowing down amid the traffic of Chapel Street—that lesser Melbourne where the shops are always crowded, and where there are inhabitants who have never found it necessary to take the four miles' journey into the city itself. Apparently it was the happy hunting ground of the baby. There were perambulators everywhere, propelled by busy suburban mothers, intent on bargain finding. Very often each perambulator held two babies, and perhaps a bigger child perched precariously upon a wooden step, and occasionally fell off. They all seemed well accustomed to shopping—the mothers had no fears about leaving them near the doorways while they sought the counters within. This frequently led to a glut of perambulators and a block in the traffic, and caused great wrath on the part of childless pedestrians—unavailing wrath, since the mothers were out of reach and the babies blissfully unconcerned. They ate biscuits contentedly, and favoured the world with a bland stare, except when their presence caused a disturbance of traffic, when they appeared to regard life as a stupendous joke, and laughed greatly. Norah found them very fascinating, and was with difficulty withdrawn from inspecting a cheerful pair of twins when the sterner necessities of shopping demanded her consideration.

To make Christmas purchases in a Christmas crowd is an exercise demanding patience and tact, coupled with more business acumen than is ordinarily the lot of the country-bred shopper. The Billabong tribe found their stock of all these admirable qualities running low long before their own vague desires were satisfied, together with Brownie's long list of commissions for the station. The shop was packed with busy people, each intent on errands like their own, and, apparently, in as great a hurry. Norah wondered if up-country express trains were waiting for them all, so wild and eager did they seem, and if she also looked as distraught; arriving at the conclusion that if she appeared as harassed as she felt she would certainly attract attention, even in that hurrying throng!

They parted company, since it was easier to work through the crowd singly than "to hunt in packs," as Wally put it; and after a time Norah emerged upon the pavement outside, a little breathless, her arms full of parcels. Behind her could be caught glimpses of the interior—a huge place, with tables and counters in every direction, behind which stood hot and tired assistants endeavouring to obtain the wants of twelve people at once. The shop seemed full of children. Upstairs was a big display of mechanical toys and other Christmas delights, and it seemed that half of younger Melbourne had been brought to see the fun by devoted mothers and aunts. In one corner a gentleman who might have been four was evidently mislaid by his guardians. He stood, a figure of bitter woe in a white sailor suit, rending the air with his howls; and a very tall and gorgeous shop walker, who bent double in an attempt to soothe him, was routed with great slaughter. Then, from afar, came the mother, thrusting her way ruthlessly through the crowd in answer to her son's voice. She had, presumably, heard those yells before. She gathered him up hurriedly, and withered the shop walker with a glance, clearly suspecting him of a wish to kidnap the lost one. The shop walker retreated, pondering on the ways of the world.

Near a counter devoted to what is vaguely known as haberdashery, Jean fought vainly for the right to purchase. Norah could catch an occasional glimpse of her square, blue-clad shoulders and the fair hair under her sailor hat. It was all too evident that she was not happy. People jostled her hither and thither, elbowing her away from the counter when it seemed that success was within her grasp. The assistants had no time for short people, when so many ladies, dressed like the Queen of Sheba, demanded their attention. Jean was not a pushing person, and only a person of push had any hope of catching the eye of the presiding goddesses. So she fought unavailingly, and Norah watched her, half in laughter and half in doubt as to whether she should go to her assistance.

From another part of the shop appeared Wally, shot out of the crowd in the manner of a stone from a catapult. He was propelled past Norah, tucked into a corner of the doorway, where she was out of the way of the throng that met in the entrance, fighting with equal vigour for exit and admittance. Seeing him thus fleeting from her vision, Norah gave a low and wholly involuntary whistle—and was forthwith overcome with confusion at her unmaidenly behaviour. Wally, however, was not given to criticism. He accepted the signal gratefully, and turned back.

"Thank goodness you whistled!" he uttered, pushing his straw hat off his forehead. "I'd never have found you if you hadn't. Great Scot, Nor., did you ever see anything like it!"

"Never," said Norah, fervently. "Is it always like this?"

"Pretty well—when it's near Christmas. There ought to be a law to make people who can shop early finish by the middle of December—then they'd leave a little space for poor wretches like us, who don't get away from school. Thank goodness, I'm about done—though I don't in the least know what I've bought. How about you?"

"Finished," said Norah, with brief thankfulness.

"Well, you ought to be," said Wally, surveying her load. "Women were given eight fingers and two thumbs, so that they could hang parcels on each! I think you've done pretty well, young Norah. Where's Jean?"

"Oh, Jean's having a horrible time!" Norah answered, much concerned for the fate of her chum. "I wish you'd go and see if you could help her, Wally—you see, she's so short, and she can't get fixed up. I'll hold your parcels."

"I feel like a knight errant," said Wally, handing over many bundles. "It takes no common order of courage to tackle that maëlstrom after having escaped from it once. However, with a damsel in distress it's got to be, I suppose. Sure you can hold 'em all, Nor.? Where is the hapless wight I've to rescue?"

"She's over there—you can get glimpses of her hat," Norah said. "At the haberdashery place."

"I've always wondered what that meant," Wally said. "It's got a sporting sort of sound about it, hasn't it? Now, I'll find out, I suppose, and probably my young illusions will be dashed to the ground—it really sounds the kind of place to buy polo sticks, but I don't fancy that's Jean's business. Well, here goes! Oh, by Jove! She's coming, Norah!"

Jean came, very red and indignant, with a knitted brow.

"I've had a perfectly awful time!" she gasped. "There isn't an unbruised bit of me! And I can't get what I want—I've been trying for ages to buy a belt buckle, and all the horrid woman has sold me is curling pins!" She held out a small parcel tragically. "And I don't even use them!" she finished—whereat her hearers shrieked unsympathetically.

"Oh, Wally, go and make them take them back," Norah begged, recovering calmness. "Go with him, Jean, and show him the buckle you want—he'll manage it."

"Not for me, thank you," said her chum decisively. "I wouldn't plunge in there for forty-eight buckles! I'll go to another shop and try. What am I going to do with those horrible pins? They were sixpence!"

"They mustn't be wasted," said Wally, with solemn joy. "I'll buy 'em from you, Jean, and put 'em in Jim's sock for Christmas. He'll be so pleased!" He pocketed the pins and repossessed himself of his own parcels. "I'd never have had the pluck to go and buy those things," he said, "but the beautiful instinct of friendship tells me that they're the articles for which my soul has longed for Jimmy!"

"Take care—he's coming!" Norah laughed. They greeted Jim with an air of innocence that would certainly have failed to deceive any one less heated and annoyed than that worthy.

"What a place to be out of!" he ejaculated. "And some people go shopping for fun! Where's Dad?"

"Coming," Norah said, watching her father's tall head in the crowd. "He likes it about as much as you do, Jimmy, judging by his expression." She smiled at Mr. Linton as he fought his way up to them. "Ready, Dad?"

"Yes, thank goodness!" said her father. "Come along—here's the car. Now, there's a poor soul!"

He stopped, looking at a little crippled hunchback in a wheeled chair; a boy who might have been any age, from child to man, so small was he, and yet so old and weary his face. He was gazing wistfully at the gay little group round the big motor. A tray of matches lay across his knees; tied to the arm of his chair was a cluster of many-coloured balloons—a pitiful contrast to the dull hopelessness of his face. Jim whistled softly.

"Poor little wretch," he said. "Can't we buy him out, Dad?"

"We'll do our best—even if the populace thinks we're the advance agents of a circus!" replied Mr. Linton. "Go and buy his balloons, Norah."

"What—all of them, Dad?"

"Yes—all of them."

He followed her across the footpath. The hunchback looked up at the grave little face.

"Balloons?" he said, half sullenly. "How many—two?"

"I want them all," Norah told him, smiling.

"Not—the whole lot!" A dull red came into the boy's white face.

"Yes, we do. My father says so."

He stared at her, bewildered.

"There—there ain't many days I sell more'n five or six all told," he said. His voice shook a little. "You ain't havin' a loan of me, I s'pose?"

"No, indeed I'm not—truly," Norah said, pitifully. "We're going to buy you out."

The boy began to unfasten the string with uncertain fingers.

"Nothin' like this ain't happened to me before," he said. "It's—it's a bit of a slow game sittin' here all day, hot or cold—an' people starin' at you. I wouldn't mind 'em so much not buyin'—but—but they look at a cove. You're sure you want the lot?"

"Yes, I want them," Norah answered—"if you're sure you can spare them all."

"Spare 'em!" he laughed. "Why, I'll be nex' door to a millionaire, bringin' off a sale like this!" He gave the string into her hand and looked at the money Mr. Linton dropped into his match tray.

"No—I say!" he said. "That's too much, sir. Can't you get change?"

"No, thanks," Mr. Linton said, with a smile. "Good-bye, my lad. Come on, Norah."

"Good-bye," Norah said. Near the car she suddenly turned back, fishing hurriedly in her little purse. The boy looked up at her with a dazed face of joy.

"Happy Christmas!" she said. She put a shilling into his hand—and fled. The car glided off into the jumble of traffic.

The hunchback sat in his corner throughout the day, selling a box of matches now and then. The busy crowds went back and forth past him, casting curious or pitying glances at his deformity. For once, the glances did not hurt him. Norah's smile yet lay warm at his heart.

"Said 'Happy Chris'mas!' she did," he muttered. "I don't believe she never even saw me back!"

The balloons proved rather exciting to the crowd until the next block in the traffic gave Mr. Linton an opportunity to present them gravely to a gaping urchin with the immediate result that his gape intensified alarmingly, and threatened to become a permanent fixture. Then they sped back to the city, with hasty visits here and there, to pick up parcels, and a hurried attempt at afternoon tea in the crowded lounge of the hotel. Their luggage was awaiting them, a big pile in the corridor, and presently it was loaded into a cab, and the motor was following it up the street towards the train.

At the big station they found themselves in another crowd—a hurrying, impatient crowd, armed with suit cases and dress baskets, and pursuing harassed luggage porters with incoherent instructions regarding trunks that appeared non-existent. Nobody had the slightest regard for anybody else—to get through the throng was to court death-dealing blows from the sharp corners of luggage, delivered with vehemence and without apology. Bells rang continually, with distressing effect upon would-be passengers, who ran very fast in divers directions at each ring, imagining it to be the final summons to trains which were very likely not even backed into the platform! Porters shouted instructions, very much in earnest, but wholly unintelligible. The shrieks of newsboys added to the clamour, together with the wails of many babies, protesting against travelling so early in life. Wild-eyed mothers clutched at wandering children, endeavouring frantically to keep them under the maternal wing. Beyond, in the station yard, engines whistled shrilly and shunting trains banged and rattled.

"It's a nice Christmassy place!" said Wally, surveying the scene. "Makes you feel no end festive, doesn't it? If you two girls hold each other's hands tightly, cling to my coat tails, and utter frequent bleats, it is possible that we shan't lose you!"

"Just take care that you don't get lost yourself," Jim uttered. "A trifle like you straying about in a crowd ought to have a bell on its neck. Take Dad's arm, won't you?"

"He'd better not," said Mr. Linton, hurriedly. "I could employ more arms than I've got, as it is." His eye, roving over the throng, caught sight of a familiar face. "Ah, there's my porter!" he said, with relief, as that functionary hastened up. "That's right, Saunders—bring another man with you. Now we needn't worry—our compartment's reserved." He sat down on an empty luggage truck and mopped his brow. "Give me Billabong!"

Then, somehow, they were all on board, the carriage overflowing with miscellaneous bundles; and presently the train was slipping out of the station, and leaving the suburban roofs behind as the wide spaces and green paddocks came in view. Further and further, until the sun went down in a red sky and the short Australian twilight faded to dusk and a star-lit night.

Norah grew a little silent. She leaned back, her shoulder against her father's, glad of his nearness: all the dear voices of the country calling to her, above the roar and rush of the train. The memory of her long homesickness came over her with a rush. She could scarcely realize that it was over, and Billabong drawing near. Until a year ago Billabong had meant all her world—all that counted. Now she had a wider horizon. But still home and home's dear ones dwarfed all the rest.

Then it was time to collect parcels hurriedly. The train stopped with a great grinding of brakes, and they all tumbled out upon the Cunjee platform. It was only a little place; the train seemed to pause just to shake itself free of them, and then it puffed away into the darkness; and Norah was pumping the hand of a big sunburnt man with a wide smile of welcome.

"Oh, Murty, I'm so glad to be back!"

"It is Billabong that's glad to have ye," said Murty O'Toole, head stockman, and Norah's friend from her cradle. "Blessed hour! Ye've grown into a young lady, so ye have."

"Indeed I haven't," said Norah indignantly. "I'm just the same. Isn't it true, Jim?"

"She's worse, Murty," said her brother, laughing. "No signs of improvement. She's lost all respect for me. It's very trying."

"Ah, g'wan wid y'!" said the Irishman. "I'll tell y' about him to-morrow, Miss Norah—wanderin' about for the last week like a lost foal, makin' believe he was puttin' on extry polish for ye! There's the dog-cart, sir"—to Mr. Linton—"an' another trap for the luggage."

"We'll need it!" said Mr. Linton dryly. "Miss Norah doesn't travel as light as she used to, Murty." He pulled his daughter's hair. Murty, however, remained unmoved.

"An' how could she?" he inquired. "Ye can't have her growin' up on y' an' expect her to go about wid a collar an' a toothbrush!"

Mr. Linton sighed.

"I don't know how much discipline they gave Norah at school, Jean," he said—"but she's sure to want an extra allowance next year, after the spoiling I foresee she's to get at home. I appear to be the only person likely to keep her in order—and what am I among so many? Neither do I see why the statement should move either of you to such ribald mirth! Here's Billy, and I hope he'll be stern."

But the black boy who held the horses was a grinning image of delight. He did not attempt to make any remarks; not, Jim said, that they were in any way necessary. You could not get beyond Billy's grin. Even the stationmaster came up with a word of welcome.

"It's very exciting—getting home," Norah said.

Then they were in the high dog-cart; Jean and herself tucked into the front seat beside her father, while the boys made merry at the back. The brown cobs were making light of the fourteen-mile spin along the country roads that were all so dear and so familiar. It was beautiful to be behind them once more—to see their splendid heads tossing the jingling bits, and their glossy quarters gleaming in the light of the lamps. Yet it seemed long until they turned into the homestead paddock—and then the mile drive, fringed with pine trees, was the longest of all.

Lights flashed out ahead as they turned a corner; Billabong, every window shining with welcome. And at the gate was a smiling group, and every one seemed to want to shake hands with her at the same moment. But behind them was Mrs. Brown, her old face half laughter and half tears, and speech wholly beyond her. She held out shaking arms to the tall girl who had been her baby for so long, and Norah went to them, hugging her tightly—not very sure of speech herself. It was not every day that one came home to Billabong.

" 'You ain't havin' a loan of me, I s'pose?' "

CHAPTER V
WALLY
But when the world went wild with Spring

What days we had! Do you forget?

—V. J. Daley.

BEFORE the homestead the lawn stretched smoothly away, its green expanse broken here and there by a gay flower bed or a mass of shrubbery. Tall palms tossed their feathery heads aloft, above lower growing roses and tumbling masses of creepers. The mellow brick of the house itself was half concealed beneath a mantle of ivy and Virginia creeper, while, on the verandah posts, masses of tecoma and bougainvillæa made a blaze of colour. Beyond the garden fence the water of the lagoon could be seen—a blue gleam, studded with lazily swimming waterfowl. Further off, the yellow grass seemed to tremble under a mist of shimmering heat.

Jim came in from the paddocks, welcoming the silent coolness of the house after the blazing sun of the parched outer world. No one was visible in any of the rooms into which he poked an inquiring head. Finally the sound of Wally's laugh guided him to the side verandah, and he made his way thither through the French windows of the breakfast-room.

It was always cool on the side verandah after the morning sun had considerately mounted so high that a great pine tree flung its shade across that part of the house. The verandah was very wide, with a low trellis fencing it in from the lawn. Just now its lattice work was covered with nasturtiums and sweet peas, which even sent intrusive tendrils creeping across the red tiles of the floor. On the posts hung clusters of climbing roses, so thick that all the verandah seemed a bower, the green of the garden blending with the ferns that were planted in tubs here and there. Rugs lay on the tiles, and here were tables, littered with books and magazines, and big rush easy chairs and lounges, made more inviting by red cushions. Altogether, the side verandah was a pleasant place, and the Billabong folk were accustomed to spend a great deal of time there in the summer days and the long, hot evenings.

Norah and Jean were at present occupying a wide lounge, the former curled up in a corner, sewing violently at a rent in one of Jim's white coats, while Jean spread herself over the remaining portion, with a book in her hand, to which she was paying very little attention. Wally, at full length on another couch, was discoursing on many topics, in his own cheerful way, to the huge delight of Mrs. Brown, whose affection for him was unbounded. A huge bowl of peas was in her lap, and Wally was resting after the fatigue of assisting her to shell them.

"Here's old Jimmy!" he said, as Jim's long form came through the French window. "You look warm, old man. Have this couch, won't you?"

"Couldn't think of turning you out, old chap," Jim answered grinning.

"I was always a beggar to struggle," said Wally, thankfully settling himself anew. "Fearful visions were in my mind of how I should bear it if you should accept my heroic offer. Is it warm outside, Jim?"

"Warm!" said Jim, briefly expressive. He dropped into an easy chair, carefully casting the cushions far from him—cushions not being part of his creed. "It's a fierce day. I don't envy Dad and the men, tailing into Cunjee behind those cattle."

"Did you go far with them, Jim?" Norah asked.

"No—only to the second gate. They didn't need me at all; only Dad wanted to give me directions about some bullocks he wants moved. We'll have to do that presently, Wal."

"Certainly," said Wally, affably. "Judging by my feelings just now, I don't think I'll be alive presently, so I can promise without any trouble. Are there many, James, and is it far?"

"Only two, worse luck," Jim answered. "Two can generally be relied upon to give more trouble than two hundred. It isn't far, but you can be pretty certain that they'll make it far."

"Cheerful brute you are!" Wally ejaculated. "Well, I'm ready any time you are, old man, though I think it would be kind to the cattle not to disturb them until the cool of the evening!"

"I like your kind forethought for the bullocks," Jim told him, laughing. "They'd appreciate it, I know. You'll end up as a philanthropist, if you're not careful, Wally. Unfortunately we've a job with the sheep for the time you mention, so the cattle must come first—it's very certain that we wouldn't get a move out of the sheep just now."

Wally sighed heavily.

"It's a laborious life I lead," he said, stretching his long limbs on the couch. "I come up here with beautiful hopes of getting fat, and I always go back about two stone lighter. Norah, I wish you wouldn't sew so hard; it makes a fellow ache to see you."

"Jim will ache if this coat isn't ready," said Norah, stitching vigorously. "His coats are in a dreadful state—there isn't one cool one that doesn't need mending. As far as Brownie and I can tell he seems to have locked them away carefully whenever he tore them. Why did you do it, Jimmy?"

"An' me ready an' willin' as ever was to mend 'em," Brownie said; "an' now Miss Norah's doin' of it, poor lamb! Why did you, Master Jim?"

"Blessed if I know," said Jim, somewhat embarrassed. "I didn't know the jolly things weren't all right. Sorry—but it's ripping practice for you, Nor., all the same. You can tell old Miss Winter I kept you up to the mark with your needle!"

"M-f!" said Norah, with much scorn in the terse remark. "In the circumstances, Brownie, does he deserve a cool drink?"

"He don't, but I expect he'll have to get it," said Brownie, laughing. She rose with the deliberate majesty that pertains to seventeen stone. "There's a new brew of lemonade coolin' in the cellar, and I'll bring a jug along."

"Bless you, Brownie, you're my best friend," said Jim. "You needn't bring any for the others—they haven't earned it."

"Haven't I!" said Wally, indignantly. "Why, I've shelled peas until my brain reeled! And I believe it's hotter to be inside on a day like this than out in the paddocks, so you needn't be superior, James." He stretched himself, letting one brown hand fall on the railing of the verandah. "I don't think——"

He broke off suddenly, twisted himself off the lounge, and was on his feet with one quick movement. Jim's stock whip dangled from the arm of his chair; Wally snatched it and struck furiously at a lithe form that slid off the railing with a sinuous wriggle, and fell to the ground beneath. The boy vaulted over the trellis as it fell, and thrashed violently among the nasturtiums below. It was all done so quickly that the others were scarcely on their feet before he hooked the still writhing body of a black snake out of the creepers, and tossed it out on to the lawn.

"You didn't lose much time, young Wally!" said Jim, approvingly. "Fancy that brute getting up here! Lucky you spotted him."

" 'M," said Wally. Something in his tone made Norah swing round sharply.

"Wally! He didn't bite you?"

"He did then," said Wally. Something of the colour had died out of his tanned face, but his voice was steady.

"Old man!" said Jim. Then he shut his lips tightly, and dived into his pocket for his knife.

Wally took the verandah steps in one stride, and was beside him.

"I'll do the chopping," he said. "Lend me that, old chap. Is it sharp?"

Jim nodded.

"Slip round to Brownie," he said, sharply, to Norah. "She knows where the permanganate is—there's some in the store, and some in the office." Norah's racing feet sounded in the hall almost before he had spoken, and he turned back to his chum.

"Would you rather do it, old man?" he asked.

Wally nodded, without speaking. There were two punctures plainly visible on the lean hand he steadied on the verandah rail.

"Parallel cuts," said Jim. "Quick, Wal." He flung a hasty command over his shoulder to Jean. "The men are at the stables—tell them I want the dog-cart with the cobs, as hard as they can tear!"

The knife was razor-edged, and Wally did not flinch. He cut deep and quickly, the blood spurting in the track of the blade. Jim was already busy with a ligature on his arm, tightening it with a stick twisted almost to breaking point. As the last cut went home, and Wally put down the knife, Jim caught his hand and bent down to it. Wally uttered a sharp exclamation, struggling.

"Get out, you old idiot! I'll suck my own blessed hand!"

He tried to wrench his hand away, but the grasp on his wrist was iron. Jim's lips were on the wound, sucking it furiously.

"Oh, Lord, I wish you wouldn't!" said Wally, miserably. "I can do it perfectly well myself; and you may have a scratch about your mouth. For goodness sake, stop it, old man! What's the good of two of us getting the dose?"

Jim, being otherwise engaged, did not answer. He continued his operations strenuously, deaf to Wally's entreaties, until Norah came flying back with Brownie in the rear.

"Here are the crystals, Jim!"

The boy caught at the little bottle. Then he saw Brownie's distressed face, and gave them to her.

"You get 'em ready," he said, briefly. "I'll go on sucking for a moment. Hurry the men, Norah!"

Almost by the time the permanganate crystals were worked into a paste and rubbed into the cut about the punctures, the horses were in the stable yard. Every man on Billabong liked the merry Queensland boy—there were willing hands at every buckle of the harness that was flung upon the brown cobs in breathless haste. The dog-cart, with Murty O'Toole on the box, clattered to the front of the house— to the little group that had been so merry when the shadow of death had suddenly fell upon it.

Wally's face was a little strained. The tightness of the ligature was telling upon him, more than the snake bite itself. But he grinned up at Murty in his old way.

"I'm giving you plenty of trouble, Murty," he said. "Silly ass, to go patting a snake at my time of life!"

"Begob, it might happen to the owldest of us," said Murty, consolingly. "Ye have that bandage tied tight, Mr. Jim?"

"He has that!" said Wally, ruefully. "Don't you worry about Jim when it comes to tying a ligature. My hand will drop off soon, I should say!"

"Y'can have it loosened just f'r a minute, presently," said Murty. "Whin it's been on half an hour it's due f'r a spell. Begob, I'll bet it hurts y', me boy!"

"Oh—some," said Wally, briefly. He glanced at his hand, swollen and purple under the bandage Brownie had wrapped about the part that had been bitten. "Pretty looking object, isn't it? Well, I do think I was a chump! That beggar must have been lying along the rail for ever so long!"

"Y' had no business to go killin' it before ye attinded to y'r hand," said Murty. "Much better have let him get away on us than wait. Never mind, there ain't much time lost, an' y'r as healthy as a rabbit. We'll have y' right as rain in no time."

"Oh, I guess so," said Wally. Then Jim came plunging out, Norah and Jean at his heels.

"Here's your hat, old man," Jim said, clapping it on its owner's head. "The girls are coming in with us. Hurry along—we don't want to lose any time." He made as though to help his chum into the dog-cart, and Wally grinned at him.

"What are you after?" he asked, swinging himself up with one hand. "I'm not a dead man yet. Come on, you old nursemaid!" He waved his hat cheerily to Brownie, whose kind old face was working with anxiety. "Don't go worrying, Brownie—I'll be back for tea! May I have pikelets if I'm a good boy?"

"You'll have everything I can make for you," said poor Brownie, tears in her eyes as she looked at the merry, defiant face. "Only come back all right, my dear!" Murty gave the cobs their heads, and they shot down the drive. It was but fifteen minutes from the moment Wally had put his hand on the black intruder lying along the railing of the trellis.

A man was waiting at each gate; there was no delay of opening and shutting. Murty swung the horses through the narrow openings, shaving gateposts by a hair's breadth, but never slackening speed. Out on the road, the brown cobs felt the unaccustomed indignity of the whip on their backs, and resented it by trying to bolt; but the hand on their mouths was rigid, and they came back from a gallop to a flying trot, that spun over the long miles to Cunjee. The shining tyres flashed in the sunlight. Now and then sparks flew from flints hard smitten by the racing, iron-shod hoofs.

Wally kept up a plucky attempt at chatter for awhile. Then he grew silent, nursing his swollen arm in a fruitless effort to relieve the agony caused by the checked circulation. Jim loosened the ligature momentarily, after a time, and the relief was great; but it had to be tightened again, and gradually the boy's set lips grew white. Once he spoke, in a low voice.

"I say, old chap," he said. "If things go wrong, you'll let them know all about it up at home, won't you? Tell 'em it was all my own stupidity."

"You shut up," returned Jim, gruffly. "Things aren't going wrong—we've got you in loads of time."

"Oh, I know. I'm not expecting them to," Wally answered. "Still, there's the chance. Don't forget, old Stick-in-the-mud." He pulled Norah's hair gently, and demanded to know why she was so quiet. "Something unusual to have you civil for so long at a stretch!" he told her, laughing—to which Norah tried to make a cheerful retort, but choked instead, and averred that she had swallowed a fly.

"Hard lines on the fly!" said Wally. "See—there's your father!"

He pointed ahead to a blur of dust on the track, which resolved itself into Mr. Linton and two men, riding slowly behind some cattle. Murty glanced over his shoulder at the same instant.

"Will I pull up, Mr. Jim?"

"Just for a moment," Jim said, hesitating. "Dad won't want much of an explanation."

Not much was needed. The racing hoofs and the grave faces told their own story, as Mr. Linton checked his horse beside the road. Jim was brief, in answer to his father's hasty question.

"What's wrong?"

"Snake," he said. "He got Wally on the hand. We're off to Dr. Anderson."

"You've done all you can, of course?" Mr. Linton asked quickly.

"Yes—everything. Haven't lost any time, either."

"Well, Anderson's not there," Mr. Linton said. "I saw his motor going out along the Mulgoa road half an hour ago. But go in; Mrs. Anderson may know what to do, or where to send for him. Murty can go for him. Meanwhile, I'll see if I can catch him now; there's no knowing where he may have pulled up. You've got stimulants?"

"Two Thermos flasks of strong black coffee," Norah said.

"That's right. Don't wait. Keep up your pecker, Wally, my boy." The big man smiled at Wally affectionately. "We'll have you all right soon, my dear lad."

"I guess it'll take a tough snake to kill me," Wally answered. "I'm all serene, sir." The buggy whirled away again as Mr. Linton wheeled his horse and went off at a hard gallop.

"Jove, old Monarch can travel!" said Wally, approvingly. A jolt shook his swollen hand, and his lips tightened again.

Mrs. Anderson could give but a vague idea of her husband's movements, nor was there any one in the township able to do more to help the patient. Murty dashed off on a fresh horse in search of the doctor; and the four from Billabong sat in the shade of a big oak tree and tried to talk—three watching covertly all the time for any new symptoms on Wally's part. After a while his eyes grew heavy, and Norah brought a flask of coffee, strong and black, and dosed him at short intervals. The boy made a brave fight to help them.

"This won't do," he said, after a while. "I'll be asleep in five minutes if I stay here. Get a pack of cards and we'll play cribbage."

They played on a rug in the shade—Jim and Jean against Norah and Wally, the latter playing with one hand and occasionally cracking a laborious joke, almost in the midst of which his head would nod to one side. He always recovered himself with a jerk, and, despite his drowsiness, he played with a keen quickness that shamed the others, who made the most egregious mistakes with a total lack of concern as to their score. It was long before Norah could ever again bear the sight of a cribbage board.

Jim flung down his cards at last, his voice shaking.

"Well, I can't stand this," he said. "Hang that man! Will he ever come? Let's walk up and down, Wal., old man."

They went up and down, up and down, along the garden path, in the hot air, heavy with the scent of the doctor's flowers—all the time fighting the fatal drowsiness that threatened to overcome the boy they loved. Mrs. Anderson kept the supply of coffee ready, and Wally took it obediently whenever it was brought to him.

"If this blessed hand would only let me do anything, I'd be all right," he said sleepily. "I'd give something to be able to use an axe! Norah, asthore, will you stick hatpins into me if I get any more stupid? I'm not going to sleep, if I have to stick them into myself!"

Then, just as they were becoming sick with anxiety and the long watching, came the far-off hum of a hurrying car, and presently little Dr. Anderson swung round the corner, pulled up with a sudden jar that would ordinarily have caused him extreme wrath, and came through his garden at a run. He cast a swift professional eye over Wally.

"Good children!" he said, approvingly. "Come along to the surgery, my boy; you, too, Jim. You girls go and let the wife take care of you."

But Norah could not talk to any one just then. The long strain had been too heavy a burden. She watched the three figures vanish within the surgery door, the doctor's hand on Wally's shoulder, and then turned and went blindly down a winding path. It ended in a fence. She put her head down upon it, swallowing hard, dry sobs. Jean put an arm round her, silent. There was not anything to say.

Within the surgery Wally had faced the little doctor.

"I say, sir," he said, moistening dry lips, "you won't let me make a fool of myself if things get a bit beyond me, will you?"

"I will not," said the doctor, sturdily. "But they won't—don't talk nonsense!" He was unwrapping the hand swiftly. "Catch this bottle, Jim."

Very long after—so it seemed to Norah and Jean—a quick step came down the path behind them.

"Your nice brown lad is all right," said Mrs. Anderson, happily. "Jack says there's no risk now. Everything was done in time. We'll keep him here to-night, just to watch him, and Jim will stay with him. Mr. Linton is waiting for you two lassies; and you can come back to-morrow, and take Wally home for Christmas. Unless you like to leave him with me for a month or so? I like that boy!"

"So does Billabong," said David Linton's voice, not quite steady. "We can't spare him to any one, can we, Norah?"

Norah shook her head. She clung to her father's hand as they went back to the house, where Jim waited on the verandah, his face still grave.

"The patient sends his love, and you're none of you to worry," he said. "And you're to tell Brownie to keep the pikelets for to-morrow!"

"Wally snatched it and struck furiously at a lithe form that slid off the railing with a sinuous wriggle, and fell to the ground beneath."

CHAPTER VI
THE CUNJEE CONCERT
And stirrup to stirrup we'll sing as we ride,

To the lights of the township that glimmer and guide.

—W. H. Ogilvie.

THEY should be home, Murty," said David Linton.

"They shud," said Mr. O'Toole, with conviction. He removed an exceedingly black pipe from his mouth and stared at it, pressing the tobacco down in the bowl with a broad thumb. "Will I be saddlin' up a horse, do ye think, an' takin' afther them?"

"Not a bit of good," said the squatter. "They may come home by any of three or four roads. I'd go myself if I were sure." He knitted his brow, staring down the twilit track. "I don't understand it—Mr. Jim is never late."

"Sure, they're young," said Murty, and propped his long form comfortably against a tree. "Ye can't never be tellin' what the young'll be after whin they gets out wid a loose leg, like. An' Mr. Jim's level-headed enough. I wud not be worryin'."

"Mr. Jim should know better than to be away so late," said Jim's father, sharply. "It's nearly nine o'clock—and they should have been in for dinner at half-past six. Wonder do they think a woman has nothing to do but keep dinner hot for them! At any rate, I've told Mrs. Brown she's not to keep anything. They can manage with bread and cheese if they can't be in in decent time!"

"Niver did I see the ould man in such a tear!" confided Murty, a little later, to Mrs. Brown—who, in flagrant defiance of instructions, was brooding over preparations for a large and satisfactory supper for the absentees. "Him that aisy-goin' as a rule, an' niver lettin' a cross word out of him—an' he's walkin' up an' down like a caged elephint, fairly rampin'. 'Tis anxious he is—that's the throuble."

"Well may he be," said Mrs. Brown, tearfully. "That new pony of Miss Norah's is that flighty and excitable—an' he's big an' strong, too, an' I know for two pins he'd buck! See him when they went off this mornin'—fit to jump out of his skin, an' dancin' little jigs all the way down the track. It's enough to make anybody anxious."

"P——f!" said Murty, with great scorn. "Miss Norah can manage Bosun as aisy as shellin' peas. There's no vice in him, nayther; he's as kind a pony as iver I throwed a leg over. Ye'd not have the little misthress ridin' an old crock?"

"I'm sure I don't know," said poor Brownie. "I never could make meself feel 'eroic where Miss Norah's concerned. All very well to be proud of her ridin' an' all that—an' you men are fair foolish over that sort of thing—but give me the contented mind as is a continual feast! An' I would feel contenteder if she rode something a little less like a jumpin'-jack than Bosun."

"That pony do be suitin' Miss Norah down to the ground," averted Murty. "Sure, 'twas something to see her face whin she caught sight of him first; an' she's that proud of him already. I did not think anny pony would ever do as well for her as poor ould Bobs, but——"

"Miss Norah'll never love a pony like she loved Bobs," Brownie said, belligerently.

"No—maybe not. But Bosun'll run him close, an' he'll carry her real well until she's growed up," Murty answered. "Sure, he's not far off fifteen hands, for all they call him a pony. An' as for worryin' about her ridin' him, Mrs. Brown, ma'am—well, ye may as well save y'r own feelin's."

"Well, I wish they were all home, that's all," said Brownie. "It mightn't be Miss Norah—there's Miss Jean, too."

"Sure, that one can take care of herself," Murty said, laughing. "She ain't one of them as talks; but I guess she won't go fallin' off on us, for all that. An' Nan is as safe a mare as there is on Billabong."

"Now, I heard you say Nan could shy!" retorted Brownie, whose soul refused to be led in ways of comfort.

"I'd not give y' a ha'penny for the horse that couldn't," said Murty, unblushingly. "Wud ye have them all rockin' horses? But Miss Jean can ride her all right. Now, wud ye be after suggestin' that it's Garryowen as'll sling Mr. Jim, or ould Warder that's goin' to market wid Mr. Wally? Ye pays y'r money an' takes y'r choice!"

"You get out!" said Brownie gloomily. "All very well for you to stand there grinnin' at me like a Cheshire cheese—but the master's as anxious as I am, an' it's no wonder! An' I would bet sixpence, Murty, me fine lad, that down inside you you're pretty anxious too!"

"Bosh!" said Murty, looking slightly confused. The sounds of hoofs saved him from further defence. He turned to the kitchen doorway with sufficient quickness to justify Brownie's accusation.

" 'Tis the Boss," he said, in tones of disappointment. "I'd thought 'twas thim young ones comin' up the thrack. Tare an' ages! he's lettin' ould Monarch out! Why wudn't he be lettin' me go, whin I asked him, I wonder? Well——" He pondered a moment, and strolled away. Five minutes later Brownie, looking out hurriedly at hearing again the sound of hoofs on the gravel of the track, saw him cantering off in the wake of his master.

"Why on earth am I seventeen stone?" queried Brownie, desperately, of the ambient air. Receiving no adequate response, she retreated to the kitchen and wept a little into her apron; then, realizing the futility of grief, roused herself to action and made scones of a lightness almost ephemeral. It was some relief to her surcharged feelings.

Christmas had come and gone, and it was New Year's eve. Summer was ruling in earnest; day after day saw the sun rise like a golden disc, to be molten brass during the long, breathless day, and finally sink into a lurid sky, a ball of liquid fire. The grass dried rapidly; paddocks that had been green when Norah and Jean came from Melbourne were now waving expanses of yellow. Rumours of bush fires all over the country districts filled the newspapers.

Despite the heat, Billabong was doing its best for its visitors. Wally's adventure was almost forgotten by the victim himself, since he had suffered no further effects from the snake bite than a rather sore hand—due, Jim said, to poor carving. No one seemed to mind the temperature much. When the thermometer was trying to eclipse all previous records, the house was always a cool refuge; or there was the lagoon, where the boat rocked sleepily in the shade of the willows; or the tree-fringed banks of the creek, where no intrusive sun rays ever penetrated. Besides, there was so much to do that there really seemed little time to think of the weather; long days out in the paddocks with the cattle, mustering, or drafting, or cutting out; boundary riding, to make sure that fences were in good order and gates secure; fishing expeditions, rides to neighbouring stations, and long, delicious bathes in the lagoon, which in themselves made the heat seem worth while. Jim had established a jumping ground during his year at home—a paddock near the homestead, where a couple of log fences and some brush hurdles made an excellent training ground for the horses. Brownie used to stand on the balcony, torn betwixt pride and anxiety, watching the four riders sailing over the jumps—with sometimes a fifth, when Mr. Linton could persuaded to add Monarch, his black thoroughbred, to the starters. The boys entertained visions of a general hurdle race, for which the entries should include Lee Wing, the Chinese gardener, on an ancient piebald mare entitled Bung Eye, and Hogg, his sworn foe, on a lean mule that was popularly supposed to be capable of kicking the eye out of a mosquito. They even planned to enter Mrs. Brown, and declared their intention of training her on Blossom, a Clydesdale mare of great antiquity. In this ambition it is perhaps unnecessary to state that they had not the support of Mrs. Brown.

To-day the quartette had ridden into Cunjee, somewhat against their inclination. As a rule the township made small appeal to them; they greatly preferred the freedom of the paddocks and the wide galloping-places of the plains. On the station, where play included work and responsibility, there was never any dullness; the interests of each day claimed them, giving even the girls a definite share in the daily business. It was the life to which Norah had always been accustomed, and which she loved with every fibre of her energetic being. That Jim and Wally should care for it was a matter of course; to them also it was a part of life. It had been added joy to find that Jean took to it with a zest little, if anything, inferior to her own. Nothing was wanting, in Norah's eyes, to complete the perfection of holidays and Billabong.

The necessity of despatching a telegram had caused the expedition to Cunjee; somewhat deplored by the boys, since they were reluctantly compelled to don coats, to which they strenuously objected in the hot weather, and to find hats of a more respectable appearance than the battered felt head gear they habitually wore. They rode away after an early lunch; four cheery figures, alike in white linen coats and Panama hats, the brims turned down to keep the sun glare from their eyes; turning at the bend in the track to wave farewell to Mr. Linton, who stood at the gate to watch them go.

Cunjee was found gasping with heat, and only mildly consoled by the fact that no such temperatures had been recorded in the memory of man.

"Now, I always think that's quite a help," Jean said. "Once it's 100° in the shade you feel almost as bad as you're going to feel—and you might just as well have the satisfaction of knowing you had every excuse for being hot, because it was 114°. That makes it so interesting that you forget to be sorry for yourself!"

"I like to hear you, New Zealand!" quoth Wally, with fine scorn. "Didn't know you ever worked up much of a temperature in those Antarctic islands of yours!"

"Well, we aren't exactly singed into chips, like the Queenslanders!" said Jean, mildly, amidst mirth on the part of Norah and Jim—while Wally, who hailed from the vicinity of the Gulf of Carpentaria, looked modestly unconscious. "But we can be just as warm as we want to be."

"Well, Cunjee is warmer than I appreciate," Jim said. "Let's leave the horses at the hotel to get a feed, and we'll go and beg afternoon tea from Mrs. Anderson."

Mrs. Anderson greeted the invasion enthusiastically.

"So lovely of you to come," she said. "I've been feeling ever so dull. And now you've come, you must stay. The doctor has had to go to Mulgoa, and may not be back to-night; and I want an escort for the concert."

"Is there a concert?" Norah asked.

"Didn't you know? Ah, well, I suppose you irresponsible people don't read the local paper," said their hostess, pouring out tea. "Cream, Wally? No? How ridiculous of you, and you so thin! Yes, we're to have a tremendous concert. I forget what it's in aid of, but it's mainly local talent, and so it's bound to be exciting. And I can't go by myself, and it's quite too hot to go out and find a companion. Personally, I think Providence has delivered you into my hands!"

"Afraid we can't, thanks very much, Mrs. Anderson," Jim told her. "We didn't say we'd be away."

"Pooh! They would know at home that you would be all right," said Mrs. Anderson. "You station folk never seem to worry about times and seasons, and I always think it's so delightful! Your father would know the others were quite safe in your care, Jim."

"I hope you children are taking note of that speech," said Jim, laughing. "I wish I could feel as confident about it as you do, Mrs. Anderson—but, unfortunately, my years don't seem to convince Dad of my common sense. I'm afraid he'd be worried if we didn't turn up for dinner."

"Rubbish!" said Mrs. Anderson. "He would know you stayed for something or other; probably he reads the local paper, if you don't, and is acquainted with the dissipated intentions of Cunjee. I'm certainly not going to let you escape now that I have you all!"

"What do you think, Nor.?" Jim asked his sister.

"Why, I don't suppose he'd mind," Norah answered. "It always seems much the same to be out with you as with him, though it's very imprudent of me to let you know it."

"He wouldn't mind if he knew," Jim said, doubtfully. "Still——"

"Oh, risk it," said Mrs. Anderson, laughing. "Consider the claims of a woman in distress—you can't leave me to face a Cunjee audience alone. Your clothes don't matter a bit—in fact, Cunjee will probably consider you clad as the lilies of the field." So Jim, against his better judgment, stayed.

Dinner at the Andersons' was a cheerful occasion, to which variety was lent by the Anderson baby, who insisted on sitting on Norah's knee, and drummed happily on the cloth with her dessert-spoon, while Norah ate on the catch-as-catch-can principle. Then, the baby being with difficulty severed from the object of his adoration, they hurried to the Mechanics' Institute, outside which the local brass band was performing prodigies of harmony, somewhat impeded by the fact that the euphonium was three tones flat.

Jim did not enjoy the concert. A shade of anxiety hung over his mind, with the conviction that it was quite possible that their absence was causing anxiety at the station. Thus the antics of the Cunjee comedian who, in private life, kept a somewhat disreputable bicycle-repairing establishment, fell flat; albeit the comedian aforesaid had bedecked himself in spurious red whiskers and a kilt compounded of a red table cloth, with a whitewash brush as sporran, and sang Scotch ditties with a violent Australian twang—a combination truly awe inspiring. They suffered from the familiar soprano, who trilled strange trills in a key very much too high, and from the confident young baritone, who warbled a ditty of the type more generally reserved for tenors, and took an encore on the echo of the first faint clap. The band master played a long solo upon the cornet, than which there is no more lonely instrument when unsupported; and on the heels of its wailing came a young lady who recited harrowing particulars of the death of "my chee-ild," whom she indicated as lying in its coffin immediately before her. She knelt by it, and apostrophized the deceased in moving terms. She wrung her hands over it; in fact, she pointed it out so definitely that to Norah, whose imagination was unfortunately vivid, it assumed actual reality, and she with difficulty restrained a cry when, in the last verse, the elocutionist forgot her previous actions, and in the anguish of her mood, stepped right into the coffin! At this point Norah decided definitely that she did not like recitations. It pained her greatly to see the young lady smirk and stroll off the stage, oblivious of her heart-rending actions.

Then the Shire President came forward and thanked everybody in impartial terms, and the concert was over. Jim hurried his party out of the hall, and as soon as possible they had said good-night to Mrs. Anderson, resisting her offers of supper; and were in the saddle, cantering along the homeward track.

Five miles out of Cunjee a shadow loomed up out of the gloom, and Garryowen gave a sudden whinney. Mr. Linton's voice followed it.

"Is that you, Jim?"

Under his breath Jim uttered a low whistle.

"Great Scott! It's Dad!" he said. He raised his voice. "Right-oh, Dad! Is anything wrong?"

"There's nothing wrong at home," said David Linton, wheeling Monarch beside Garryowen. "What has kept you?"

"Went to a concert," said Jim, briefly, feeling suddenly very small and young.

"We never thought you'd be anxious, Dad!" Norah said.

"Not anxious!" said her father, explosively. Then he shot a glance at Jean and Wally, uncomfortably silent.

"You've given us a pleasant evening," was all he said. But Jim winced as if he had been struck, and the blood surged into his face.

"I'm sorry," he said curtly.

"It was my fault, just as much, Dad," Norah began. But her father stopped her.

"Jim was in charge," he said. "There isn't any more to be said about it. We'd better hurry. Mrs. Brown is picturing all sorts of things." He put Monarch into a canter, and they rode on in silence. Two miles further on a dim figure at the roadside turned his horse beside Wally.

"Is it all right, ye are, all of ye?" asked Murty in a hoarse whisper.

"Some one else out hunting the lost sheep?" Wally asked. "Yes, we're all right."

"Thin I'll not let on to himself that I kem out," said the Irishman. "Wisha! he was wild!" He dropped behind the riders, vanishing into the gloom.

Billabong was slow in appearing; to the silent riders the miles had never seemed longer. At last the lights came into view with Brownie's massive figure silhouetted against the light of the doorway.

"Run in, you and Jean, and tell Brownie you're all right," Mr. Linton said to Norah, as they pulled up. "We'll see to the horses."

In the harness room, while Wally took off bridles outside, Jim's eyes met his father's. Both had been thinking.

"I'm sorry we made you anxious," said the boy, stiffly.

"You made me very anxious," said David Linton. "Still——" He hesitated, memories of his own early manhood coming back to him as the big fellow faced him. "Perhaps I forget that you're not a child any longer," he said, with an effort. "If I hurt you, Jim, I'm——"

"Don't!" Jim's hand went out quickly. "I deserved a jolly sight more than I got. But I'm sorry, Dad." They shook hands on it, gravely.

"Bring in those bridles, young Wally, and be quick!" sang out Mr. Linton—and Wally appeared, his face comically relieved at the tone. They walked over to the house—a laugh from Jim at some futile remark of his chum's coming to Norah's ears as they neared the verandah, and greatly relieving that distressed damsel, to whom it had appeared that the skies had fallen.

Later, when supper had been discussed cheerfully, and the household had scattered, David Linton smoked a last pipe on the balcony, thinking.

A slender figure in blue pyjamas came softly to him.

"Dad—I'm sorry!" said Norah.

"Right, mate!" said her father. He saw the quick lift of her head, but she hesitated.

David Linton laughed, kissing her.

"And Jim's all right," he said. "Off to bed with you!"

CHAPTER VII
MORNING
That loving Laughing Land, where life is fresh and clean,

Where the rivers flow all summer, and the grass is always green.

—Henry Lawson.

NORAH!"

"James?" said Norah, with polite inquiry. She paused with Jean, and turned a questioning eye towards the window whence Jim's voice had reached her.

Jim, in his shirt sleeves, his face obscured by lather, looked out, razor in hand.

"Don't go over to the stable just now, if that's where you two are going," said he.

"Right-oh, Jimmy. For how long?"

"Don't quite know," Jim said, grinning through the suds. "Dad's having words with one of the men, and you'd better wait until he comes over. You mustn't risk interrupting the flow of his eloquence."

"Is anything wrong?" Norah asked.

"It's that blithering ass, Harvey," Jim answered. "He's a useless loafer at the best of times; and he's let us in for a nice game now! Dad has been sending him out to look round those new Queensland bullocks in the Bush Paddock, and he's left the slip-rails down, and they've all boxed with the cattle next door, in the Far Plain." At this point Jim's wrath, or an unconscious movement, led him to take a mouthful of lather, and his head withdrew abruptly, spluttering. Incoherent sounds came from the interior of the room.

The girls laughed unfeelingly.

"He's so funny when he shaves, isn't he?" said his sister. "Jean, it's an ill wind that blows nowhere!"

"Why?" asked Jean.

"Well, if those cattle are boxed it means a big muster," said Norah; "and mustering the Bush Paddock is better fun than anything else. I don't feel nearly as sorry as I might."

"More shame for you!" said a voice above their heads, at which both girls jumped. Wally's face emerged from the concealment of the dark green leaves of a cherry tree. A big black cherry bobbed temptingly near his nose, and he ate it, still keeping a severe eye upon his audience.

"I never knew any one with your ability for appearing in unexpected places," said Norah, laughing. "Come down, Wally; I know quite well your mother doesn't let you climb!"

"I come," said Wally; "but more because the cherries are scarce than because of you, young woman. Funny how few ripe ones there are this morning."

"Not a bit. Jean and I have been up there," said Norah, with calmness. "That's what comes of being early birds. If you'd only get up in the morning instead of snoring in a loud voice——"

"Never did," said Wally, swinging his long form to earth. " 'Twas Jim you heard."

"Jim never snores!" said Jim's sister.

"Then 'twas the Boss. Or probably you weren't up at all, and heard yourself snoring in your sleep, which is far more likely. Certainly, the cherries have disappeared in a manner only possible to you and Jean; but that might have been while I swam peacefully in the lagoon. In any case, you're a shocking hostess!" Wally paused for breath, while Norah grinned amiably and remarked that, at any rate, she had suited Jean!

"Given up to greed, both of you," said Mr. Meadows, "while I, alas, am given up to hunger. Here comes your father, and he looks pretty wild. Wonder if he's sacked Harvey?"

"We'll want all hands to-day," said Mr. Linton, pausing to greet them as he came up with quick strides. "Harvey's boxed half the cattle on the place, and we'll have our work cut out to get them all in, short-handed. You see, I gave the other men permission to go to the races, and they left about sunrise. And now Harvey's leaving too, in haste!"

"Did you sack him, Dad?"

"I did," said his father. "I don't know that I would have done so, though he's a most useless man on the place, but he chose to be insolent about it. In fact he told me just what he thought about me for oppressing the labouring man. I wished Murty and Boone and the rest had been there to have learned how down-trodden they are. They would have enjoyed it!"

"I believe Murty would have fought him," Norah said, indignantly.

"It's not unlikely," her father answered. "Murty's a loyal old soul. According to Harvey, they are all worms, and I am a callous tyrant, and Jim's a whelp!"

"Oh, am I?" said that gentleman, with interest, looking out. "What have I done to the noble Harvey?"

"Well, you've existed. I can't quite gather that you've done anything else, and I fancy Harvey would have mentioned it if you had. At times he seemed hard up for things to mention. Still, on the whole, he was very eloquent. I've known politicians tarred with the same brush; the less they have to say, the more fluent they become! Judging by present indications," said Mr. Linton, "Harvey will develop into a Prime Minister, and probably afflict me with a special land tax. And all because I asked him why he'd left the slip-rails down."

"Well, I'm glad you've sent him away, Dad," Norah said. "I always thought he had a horrid face."

"Oh, he's a miserable type," her father answered—"the kind of man that never ought to come to the country. He's absolutely useless, and I don't think he ever did a day's work in his life—if he did, it wasn't on Billabong. We've put him at various kinds of work, and found him worthless at each; his one idea was to 'knock off,' and he shone at that. And, as you say, he's a low-looking brute, and I shall be glad to have him off the place. But I don't like sacking a man."

"Don't know why we ever put him on," said Jim, through the window.

"Well, he said he hadn't a penny, and wanted work. One doesn't like to send a man away without giving him a chance. But I'm sorry I kept Harvey. However, he's off, or he will be shortly, so we needn't bother our heads about him. The bullocks are likely to need all our energies. Jean, can I rely on your assistance?"

Jean nodded vigorously. It was clear that the prospect afforded her undiluted joy.

"That's right. And Wally?" Wally grinned, disdaining further answer.

"Then," said Mr. Linton, "as I presume I can count on Jim and Norah———"

"Not that they're much use," said Wally, despondently. A large boot hurtled from Jim's window, took him in the rear, and he uttered a startled yell. Recovering his composure, he possessed himself of the missile and proceeded to swarm up the bare trunk of a tall palm, going up hand over hand, much like a monkey on a stick. Arrived at the crown of leaves, he clung with his legs while he tied the boot firmly in with the laces.

"Bring that down, Wally, you reptile," sang out Jim. He made a dash for the garden, one foot encased in a sock, and, seizing a hoe, prodded vainly upwards in the climber's direction.

"Not if I know it," said Wally, happily. "Looks lovely up here—like some strange tropic blossom. Orchid Kangaroohides Jamesobium Wallistylis. Exquisite new species, flowering once a century. Look out, Jimmy, I'm going to slide."

"Are you?" said Jim with vigour. His eye, roving round in search of a weapon, had caught sight of a fragment of barbed wire—the remains of a device of Hogg, the gardener, to keep greedy 'possums from devouring his rosebuds. It was but a moment's work to seize it and coil it round the palm trunk in a long spiral. He stood back, grinning.

"Better not slide too suddenly, old man!" he said, pleasantly.

Wally had already begun to move, but he checked himself quickly. There were not many intonations in his chum's voice that he did not understand. He leaned sideways and surveyed the trunk, his face lengthening involuntarily.

"Oh!" he said, and paused, apparently seeking for inspiration. "Beast!"

Jim sat down in a leisurely fashion on the grass and nursed his unshod foot.

"It's a nice morning," he remarked, conversationally. "Garden looks jolly well before the sun gets hot, doesn't it? Tropic blossoms well out, and all that—including the climbing novelties! And there's breakfast," as the gong sounded. "What a pity to leave it all!" He gathered himself up, slowly. "So long!"

"Brute!" said Wally, with fervour.

"Aren't you happy?" asked Jim, surprise in his tone. "You ought to be—I've never seen you look so nice! Will you bring me my boot, young Wally?"

"I will not," said the victim, firmly. "Not if I stay here for a week!"

"The barbed wire will last longer than that," said Jim, grinning. "Does it strike you, Dad, that the climbing novelty looks dry?"

"It's more evident that it's annoyed with you," said David Linton, laughing. "Better bring him his boot, Wally—it's his game, I think."

"Never!" said the captive.

"Told you he was dry," said Jim. "Look at that purple flush—doesn't that indicate a need of cooling down?" He disappeared behind a clump of laurustinus, and returned armed with a coil of hose.

Norah gave a fresh burst of laughter. "Oh, Jimmy, you won't!" she cried.

"Will I not?" grinned her brother, turning on the tap. A light shower of drops spattered the trunk near the victim's head—with due regard for the safety of the dangling boot.

"My hat, Jimmy, when I get within reach of you——," said Wally, laughing. "Put that down, you fiend, and fight fair!"

"Bless you, I'm not fighting," said Jim blandly. "I'm watering the garden!"

"Yes, you're Daddy's useful little son, I know," returned Mr. Meadows. "I'll deal with you when I get down!"

"Told you water was necessary," said Jim to his audience, two-thirds of which had collapsed on the grass, helpless. "Parched, that's what he is. Turn on that tap a little harder, Dad, and I'll give him a really nice tropic downpour!"

Mr. Meadows capitulated.

"Take off your beastly barbed wire," he said, his tone expressing anything but pious resignation. "And put on your beastly great boot!" The boot descended with some force, and caught Jim on the shoulder as he stooped over his spiked entanglement. "Nice shot—there's some balm in Gilead!" said Wally. He slid down, arriving at the ground with some force, and immediately gave chase to Jim, who had gathered up his property and fled.

"No one would think there was any work waiting on this place!" said Mr. Linton, laughing. "Come to breakfast, all of you—hurry up, Norah!"

Wally joined them in the breakfast-room, somewhat dishevelled.

"He'll be in in a moment—he's putting on the boot!" he said. "Isn't he an uncivilized ostrich? I don't know how you brought him up in his youth, sir, but he's no credit to you. I'd sooner have old Lee Wing, pigtail and all."

"You look a little damp, Wally," Norah said, kindly. "I hope you won't take cold!" To which the injured one returned merely a baleful glance, before devoting himself to his porridge.

Jim slipped in unobtrusively, wearing an air of bland composure.

"We'll take lunch out, I suppose, Dad?"

"Yes, I sent Brownie a message some time ago," said his father. "You'll have to run up the horses after breakfast, Jim, and when you've caught ours turn the others out into the big paddock."

Jim glanced up inquiringly. It was an unusual command.

"I wouldn't trust that beggar, Harvey," his father said, answering the glance. "If the horses were close at hand the temptation to borrow one to get as far as Cunjee might be too strong; but he couldn't catch one in the big paddock. It won't take long to put them back when we come in."

"You're not going to send him in to the township then?"

"I'm not," said Mr. Linton, firmly. "He came carrying his swag, and he can carry it away—after the flood of bad language and insolence I had from him this morning, I really don't feel any obligation to have him driven in. The walk may give him time to get a little sense—not that you could put sense into a man of the Harvey type by any known means."

"Well, it won't hurt him—and I don't see who would have driven him, anyhow," Jim said. "Are you letting him have any tucker?"

"Oh, yes; I said he could get some from the kitchen."

"Then he's got nothing to grumble at," Jim declared. "Not that that is in the least likely to keep him from grumbling. I expect it wouldn't be a bad precaution to lock up pretty carefully at the stables, Dad."

"Certainly, lock up everything," his father answered. "I'd have been glad to see him fairly off the place, as Murty and Boone are away—still Hogg and Lee Wing are about, so there's really no need—and we can't afford the time."

"Lee Wing would be sufficient guardian for any place," said Wally, who cherished an undying affection for the stolid Chinaman, who did not return the feeling at all. It was not certain that Lee Wing loved any one, though Norah was wont to declare that he wrote sonnets to a girl in China. So far as Australia was concerned, his heart seemed to be given to his onions, and he regarded Wally with a dubious eye.

Mrs. Brown came in, favouring the company impartially with her wide and beaming smile.

"Will you be boilin' the billy, sir?"

"Yes, decidedly," said Mr. Linton. "It is going to be hot enough to make tea a necessity, I fancy. And Wally is aching to carry the billy—aren't you, my boy?"

"Personally," said Jim, "I should have thought it was the breakfast he's eaten, on top of about a hundredweight of cherries. Give him some more coffee, Norah—he looks pensive!"

"That's because he has had two cups already—and I don't allow him three, as a rule," said Norah, callously. "However, he's had a hard morning, so I'll be weak—and so will be the coffee. Pass his cup, Jean."

"I don't know why I come to stay with the Linton tribe," said Wally, surrendering his cup and sighing heavily. "I'm not appreciated, and it's blighting my young life. Mrs. Brown, may I stay with you to-day and hold your hand?"

"You can't. I got a fair amount to do with it," rejoined Brownie. "Not but I will say, Master Wally, you're the good-temperedest ever I see! And gimme a boy as laughs!"

"Well, I've thrown myself at your feet often enough, but you won't pick me up!" said Wally, much aggrieved. "Some day I will wed another, and then you'll know what you've lost!" At which Mrs. Brown bridled, and said, "Ah, go along now, do!" and aimed a destructive blow at him with her apron. Murmuring something about lunch, she retreated to the kitchen.

"I'll go and run up the horses," said Jim, pushing back his chair. "Young Wally, see that you have the saddles out by the time I get them in, and bring the bridles down to the yards."

"Be it thine to command," said Wally, with meekness. "Mine to obey—when I'm ready."

"Better make it convenient to be ready quickly," warned Jim. "Otherwise——"

He left the sentence dramatically unfinished, and, finding a halfpenny lying on the mantelshelf, deftly inserted it into his friend's collar as he passed him. Wally choked over his coffee, and fled in hot pursuit, clutching at his backbone as he went.

"Aren't they cheerful babies!" said Norah, laughing. "I guess I'll be grey-haired long before they grow up. Come on, Jeanie—I'll race you getting ready!" The sound of their flying feet echoed down the corridor.

" 'Bless you, I'm not fighting—I'm watering the garden!' "

CHAPTER VIII
NOON
Ah, . . . I remember

The muster of cattle away outback,

The thunder of hoofs and the stock-whip's crack,

The panting breaths on the warm sweet breeze,

The tossing horns by Rosella trees,

And the whirl of dust, and the hot hide's reek!

—M. Forrest.

ALL aboard!"

"Are you girls ready? Hurry up." From the direction of the garden came a faint hail, which might have been taken to mean anything.

"Curious things, girls," said Jim sapiently. Wally and he were leaning over a fence, five horses ready behind them. "When young Norah's alone, she gets dressed as quickly as you or me; but now she has Jean, they spend ages in getting togged up. And they don't look any different, no matter how long they take."

"No," agreed the other masculine observer. "They always look jolly nice, anyhow. I never can make out what they do, to keep 'em so long."

"Oh, tie each other's hair ribbons, and swap neckties, and things like that," said Jim, vaguely. "Nobody ever knows what girls are up to. Of course, Norah never seemed quite like a girl until she went to school. But you can see there's a difference now."

"Well—a little," Wally answered. "But she's up to all sorts of larks yet, thank goodness."

"Well, I should say so," said Jim, staring. "They'd have to boil Norah before they made her prim; and that's a comfort. I rather fancy she must have had a pretty woeful time when she went to school first."

"Pretty rough on her," Wally agreed. "She'll be growing up next, I suppose—worse luck."

"Norah—oh, rot," said Jim, firmly. "She's only a kid yet—and will be for ages. Don't you go and put ideas like that into her head, Wal."

"Me?" rejoined his chum. "What do you take me for? But she'll get 'em put in at school, you'll see, quick enough." And Jim glowered, muttering something unkindly about school and its by-paths of learning.

"Well, I wish they'd hurry up, anyhow," he said. "Wonder what's keeping them."

From behind them came a faint snore, and he swung round. Jean and Norah were already mounted, their heads drooping on their horses' necks, in attitudes of extreme boredom. They gave the impression of having sat there for many hours, and finally succumbed to fatigue and slumber. The boys burst into laughter.

"Well, of all the idiots," said Jim, ungallantly. "How did you get there?"

"Came round the back of the stables," laughed Norah, waking up. "You two old gossips were muttering away with your heads over the rail—I believe we could have stolen all the horses without your knowing anything about it. It's just extraordinary how boys will gossip—Jean and I never get lost in our own eloquence, like you and Wally. What were you being eloquent about?"

"Never you mind," said her brother, shooting an amused look at his chum. "Matters of State too high for your little minds. But you're not going to ride Warder, are you, Norah?"

"No," said Norah, slipping off Wally's mount. "I knew it was no good trying to be quiet if I got on Bosun, bless him!" She patted the brown pony's neck, and fished a lump of sugar out of her pocket for him.

Mr. Linton came hurriedly over from the house.

"Sorry to keep you all waiting," he said, taking Monarch's bridle. "I had to give Brownie some directions; and Hogg is in tears because something's wrong with the longest hose—I left him trying to mend it with bicycle solution and strips of rubber cut from one of Brownie's old goloshes, which she nobly sacrificed on the altar of the garden."

"There are always excitements in being out of reach of shops," Jim said. "I hope it's not the hose I used this morning?"

"Oh, no; your skin's safe this time!" said his father, laughing. "That was a shorter one. I don't like the big one being out of order, in case of fire; not that a fire at the house is likely—but it's as well to be prepared. Stirrups all right, Jean?"

"Yes, thank you," Jean answered. Nan, staid stock horse though she was supposed to be, was impatient to get away, and Jean was walking her round in a circle, pursued by Wally with anxious inquiries as to whether she were qualifying for the circus ring. Bosun's eagerness to start had been manifested so strongly that Norah had at length given up trying to restrain him, and was some distance across the paddock, the pony fretting and sidling, and trying to break into a canter.

Mr. Linton and Jim mounted, and they all cantered after Norah. She gave Bosun his head as they came up to her—a liberty he acknowledged by executing two or three tremendous bounds in mid-air.

"Mind him, my girl," her father cautioned. "Don't let him get his head down; he's quite happy enough to buck this morning."

"I'll watch him, Daddy," Norah panted. The big pony was reefing and pulling double. She patted his arched neck. "Steady, you old image—steady!" and Bosun came back to a jerky canter, still longing for unchecked freedom to put his head down, kick up his heels and race across the paddock without any handicap of saddle and bridle and rider. For Jim's weight he had some respect—but this new featherweight, to whom he was not yet accustomed, was a different matter; it was difficult to realize that she had wrists like steel and a curious comprehension of his moods and high spirits. Yet already Bosun understood that his new rider was not at all afraid of him; and that is the best foundation of friendship between rider and horse.

The gate into the bush paddock was on flat country—the end of the wide plain on which Billabong homestead was built; but within a few chains after entering the paddock the ground began to slope upwards until the flat had given place to a range of low hills, sparsely timbered, and interspersed with green and quiet gullies, where thick bracken grew. A week or so back cattle had been grazing all through the hills; big, scraggy Queensland bullocks, new arrivals from "up north," and still wild and shy. Now, thanks to the vagaries of Harvey, there were none to be seen. They had scattered into the next paddock, where the grass was shorter and sweeter, and "boxed" thoroughly with the other cattle already running there.

"It's maddening," said David Linton, scanning the hills with keen eyes. "I came out here ten days ago, and the bullocks were settling down splendidly—not half as wild as they were when we drafted them into this paddock. Now they won't want to come back, off the clover they are on now. I'd like Harvey to have the job of mustering them alone on foot!" Jim whistled.

"Jolly for the bullocks—to say nothing of Harvey," he said, laughing.

"Jollity for Harvey isn't part of my idea," his father responded. "But the bullocks would be dying of senile decay before he completed the job, I'm afraid; and I'd rather fatten them while they're young."

"I expect you would," Jim agreed. "Well, I don't believe there's a hoof left in this paddock, anyhow, Dad."

"Doesn't look like it," Mr. Linton answered. "We'll scatter a bit and ride round. Jean had better keep fairly close to me; the rest of you know where the slip-rails are, and we can all meet there. Be as quick as you can, all of you."

So they scattered into the timber, Jim taking a line to the extreme left, with Norah nearest to him, then Wally, and, on the right, Mr. Linton and Jean. Jean had not quite the appearance of having been "born in the saddle," as had the others, who had certainly ridden almost as soon as they had walked; nevertheless, she could be depended upon to give a very good account of herself on Nan, who combined a cheerful spirit with great common sense, after the manner of stock horses, and was quite capable of correcting any mistakes made by a rider unversed in the ways of cattle. Jean's experience had been chiefly gained after sheep in far-off New Zealand, and to muster cattle is very different work.

But, like many other silent people, Jean was observant, and even since coming to Billabong she had picked up a good few points about cattle and their ways—not a difficult matter where station matters, and the stock generally, entered largely into the life of every day. She was, moreover, greatly afraid of making mistakes, and not at all above asking questions where she needed guidance—two excellent characteristics in a "new chum." The man of the Bush is nearly always tolerant to beginners, and kind in "showing 'em how." The one individual for whom he has no time and no mercy is the ignoramus who is cocksure.

Jean was not exactly a beginner—she had ridden by her father's side in New Zealand much too often for that. Her blue eyes were alight with keenness as they trotted through the timber—now swinging into a canter where the going was clearer, or pulling up when a stretch of crab-holey ground threatened risk to horses' legs. It was very pleasant in the chequered shadows of the trees, and in the deep gullies where the night-dews still spangled fern and tussock, and the wild convolvuli nodded blue and white bells as if in greeting. Pleasant to give a good horse his head—to let him swing in and out amid the timber, dodging low-hanging limbs by instinct, and skirting the rough barked trunks closely. Pleasant to smell the sweet bush scents; to catch the strong beat of wings overhead where black swans sailed southwards towards the reed-fringed lagoon; or the shrill scream of parrakeets, swooping into a wild cherry tree in a green, flashing, chattering crowd. Pleasant, too, to think of school—very far away, with shuttered windows and great empty classrooms, with dust lying thick on the desks that were symbols of hated toil! Quite possibly the caretaker did not permit dust to linger at all. But it was undeniably cheering to picture it.

A white blur in a deep gully caught Jean's eye as they rode, and she called to Mr. Linton.

"Is that a bullock lying down?"

"Good girl!" said her host, approvingly. "Yes, it's a beast down, and I should say he can't get up. Perhaps you'd better not come down, lassie; just keep straight along this ridge, and I'll catch you up presently." He turned his big black's head down into the gully.

It was ten minutes before he rejoined her—by which time Jean had come to a standstill, partly because she was uncertain as to which way to go, and partly because of a queer sound that might have been a stock-whip crack, but sounded somehow different. She looked inquiringly at Mr. Linton as he rode up. His face was grave and angry.

"Poor brute! I had to put him out of his misery," he said. "He'd been caught in a little landslip and fallen, and his leg was broken. Come on, Jean, we're not far from the slip-rails, and the others will be waiting."

Norah and Jim and Wally were sitting on a log near the rails, letting their horses have a mouthful of grass. They mounted as the late-comers rode up.

"We didn't find a hoof," Jim said. A glance at his father's face had told him that something was wrong, and he brought Garryowen beside Monarch as they rode into the next paddock, over the rails that Harvey had flung down the day before. "Did I hear a shot?" he asked, dropping his voice.

Mr. Linton nodded.

"Yes," he said, curtly. "A beast down in a gully—leg broken. I was very glad I'd brought my revolver; it's always best to bring it in country like this, when you never know if it will be necessary to put an injured beast out of pain. The sickening part of it is, that the job should have been done a week ago."

"A week!" Jim whistled.

"I should say so. The poor brute must have lain there in agony for a good many days—the ground about him was ploughed up with his struggles, and the leg was in a fearful state. He was nearly dead; the bullet only hastened things a very little."

"And Harvey's been out here every day," uttered Jim.

"Yes—with nothing to do but ride round and see that those cattle were all right. Of course he couldn't have helped the accident, but he could have saved that poor helpless brute days of agony. It's quite near one of the tracks, too; there can be no excuse for missing it."

"I don't think Mr. Harvey ever did much riding round," Jim said. "Going to sleep under a log is more his form."

"Or if he did see it he wouldn't bother his head about it," his father answered. "Well, I'm not likely to see Harvey again, thank goodness, and that is fortunate for him!" In which, as it happened, David Linton was very far from the truth.

There were plenty of cattle to be seen in the paddock they had now entered. The ground was gently undulating, with clumps of trees here and there, and in two or three places a blue flash that spoke of water. Bullocks were feeding in every direction—some quiet and half fat, while others were raking, long-horned fellows, gaunt and shy, who threw up their heads and their heels and lumbered off at a gallop at sight of the intruders. This had generally the effect of making the quieter bullocks gallop too, and Mr. Linton groaned at the spectacle of so much good beef deteriorating by unseemly and violent exercise.

"I had cherished foolish hopes of cutting them out here and coaxing them back to their own home," he said. "But there's not a chance of that—it will have to be a general muster."

"Where do we take them, Mr. Linton?" Jean asked. It was evident that she did not share any of her host's troubles—her face was eager and merry, her eyes dancing as they met Norah's, who, needless to say, was equally cheerful over the prospect before them. Mr. Linton laughed as he looked from one to the other.

"Pretty sympathizers you are for a worried man," he said. "I believe you're in league with Harvey—are you sure you didn't bribe him to leave down the rails? Does it matter at all to you that I drafted out these bullocks very carefully not long ago—and that now I've the job all over again?"

"It would matter to me horribly if I were at school and heard about it in a letter," said Norah, laughing. "I would be awfully worried and cross over it—to think of you having such a time! And I would tell Jean all about it, and she'd be cross and worried, too. But as it is—when we're both here, and can relieve you of quite half your anxiety by helping——!" Whereat Jim and Wally became a prey to great laughter, in which Jean and Norah joined after a fruitless attempt to ignore them haughtily.

"Since it's no use to expect decent sympathy from you, you can certainly do all the helping you like," said Mr. Linton, smiling broadly. "We'll muster all the cattle down towards the far end of the paddock, and take them out through the gate there—we might have a pretty hard job if we tried to take them through the Bush Paddock. Wally, my lad, just canter back and put up those slip-rails, will you? Jean, you can't get bushed in this paddock, because there isn't enough timber; we can't get out of sight of each other for any length of time. Now we'll each take a line and get hold of the bullocks in front of us, and hope as hard as we can that they'll go quietly. I believe much is said to be done by hoping, though I don't know what happens if the cattle are hoping to stay where they are!"

It was soon distressingly evident that such was indeed the high ambition of the bullocks. They were very contented on the short, sweet clover and rye grass; they saw no reason whatever to justify being driven towards some unknown region. For a good many weeks they had been on the roads, these long-horned Queenslanders, travelling through regions that were all unknown. Most of them had been very comfortless—bare roads where scarcely a picking could be obtained, or through runs where fierce stockmen and unpleasant dogs were jealously indignant if they took so much as a bite of grass or failed to cover each day the prescribed number of miles for travelling stock. Now they had come at last into a peaceful haven, where clover grew thickly, and a creek flowed for their special benefit. Was it to be expected that they should tamely leave it? On the whole, the bullocks thought that it was not, and that whoever was so weak as to expect it must be taught by painful experience the futility of so hoping.

The half-fat cattle went readily enough. The tracks were familiar to them—the crack of a stock-whip was sufficient to start them lazily along the way towards the gate. They had grown philosophic as they attained weight; it was known to them now that when mounted people, with dogs, express an inclination for bullocks to move in a particular direction, it is as well to be acquiescent and move. But the Queenslanders had learned no such lesson, or, if they had learned it, it had been forgotten since they had exchanged the roads for Billabong. Tracks meant nothing to them; they galloped madly hither and thither, made off for the farthest corners of the paddock, with tails wildly streaming in the air, and dodged back with a persistence calculated to reduce the most patient drover to wrath and evil words. Their spirits infected some of the staider cattle, and they also fled to the four winds, with a lumbering agility wonderful in such mountains of beef. It was quite too hot a day for such pranks, and their owner groaned as they fled.

"You can see the condition simply evaporating from them," he declared.

The heat did not seem to affect the Oueenslanders at all. But the horses were soon sweating and the riders almost as hot, while the dogs became almost useless, and sneaked off to the creek to wallow luxuriously in the fern-fringed pools. Wally looked after them eagerly.

"Lucky brutes," he uttered, "wish I could follow their example."

He was tailing behind a dozen bullocks—eight of the quieter section and four of the "stores." For once they seemed inclined to go quietly, and Wally began to breathe more freely, with visions of handing them over to augment the little mob he could see Jim bringing alone, away to the right. Then came a sudden descent before him, where a little hill ran down into a grassy hollow. The Oueenslanders began to trot down it; then the slope proved too much for them, and the trot broke into a canter and merged to a stretching gallop, striking across the plain. There was no chance of catching them—Wally could only bring up the rear, sending the spurs into old Warder in his fruitless hope of heading them before they should reach Jim's mob, and upset their serenity.

The cattle had all the best of it. Here and there one dropped out of the chase, panting, or broke back to try to reach the open country they were leaving; but the leaders made for Jim's little mob, even as the swallows homeward fly. They scattered it hither and thither; heels flew up, and hoofs pounded, as they tore in different directions, and not one the right one. Jim's eloquence failed him. He could only give Garryowen his head in somewhat vague pursuit, since it could not be definitely said which beast to pursue.

"Hard to know which has most call on a fellow's time," Jim muttered grimly as he galloped.

Further across the paddock, Jean was having troubles of her own. The width from fence to fence was all too great for five to guard; although Mr. Linton had said she could not get lost—which she knew very well—it was lonely enough in the wide space, catching only an occasional glimpse of fellow-musterers to right and left across the undulating ground. The bullocks had no sense of chivalry; they treated her with scorn and derision, and her hopes of being of definite use in the muster faded swiftly.

It seemed easy enough to bring along the bullocks directly in front, but when Jean came to put the instruction into practice it was not nearly so simple. Some went quite calmly, insomuch that swift affection kindled for them in her breast; others merely looked at her, walked a few steps, and began feeding again. Pressed more closely and shouted at very energetically, they departed in divers ways, making it quite impossible to pursue them all. She could only hope that they came in the path of the other musterers and meet their due fate. Finally, a big spotted brute, with a great raking pair of horns, doubled when, in her ignorance, she failed to "keep wide" near him, and slipping past her, made for the open paddock behind her. Jean dug her heels into Nan with all her energy, wishing to her heart that they were spurred—a wish slightly unfair to the brown mare, who was only too ready to do her best. They fled in hot pursuit.

The bullock had made all possible use of his start, and he redoubled his speed as the hoofs pounded in the rear. A rise ahead prevented his seeing any fence. He pictured safety in the way he was going, could he but outstrip pursuit—safety and peace, and good grass, away from worrying humans and the rattle of stock-whip cracks. So he topped the rise and raced on; and behind him came the brown mare, entirely beyond Jean's control now. Nan knew precisely what should be the duty of any self-respecting stock horse, and she was very certain that no featherweight upon her back should prevent her from doing it. She swung outward just at the right moment—a movement which very nearly disposed of Jean, who felt the saddle fleeting from under her, and only saved herself by grabbing at the pommel. It taught her caution. She realized that she could not at all tell what this determined steed was going to do. Therefore she sat very tightly and kept a hand close to the kindly pommel as they raced past the bullock. And it was as well she did.

Nan swung in sharply, and headed the bullock off. For a moment it seemed as if he would race away diagonally across the paddock. Then he propped uncertainly in his gallop for a moment, and immediately the brown mare propped too, turning "on a sixpence" in a way that would certainly have disposed of Jean but for her timely grip. As it was, she went forward upon Nan's neck, losing both stirrups as she went—and had barely wriggled back into the saddle with a violent effort when the bullock was ready for further action. He uttered a low bellow, moving his head uncertainly.

"Shoo! Shoo!" cried Jean, wildly. "Get along! Oh, I wish I was a man, or a dog, or a stock-whip!"

Something in the shrill voice checked the bullock, or else the sight of the brown mare, eager to do battle again, made him realize the vanity of bovine wishes. He turned sharply, and raced back along the way he had come, with Jean in hot pursuit—atop of Nan, clinging for dear life, with both feet out of the stirrups—Jean, oblivious of all save the joy of conquest, and uttering spasmodic and breathless shouts of "Shoo!" The bullock raced as though the end of the world were approaching for him. Ahead was a group of other cattle; he shot into the midst of them and pulled up, uttering an indignant bellow.

Nan slackened, visibly uneasy at the dangling stirrups, which had, indeed, acted as flails, beating her with great ardour throughout the race. Jean managed to pull her up, and to get her feet in again. Pride rested on her crimson brow.

"Oh, I hope Norah saw!" she uttered.

Then, from some unseen part of the paddock she saw a riderless horse top a ridge and race towards her.

"Oh!" said Jean, "oh! it's Bosun!" Her voice was a little wail of distress. She dug her heel into Nan, and cantered out to meet the runaway, her heart in her mouth.

It was not Bosun, however, but Warder, Wally's mount. He came to a standstill as the brown mare and her rider appeared across his path, and looked considerably ashamed of himself, since it is no part of the duty of a stock horse to run from his rider, should misfortune overtake that luckless wight. Then from the same direction came Jim, galloping, with a broad grin on his face. He changed his course and came round when he saw the two horses close together.

"Good girl, Jean!" he sang out. "I'll catch him." And Jean swelled with joy at the carelessly given word of praise.

Warder stood quietly enough while Jim came gently on Garryowen, speaking soothing words until he was near enough to grasp his rein.

"Thought I'd have a lovely chase after him," Jim said.

"Is Wally hurt? Warder didn't buck with him, did he?" Jean asked anxiously.

"Not he—Warder's no buckjumper," returned Jim. "No—the silly old mule—it was all his fault!"

"Whose—Wally's?" Jean asked, as he paused.

Jim laughed.

"No, Warder's," he said. "Put his foot into a crab-hole and turned a somersault—neatest thing you ever saw! Wal. shot about a hundred yards; luckily he landed on a soft spot, for he's not hurt. There he is, lazy beggar; he ought to be coming to meet us."

Wally held no such view. He was stretched at full length on the grass, his felt hat pulled over his face. As they rode up he came slowly into a sitting position.

"Bless you, Jimmy! Much trouble?"

"Don't bless me," Jim said. "Jean had him nearly caught." At which Jean flushed with embarrassment and pride, and said something entirely incoherent.

"Come along, you lazy rubbish! I say!" said Jim, in sudden alarm, "you're not hurt, really, are you, old man?"

"Not a bit," grinned his chum, jumping up. "Merely lazy, as you truthfully remark, and besides, you were so busy that there didn't seem any need for me to be more than ornamental." He dodged a flick from Jim's stock-whip, and swung himself into the saddle.

Far across the paddock they could see Norah in hot pursuit of a bullock. Bosun was hardly trained after stock yet; so far he lacked the amazing instinct that comes to horses, making them understand precisely what a bullock will do next—often some time before the bullock himself knows. The brown pony was only too willing to gallop; that was simple; but he was weak in the delicate science of checking and heading a beast, of propping and swinging so as to anticipate every froward impulse in his bovine brain. It made Norah's task no easy one, for the bullock was a big, determined Queenslander, with a set desire for peace and freedom. There was no chance of using a stock-whip, since Bosun was far too excited to permit such a liberty. She could only gallop and try to head him, and shout—her clear voice came ringing across the grass. Finally determination in the pursuer proved stronger than the same quality in the pursued, and the bullock gave in. He turned and trotted sulkily back, with Bosun dancing behind him.

So they galloped and shouted and raced through the long hot morning until they were all hoarse and tired, with tempers just a little frayed at the edges. Even Jean and Norah were of opinion that there may be less fun in mustering than they had dreamed. Bosun was a distinctly tiring proposition in such work as this, his lack of training, coupled with his excitability, making him anything but easy to ride. Many times a bullock got away from Norah because she had been unable to turn her pony—since Bosun saw no reason why he should not sail on to the end of the paddock when once he got going. On one occasion he did actually get out of hand, and bolted a long way, scattering the cattle in his mad career. Altogether it was a strenuous morning, and they were all very thankful when persistent effort succeeded in getting all the bullocks together and through the gate, and so across the next paddock to a set of yards built for just such emergencies, to save driving stock the long distance back to the homestead.

"Eh, but I'm thirsty," said Wally, slipping Warder's bridle over a post and turning to take Bosun. "Norah, you look jolly tired."

"I'm all right," Norah answered. "I only want tea, and buckets of it. But this fellow makes your arms ache; he's been trying to bolt all the time. I'd have been more use riding an old cow, I believe."

"Don't you talk rubbish," said Jim, leading Nan and Garryowen up to the fence. "But I tell you what, old girl, you're going to ride my neddy after lunch. He's quite a stock horse now, and won't be nearly so hard on your arms."

"Well, I don't like shirking," Norah said, looking doubtfully at Bosun. "He's such a beauty, too, Jimmy—only he doesn't understand yet."

"Of course he doesn't—you can't expect it," said her brother. "You wouldn't care for it if he went like an old sheep, naturally. He'll be all right after a little regular work with the cattle. Anyhow, you want a rest."

"And you're sure you're not too heavy for Bosun?" said Bosun's owner, doubtfully, looking at Jim's long figure.

"I thought that had something to do with it," Jim grinned. "Don't you worry, my child; I won't squash your pretty pet!" To which Norah responded by turning up an already tilted nose, and proceeding to unpack the lunch valise, which had bumped somewhat cruelly on Warder's saddle all the morning, considerably to the detriment of the hard-boiled eggs.

Lunch was simple; they boiled the billy at a little fire in a green hollow where there was no grass dry enough to risk burning, and drank great quantities of tea in the shade of a big she-oak tree. At first Norah and Jean declared that they were too hot to eat; but they revived considerably after the first fragrant cup, and found Brownie's sandwiches very good. Then Jim emptied the inconsiderable remains of the tea over the fire and stamped it out carefully, separating the embers; and the two boys took the horses for the drink that could not be allowed them until they had cooled down. After which the girls professed themselves ready to start; but Mr. Linton ordered half an hour's "smoke-oh," with a keen eye on two faces that were quite too sun-kissed to look pale, but were certainly a little weary. So they all lay flat in the shade, and all but the squatter went to sleep almost immediately, while he sat propped against the she-oak trunk and smoked lazily. The half-hour had stretched almost to an hour before he woke them.

"Come on, you sleepy-heads!" he said, smiling at them. "Time to get busy."

"Ugh-h—I'm stiff!" uttered Wally, wriggling, with an agonized countenance. "I think I've been tied in a tight knot, judging by my feelings." A small twig caught him neatly on the back of the neck, and, forgetting his stiffness, he sprang up and gave chase to Jim, who was already at the horses.

"Oh, I'm so hideously hot!" Norah grumbled.

"Or hotly hideous?" called out Jim, who looked provokingly cool.

"Both, I think. All the same, that was a nice sleep. Don't you feel better, Jean?"

"Heaps," said Jean, who was busy in removing burrs and fragments of grass from her divided skirt. "At least, I will feel heaps better after I've got over feeling as horrible as I do just now." She pushed the hair away from her eyes. "If only one could have a bathe!"

"We'll have one to-night, in the lagoon," Norah told her.

"You won't have much chance of anything to-night except supper and bed, if we're not quick," said Mr. Linton. "Come along—you've rubbed that pony long enough, Jim. Get in behind those bullocks."

He took his place at the drafting gate at the end of the race—the narrow lane, high fenced, connecting the big yard, where the cattle had been put, with two smaller yards. The boys whistled to the dogs and slipped in through the fence, urging the bullocks down the race. There Mr. Linton, with a quick turn of the gate, directed their further progress—the Queenslanders into one yard, the older bullocks into the other. Norah and Jean, debarred by the distinction of sex from active participation in these joys, took up a commanding position on the cap of the fence, occasionally emitting a warning yell when a bullock turned back at the very moment when he should have been entering the race.

Drafting cattle is far more pleasant work after a shower of rain. Even mud is better to work in than dust, which rises, and chokes and blinds you, and annoys the bullocks, and makes the entrance to the race puzzlingly obscure. Luckily these yards were not very often used, and had a thin carpet of grass, otherwise the job would have been a more difficult and lengthy one. As it was, when the cattle were finally divided into their respective mobs, and the boys came out of the yard, their features were somewhat indefinite, thanks to the coating of dust that covered each cheerful countenance.

Mr. Linton rammed home into its socket the peg that secured the drafting gate, and rejoined his assistants. They mounted—Norah this time on Garryowen—and Jim let out the Queensland cattle, which immediately made off in the direction of water. Withdrawn from the creek, not without difficulty, they were hustled into the Far Plain and driven along the way they had come that morning, with no chance of nibbling the sweet green clover that was provokingly soft under their feet.

Near the slip-rails Mr. Linton turned to Norah.

"We won't have any more trouble," he said, "they're tired, and will go through into the Bush Paddock quietly. You and Jean can cut back if you like, and let out the others."

"All right, Daddy," said Norah, happily. "And bring them along into this paddock?"

"Yes, it will save time. You'll find they'll be only too ready to come."

So Jean and Norah cantered back over the springy turf. The sun was setting, and the trees sent long shadows far across the paddock. A little breeze had sprung up from the west, swelling gradually to a cool wind, that fanned their hot faces—it was quite easy to forget the heat and burden of the day.

The big yard gate swung open—it was one of Mr. Linton's "notions" that there should be no gate on Billabong that should not open easily, without forcing a rider to dismount. The cattle came out gladly, stringing across towards the clover of their own home, Jean and Norah behind them, happy in the certainty of really being able to render service. Just as the last slow beast had wandered through the open gateway, the three masculine workers came cantering back.

"Well done!" said Mr. Linton, with approval. "Did they give you any bother?"

"Not a bit, Dad."

"That's right. But I'm afraid it's going to be too dark for that bathe, Jean."

"Can't be helped," said that lady, philosophically. "There are tubs!"

"And there's tea!" said Wally, thankfully. "I don't know which I want more at this moment."

"I do, then," said Norah, surveying him with critical eyes. "There isn't a doubt!"

"Your face, my thane, is as a book, where men

May read strange matters,"

quoted Mr. Linton, smiling. "Not fair to jibe at you, Wally, old man, when you earned your stripes in a good cause."

Wally put his hand up to his face, where little runners of perspiration had made streaks in the grimy surface.

"I'm used to ingratitude," he declared. "I've a good mind to make a non-washing vow, like those Indian Johnnies and keep off soap and water for seven years!"

"Then you'll certainly have your meals out in the back yard!" Norah assured him. They shook their tired horses out of a walk and cantered home across the paddocks through the gathering dusk.

CHAPTER IX
A LITTLE YELLOW FLAME
There's rest and peace and plenty here, and eggs and milk to spare;

The scenery is calm and sane, and wholesome is the air;

The folk are kind, the cows behave like cousins unto me—

But, please the Lord, on Monday morn I'm leaving Arcady.

—Victor J. Daley.

AS she had predicted, Mrs. Brown had not found idleness during the morning hours. The individual who is popularly supposed to supply mischief for unoccupied hands could never be said to number Brownie among his clients. Jim was wont to say that she was a tiringly busy person—with a twinkle in his eye. Her huge form moved with a quite amazing lightness, and she was rarely to be seen sitting still. On the infrequent occasions that she subsided into a chair she produced wool and needles from some unseen receptacle about her person, and knitted as though her life depended on it.

There had, however, been no time during this long, hot morning for such gentle arts as knitting. Brownie was short-handed, the races having taken away some of her helpers; in addition, it was baking day, and that in itself was sufficient for any ordinary woman. The bread had gone into the great brick oven comparatively early. By the time it came out there were other things ready to go in—mammoth cakes and pies, and kindred delicacies. No oven cooks with the perfection of a brick one. Brownie never allowed its heat to be wasted on the days that it was lit for the bread baking. Then "her hand being in," she proceeded to compound lesser matters— little cakes, cream puffs, rolls, whatever might be calculated to appeal to the healthy appetites that would return to her that evening. "They do take some cookin' for, they do—bless them," she mused.

She was outside the kitchen, rooting in the dark recesses of the brick oven with an instrument resembling a fish slice made into a Dutch hoe, when an unfamiliar step sounded on the gravel behind her. At the moment her occupation was quite too engrossing to be relinquished for any step. She did not turn until her explorations had been crowned with success, and she had backed away from the oven door, bearing on her weapon a delicately-browned pie. She deposited it carefully on a little table placed handily, shut the oven door, and faced round.

"Oh, it's you," she said. "I thought you'd gone, Harvey."

"Wasn't any 'urry," said Harvey, a short, weedy individual with a crafty face. "Boss said I could 'ave some tucker."

"He thought you was goin' to get it hours ago," said Brownie. "What have you been doin', hangin' about like this?"

"Haven't been doin' anything," the man answered sulkily. "Been campin' on me bed; there's no points in tearin' off in this sort of weather. It don't hurt you, I suppose?"

Brownie stared at the insolent face much as she might have regarded some weird curiosity among the lower animals.

"No," she said, after prolonged contemplation, during which Harvey had shuffled uneasily. "It don't hurt me at all; only I happen to be in charge of the place, and it's my business to see Mr. Linton's orders carried out. So I think the best thing you can do, an' the most comferable for all concerned, is to take yourself off as soon as possible."

"Oh, I'm goin'—don't you fret," Harvey said. "Wouldn't stay on the beastly place, not if I was paid. A nice name I'll give Linton in the township—an' the Melbourne registry offices, too! He'll know all about it when he wants to engage new men."

"You poor little thing!" said Brownie, pityingly. "Funny now, to see you that full of malice an' bad temper—and to know how little notice any one'll take of you! All the districk knows the sort of employer Mr. Linton is—he don't never need to send to Melbourne for his hands. Why," said Brownie, becoming oratorical in her emotion, "there's alwuz men just fallin' over themselves to get work on Billabong—an' better men than you'll ever be! You go an' talk just as much as you like—it'll never hurt my boss. But I wouldn't advise you to get into Master Jim's way—him bein' handy with his hands!"

"That pup!" muttered Harvey, malevolently; "why, 'e's only a kid; I guess I could manage him pretty easy if I wanted to."

"If you want any tucker off me, I'd advise you to keep a civil tongue in your head," warned Brownie. "Master Jim ain't to be discussed by you, not near my kitchen anyhow. If you ask me, I'll tell you straight I don't think you're fit to menshin his name!"

Harvey took a step nearer, almost threateningly. But Brownie had handled too many insolent swagmen in her day to be in the least afraid of this undersized little man, with the rat face.

"Now, don't you be foolish, Harvey," she advised. "I'm not likely to be scared of you, or any one like you; and if I was, there's old Hogg just over the fence in the garden, an' Lee Wing in the onions, an' they'd put you into the lagoon as soon as look at you if they caught you givin' me any cheek. That sort of thing don't go down on Billabong."

Harvey's answering snarl might have signified anything unpleasant. Brownie regarded him reflectively.

"Fact is," she remarked confidentially, "I'm really a bit sorry for you. I don't know what kind of a mother you had, but it's me certain belief that she never spanked you half enough as a boy. You don't strike me as having had much spanking, an' I'm not too sure as you wouldn't be the better for it now. What's the good of goin' on like this?—just a useless waster! Whatever on earth do you think you're goin' to make of your poor little life?"

"Ah, get out!" said Harvey, not at all impressed by this impassioned oration. "What's it got to do with you or any one else?"

"Very little," said Brownie, majestically. "You ain't likely to be in danger of any one here breakin' their hearts with worryin' over you, anyhow. Deary me! I hope Providence is with them turnovers in the oven, or else they'll be burnt black on me!" She waddled hurriedly into the kitchen and rescued the tarts—not too late. Rising with some difficulty from shutting the stove door, she found Harvey behind her.

"You'll have to be off, Harvey, you know," she said, firmly. "I ain't got time to talk to you, even if I wanted to, which I don't; an' Mr. Linton'd be annoyed if he came home an' found you still encumberin' the place. Take my advice an' try an' get another good job, an' stick to it this time. You're young yet, you know, an' there's no reason why you shouldn't turn over a new leaf an' do well." ("Only, his face is agin it!" she murmured to herself.)

"Aw, don't go preachin'," Harvey muttered. "There ain't no chance for a poor beggar of a workin' bloke in this country——"

"Don't you talk that kind of silly nonsense to me," returned Brownie, warmly. "If ever a country was God's own country for a man not afraid to use his hands, an' with pluck to tackle the land, it's Australia! I got three sons on the land—an' if I had thirty-three I'd put 'em all there! But unless the Angel Gabriel came along an' took you by the back of the neck an' shoved you, you'd never work—an' I think even Gabriel 'ud have his hands full. There, I ain't got time for you. Your tucker's here; I got it ready early this morning."

"Can't I stop an' have dinner?" he whined.

Brownie hesitated.

"No, you can't," she said at length. "Dinner's not for an hour, and Mr. Linton left pertikler directions that I was to have your tucker ready so's not to keep you from makin' a start. He wanted you to get off the place, an' I won't take the responsibility of keepin' you when you ought to have been gone hours ago. There's enough tucker there for three meals—the meat'll only go bad on you, in this weather, if you don't use it." She thrust the parcel of food—a generous bundle—into his hands. "I'll give you a bottle of milk, too, if you like," she added.

"Milk be darned!" said Harvey, savagely. "I'll let the distrck know you turned me out without a meal!"

"The districk'll be interested," responded Brownie, with great composure. "Now, be off, or I'll call the men—an' Hogg's temper's none too good these warm days!"

Harvey's snarl was not a pleasant addition to an unpleasant countenance.

"Mark my words, I'll——" he began.

"Mark my words, you'll find the hose turned on you if you don't go out of here politely!" said Brownie, her good-tempered old face flushing. "Get along with you, an' don't be a silly young man!" She turned her back upon him decisively, and opened the oven door with a snap. Harvey stood still for a moment, his evil features working furiously. Then he shambled out of the kitchen and across the yard, pursued hotly by Puck, the Irish terrier, who barked at his heels in extreme wrath.

"Wonderful how that blessed dog hates vermin!" uttered Brownie. She watched Harvey until he was out of sight—seeing him pick up his swag outside the gate and shuffle away down the track. Even the swag was typical of him—badly rolled and lumpy, with ends sticking out of the straps in various places. Puck came back presently, apparently disheartened by this species of quarry, that was not even sporting enough to show fight; and presently a bend in the tree-fringed track hid the shambling figure.

"A good riddance!" uttered Brownie, turning from the window. "Wonder if he favoured his pa or his ma?" Ruminating on this important point, she returned to cleaner matters.

Harvey, however, did not go far.

It was very hot, and his swag, although it contained little enough, was heavy upon his weedy shoulders. Even the bundle of food bothered him. It took up his free hand, and made it hard to keep away the flies that buzzed persistently about his face and crawled into the corners of his eyes in maddening fashion. He tried balancing it upon his stick across his shoulders, but the pressure of the stick hurt him, and the parcel kept slipping about, and nearly fell more than once. He abused it with peevish anger, including the heat, and Mr. Linton and Billabong generally in his condemnation. Finally, he stopped and kicked the dust reflectively.

"Blessed if I start in this darned heat!" he uttered.

He looked about him. To return to the house was clearly unsafe. He scowled, remembering Brownie's determined face, and her evident resolve to rid Billabong of his presence. Ahead, there was very little cover for a few miles, and Harvey was rapidly sure that he did not intend to walk so far in the heat. Clumps of box trees were scattered about, but a man sheltering in their shade was easily visible from the house, and he had no mind to be visible. Where could a lone wayfarer dispose of his unobtrusive presence?

Looking back, a little to the west of the stables, a thick clump of low-growing trees caught his eye—lemon gums, planted by Mr. Linton as shade in a little paddock where a few horses could be turned out when it was necessary to keep them close at hand. They grew in a corner, hedged in on two sides by a close-growing barrier of hawthorn. It was a tempting place, cool and shady. A man might lie there unseen of any one, although it was but a few chains' distance from the stables.

Harvey glanced round. No one was in sight. Behind him the homestead slumbered peacefully, its red roofs peeping from the mass of orchard green. That abominable dog had retreated, much to his relief. Puck always caused him to feel uneasy sensations in the calves of his legs when he rent the air behind him with yelps. It occurred vividly to Harvey that it would have been gratifying to have been able to kill Puck before he went away. Then he left the track, and hurried across the long grass to the little clump of trees.

He reached it unseen, and flung himself on the grass, dropping his swag and bundle thankfully, and tucking himself as far back into the shade of the hedge as the hawthorn spikes would allow. It was the only green thing; the lemon gums looked dry and parched, and the long grass of the little paddock was quite hard and yellow. Still, it was a good nook for a lazy man; the trees hid him from the stables and the house, and the hedge from any other point of view. He stretched out luxuriously— and then jumped up with a nervous start, as an old kerosene tin, nearly hidden under the hedge, rattled and banged as his boot caught it. Harvey told the kerosene tin just what he thought of it, flinging it further away in childish anger. Then he lay down again, and went to sleep, his mean little face half hidden under his battered hat.

When he awoke it was long past the usual dinner hour, and he was hungry. He unpacked Brownie's parcel, abusing her in a muttered snarl as he did so, and fell to work eagerly on the provisions. Then he dived into the recesses of his swag, and produced a whisky bottle which he had already visited several times during the morning, and washed the meal down with the raw spirit. He tried to sleep again, but sleep would not come, so he propped himself against the trunk of a lemon gum and smoked cigarettes during the hot afternoon, occasionally seeking solace from the bottle. After a time the latter gave out, which annoyed him greatly; he flung it into the hedge, and continued to smoke.

As long as the whisky lasted Harvey had no complaint to make about his day, which was, indeed, a picnic of the kind his soul most desired. He considered that a man not compelled to work, and supplied with food, whisky and cigarettes, has very little more to ask in this troublesome world. It was regrettable that, even to obtain these, it had been necessary to perform something even faintly resembling work. Still, work did not exist on his present horizon; his cheque would last a little while, and beyond that he did not trouble to think—at least, while the whisky yet remained to him.

But when the bottle ran dry his contented mood rapidly fell away from him. He had been dreaming gentle, whisky-assisted day-dreams of suddenly rising to fame and fortune—the means he most favoured consisted in buying a horse out of a costermonger's barrow, for, say, 2s. 11d. and training it in secret until he won the Melbourne Cup with it. It made him very happy, but he could not dream it unassisted; and the bottle was empty, leaving him not quite sober, yet a very long way from drunk—an unpleasant position. Instead of such joyous visions, cheerless spectres came to him—work, and policemen, and bosses; all three equally distasteful. He went over and over the recital of his woes—of Mr. Linton, bloated capitalist and slave-driver, rolling in wealth and grinding the poor beneath his large boot; of himself, Harvey, toiling heavily for a pittance, his lot unredeemed by kindness or fair treatment. Put in that way, it made quite a pathetic case. Harvey grew sorrier for himself with every minute and more and more convinced of the injustice of his lot. That Mr. Linton worked harder than any man he employed, and that he himself had not made the smallest effort to earn his wages, mattered to him not at all. The squatter represented the hated class that owned money, while he had none; and the fact was sufficient condemnation in Harvey's eyes. He passed from the stage of whining to that of showing his teeth—somewhat hampered by the fact that no one was near to be impressed by the exhibition.

He had worked himself into a sullen fury by the time the sun suddenly dipped behind the western pines, and he realized that it was late—that he should have been on the track long ago. It made another item in his list of grievances. Harvey hated walking—the fourteen miles to Cunjee seemed a hundred as he sat on the grass and thought about it. Still, he did not dare to remain until the others should come home—willing enough to hurt them, could he find a secret chance, he was as little anxious to face Mr. Linton and Jim as he was to meet Murty and the stockmen, whose criticisms, he felt, would be pointed.

He lit a cigarette, letting the match drop carelessly, and a little trail of fire sprang up in the grass in quick answer. Harvey put it out with a casual blow from his hat; even he knew a man must not play tricks with matches in summer. And then the whisky, working on his own evil mind, put a thought into him, and he bit off the end of his cigarette in sudden excitement.

It was a mad thought, but he toyed with it as he sat there, smoking fiercely, until it did not seem so mad after all. Other men had been punished for oppressing the poor. Other squatters had known what it meant to offend the working man— had seen their sheep go unshorn, their lambs undocked, their bullocks left untended. Other swagmen had done what was in his brain to do—had left a fire carefully smouldering near a station boundary so that it should get away into the long grass. It had always seemed to him a particularly smart thing to do—the sort of thing to serve a squatter jolly well right, and prove to him that he was not going to ride rough-shod over every one. There would be exquisite enjoyment in administering just such a lesson to Billabong's owner. Yet, how to do it?

He was not devoid of cunning. Risk to his own skin was the only thing that really mattered to him. He turned over in his mind various plans, and rejected all of them because he could not quite see his way out. Once started in the long, dry grass, a fire would travel like a flash. There would be no time for the man who lit it to make his escape, for the alarm would have been given before he had gone half a mile. He could not even plead an escaped spark from a camp fire. He had no billy, and with the thermometer at 110 degrees in the shade, there was no possible excuse for a man to light a fire, unless he wanted to brew tea. And short shrift would be given to the "swaggie" careless with pipe and matches in such weather, with the grass like a yellow crop over the sun-baked district. It was really very difficult to be an incendiary, with a due regard for your skin.

Then the old kerosene tin he had kicked away earlier in the afternoon caught his eye, and he gave a low, triumphant whistle. There was an old trick; he had heard of it in Gippsland, if a man wanted to light his cut scrub before the law allowed him to burn it. You put a candle, alight, under a tin, and then rode away, leaving the little sheltered flame to burn slowly down until it came to the tinder-like grass. By that time you were probably inspecting cattle at a farm ten miles off, so that no one could say you had been near your own property to start the fire. It was a very happy way of proving an alibi, and, whatever the neighbours might think, particularly if your burn had spread to their paddocks and involved them in loss, the police could say nothing to you.

"Why not?"

Harvey asked himself the question quite cheerfully. He had a candle. It had occurred to him that the one in his room might be useful, so he had packed it in his swag. The tin appeared to have been put there by a thoughtful Fate. Everything was playing into his hands. Already it was almost sunset. The candle was nearly new, and it would burn long enough to let him get a long distance away. Even if the cracks of the old tin should show a faint glow, no one would notice it behind the clump of gum trees. And once burned to the grass—well, the grass would do the rest.

He took out the candle, and made a little hole in the ground to act as a socket, pressing it tightly into position. Round it he cut the tall tops of the grass, so that the blaze should not come too soon, laying them round the base—a carefully-prepared little mat of tinder. Then he rolled up his swag and made quite ready to start.

He lit the candle. The flame burned steadily in the still, hot air. Then, gently, he inverted the kerosene tin over it, peeping through a hole in the side to make sure that the little yellow flame was still alight. It seemed a little weak—perhaps there was not enough air. So he slipped a stick under one edge, tilting it very slightly, yet enough to admit a breath. He nodded, pleased with his improvement.

"I guess that'll about fix you, Mr. David Linton!" he muttered.

There was a hole in the hawthorn hedge near him. He pushed his swag through and crawled after it. No one was in sight. He cast a hurried look round. Then he rose and almost ran from the spot—from the rusty kerosene tin and the little yellow flame. The twilight shrouded him—a mean figure, slinking in the shadow of the hedge.

CHAPTER X
MIDNIGHT
When the north wind moans thro' the blind creek courses,

   And revels with harsh, hot sand,

I loose the horses, the wild red horses,

I loose the horses, the mad red horses,

And terror is on the land!

—Marie E. J. Pitt.

DUSK fell, and the stars came out to ride in a blue-black sky, before the sound of horses' feet, galloping, floated to the quiet house at Billabong. Mrs. Brown came out on the verandah, one hand at her ear, listening.

"Here they are—an' thank goodness!" she uttered. "I'm never easy in me mind when they're out on them young horses—not as anything ever happens, but who's to say it isn't goin' to? It's always a relief, like, to see them come scrimmagin' in!"

Hogg, a dim figure in the gloom of a big clump of hydrangea, merely grunted. Norah considered that a serious realization of the claims of his name had induced Hogg to practise grunting. It was a fine art with him, and capable of innumerable shades of expression.

Just now he was hunting snails—his dour face occasionally revealed in an almost startling manner by gleams from the tiny lantern he carried.

"Watter will always bring them," he remarked.

"Eh?" asked Brownie, sharply.

"Ay. The place was free a week back—an' noo they're crawlin' all through it—rapacious beasts!"

"What on earth are you saying, man?" demanded Brownie, bristling.

"Tes the snails, Mistress Broon. Whiles, 'a wes thinkin' there wes none; but sin' 'a've been soakin' this pairt o' the gairden they've made ma life a burrden. 'A ken fine there's nae gairdener wull get to heaven gin he has to deal much in life wi' snails!" said Hogg, desperately.

"Nasty beasts!" said Brownie sympathetically. She shuddered as a crunching sound came from under Hogg's boot, and fled indoors; and the Scotchman worked on, pondering upon the peculiar and painful susceptibilities of women. "It makes ma heart glad to scrunch 'em!" he reflected, demolishing half a dozen of his enemies with a massive boot.

The riders trotted into the stable yard, tired, but cheerful.

"Coming home was the best part of the day," said Norah, happily, slipping off and beginning to unbuckle Bosun's breastplate, leaving Garryowen to Jim. Garryowen had carried her like a bird; but Norah had a fancy for letting her own property go.

"I think you can put Bosun in the stable to-night," her father said; "Monarch and Garryowen, too; they deserve a bit of hard feed."

"And don't Nan and Warder?" protested Jean.

"Yes—but they aren't used to it," said Mr. Linton, laughing. "These three are pampered babies, and the others are matter-of-fact old stagers."

"Nan's a dear!" said Jean, indignantly. She caressed the brown mare's long nose.

"I'll slip over after tea and feed them," Jim said. "They're a bit hot now."

"Very well," his father answered, leading Monarch into the dark recesses of the stable and returning for Bosun. "Better leave the others in the yard, too, until you come over; then you can give them some chaff, just to set Jean's mind at rest." He pulled that lady's hair gently. "Make haste, we've kept poor Brownie unconscionably late."

Brownie showed no signs of having been delayed. She met them smilingly, and called Wally "poor dear!" when he simulated extreme fatigue. Tea was a mighty meal, and before it was over Norah and Jean felt their eyelids drooping. It was still very hot in the house. Outside, a wind began to blow fitfully from the west.

"Go to bed, both of you!" ordered Mr. Linton, as they rose from the table and went out through the long windows upon the verandah. "You're both knocked up. What's that light moving?"

"That's Hogg, snail hunting," Jim answered.

"I'll be fined for working him overtime some day," said his father. "Most of them are only too glad to knock off, but Hogg's a demon to work."

"This isn't work, it's sport!" grinned Jim.

"I should think Hogg's dreams would be haunted by the screams of slaughtered snails!" Wally said. "Wonder how many of their scalps he's entitled to wear at his saddle bow—slain in gentle and joyous combat! He's a mighty hunter." He yawned, cavernously. "Jim, if you want me to help you feed those horses before I go to sleep you'd better hurry."

"Come on," Jim said, swinging himself over the low railing of the verandah. "Then I'll race you to bed, if you like. Good-night, kids!"

"Kid yourself," said Norah, in great scorn. "Jean, first into the bath gets it!" Uttering this mystic prediction, she kissed her father hastily, and fled upstairs, with Jean toiling in her wake. Sounds of much splashing kept the bathrooms lively for some time. Then Billabong, clean, refreshed and profoundly sleepy, tumbled into bed and became oblivious of the world.

* * * * *

Norah woke from a confused dream of Hogg, mounted on an immense Queensland bullock, and chasing a battalion of snails down Mount Kosciusko. Variety was lent to the vision by the fact that Kosciusko had become an active volcano, and was in wild eruption behind the Scotchman, who was silhouetted blackly against a background of burning lava. And the snails were screaming.

For a moment she did not think she could be awake. The ridiculous dream had been vivid, and still the glow filled her room. Then again came the sound she had dreamed, and Norah was suddenly broad awake, and, flinging herself out of bed, fled to the window. She uttered a cry, and tugged at Jean frantically.

"Whatever's the matter?" asked Jean sleepily.

"Quick, tell Jim! Call him! Oh, hurry, Jean, the stables are on fire. I'm going—the horses!" She was groping for shoes and flinging on a coat. Then she tore downstairs, shouting as she went. From the stables, as she stumbled out upon the verandah, came again the sound of her dreams, and she caught her breath in a sob. For no one who has ever heard it can forget the horror of a horse's scream.

The stables were burning fiercely. One end, the westward end, that held the buggy house and harness rooms, was a sheet of flame; but the fire had not yet fairly seized upon the whole, although the door of the loose boxes showed trails of smoke coming from within. She could hear the trampling of hoofs, jostling, terrified, and then a long whinny of utter fear, rising again to a scream. Sobbing, she wrestled with the stiff bolt of the door.

Across the garden came a shout—Jim's voice.

"Come away from that, Norah! Come back, dear. They'll trample over the top of you." He was running desperately towards the little figure against the lit building.

"They're burning!" said Norah, sobbing. The fastening yielded, and she flung one door back, unable to see anything for the dense smoke. She called the horses by name, pushing open the lower door, and had barely time to jump aside when Monarch and Bosun bolted out, frantic with fear. Further back, the scream came once more.

"Oh, it's Garryowen!" Norah gasped, "and his door's shut; and if I don't go in, Jim will." She took a long breath, a child's fear fighting against pity and love. Then she put her arm up, as if to guard her eyes, and stumbled into the smoke.

Within, it was almost impossible to breathe. Fierce little shoots of fire came through cracks in the wall that showed a mass of flame beyond; and the heat was choking and deadly. Already the roof was burning; the hay in the loft above had caught, and the flames were shooting fifty feet above the stables. In his box, Jim's big bay thoroughbred was rearing and kicking, mad with terror. Even when Norah had managed to open his door, he would not come out to face the unknown horrors. She called him, trying to steady her voice—knowing that to venture within his box in his maddened state was little short of suicide. From outside she could hear Jim's voice, shouting for her, sharp with anxiety.

"Oh, I'll have to leave him!" Norah sobbed. "The fire's coming through the roof. Oh, Garry, dear, do come out!"

Above the loose box the ceiling split open for about a yard, and a shower of burning fragments came down. They struck Garryowen on the quarter—and the great horse, screaming, plunged through the open door and out like a whirlwind to the glimpse of star-lit sky that showed through the further doorway. Behind him Norah staggered feebly, brushing burning particles from her hair—holding one hand across her mouth in the vain effort to keep out the choking smoke. Within sight of safety, consciousness left her; she tripped, falling face downward on the wooden blocks.

Jean's terrified voice at his door had awakened Jim almost before Norah had flown downstairs. The glow in his room did not put the fear into his heart that flashed there at the stammering words—

"Norah's gone over!"

"Norah—she mustn't!" the boy gasped. He flung himself past Jean, shouting to her to warn the rest of the house, and raced across to the burning stables. At the gate of the yard Monarch and Bosun almost were upon him—they swerved in their maddened gallop, missing him by a hair's breadth as he ran. But there was no sign of the little sister.

He peered through the smoke wildly, calling to her. For all that he knew, his own horse was already out, safe in some dark corner of the yard; that Norah had gone into the burning building did not enter his head. He searched for her, shouting her name more and more loudly. A sudden terror came upon him lest the horses should have knocked her down as they rushed out—he sprang to the open doors, in sick fear of finding her hurt—senseless. But nothing was visible—nothing but the rolling clouds of flame-shot smoke. He paused, irresolute.

Then he heard Norah's voice at Garryowen's box, and even as he leapt forward, amazed and despairing, came a clatter of hoofs on the wooden pavement, as the bay horse bolted out in his last wild dash for safety. His shoulder just brushed Jim as he plunged through the doorway, but the touch was enough to send the boy staggering back, almost falling. He recovered himself with an effort, dashing into the stable.

Beyond him, above Garryowen's loose box, the roof split gradually, and the roar of inrushing flames filled his ears. They lit up the dark interior, for a moment even stronger than the cruel smoke. Then he saw Norah at his feet. He picked her up, holding her with her face pressed against him to save her from the burning fragments that filled the air—staggering out, grim and determined, with his breath coming in choking gasps. Then his father's voice rang in his ears, and he saw Wally's face dimly and felt their hands as they drew him and his burden to safety.

He put Norah down on the grass gently, a limp, unconscious figure. A voice he did not recognize as belonging to him was gasping something about water, and he heard Wally's swift feet, that seemed to go and come all at once——. They were splashing water on Norah's face, but she did not move; and suddenly he heard a dry sob break from his father, more terrible in its agony than any sound could ever be again. Perhaps it was in answer to it that Norah's eyes flickered a little and presently they opened more widely—red-rimmed eyes, half blind—and she smiled at them faintly. Her smoke-grimed lips moved in words that sounded like "all right."

Jim got to his feet and moved over to the fence, his shoulders shaking as he gripped the pickets.

"I thought she was dead," he said; "I was jolly well sure she was dead."

Voices and shouting were coming from the men's hut. Behind him a long, thundering crash echoed to the sky as the stable roof fell in. Then his father's hand was on his shoulder.

"Steady, old chap," said David Linton, "she's all right. Get to the hose in the garden quickly, Jim. The house has caught."

CHAPTER XI
THE BATTLE UNDER THE STARS
This is the homestead—the still lagoon

    Kisses the foot of the garden fence,

Shimmering under a silver moon

    In a midnight silence, cold and tense.

—W. H. Ogilvie.

SARAH, the housemaid, was at the big bell of the station, ringing it wildly. Long after every man and woman on Billabong was awake and busy, Sarah continued to ring. She said afterwards that it seemed to ease her!

A flying fragment from the burning loft had been carried by the wind across the gardens to the oldest part of the homestead—wooden rooms that were now used as storerooms and out-offices. In five minutes they were blazing fiercely.

Jim and Wally had raced for the garden fence, vaulting it, and landing in the midst of a bed of pansies.

"Lucky for us they weren't roses!" gasped Wally, picking himself up out of the soft soil. "A fellow wants to have on more than pyjamas for this sort of a lark!" They tore on, ploughing over Hogg's most cherished flower beds.

"Where is that blessed hose?" Jim uttered, wrathfully. He dived into various dark corners where taps existed. Then he stopped, frowning.

"Hogg was mending it. Confound the delay!" he said. "Start with the little one, Wal.; you know, it's near that palm you were climbing. I'll find Hogg." Shouting, he ran round the corner of the house, and collided violently with the gardener, hurrying to meet him with the great rubber coil in his hands. The shock sent them both staggering, and Hogg sat down abruptly.

"Ye took me—fair i' the wind!" he gasped. "Run on, laddie. A'll get ma breath presently."

Flames were shooting from half the windows upstairs when Jim at length got his hose to work. The fire had caught the wooden balcony, spreading from it to the upper rooms, and downstairs the kitchen was burning, and the back verandah had caught. Mr. Linton, running over after carrying Norah far out of the way of heat, and leaving her in Jean's care, saw how the flames were being sucked into the house through the wide-open back door.

"Won't do!" he muttered. Dashing in through the smoke, and gripping the almost red-hot door-handle with his felt hat, he managed to slam the door. He staggered off the verandah just as the flooring collapsed.

Black Billy, his eyes apparently starting out of his sable face, was at his elbow.

"Run round and shut the front door, if it's open, Billy!" Mr. Linton said, coughing.

"Plenty!" murmured Billy. He disappeared round the corner of the house, a black streak of fear.

On the eastern side the window of Mr. Linton's office stood open. The squatter swung himself through it with the lightness of a boy, and ran to his desk, which stood open, its roll-top flung back. It held papers that must not be risked—he thrust them into his overcoat pockets hurriedly; then, spreading the cloth from a little table on the floor, he emptied the drawers upon it, working by the dancing glow of the flames that lit up all the surroundings. Already the heat and smoke were almost unbearable.

"The safe's fireproof," he muttered, glancing towards its corner—"that's a comfort, anyhow!"

The room was becoming untenable. Clouds of smoke rolled in from the windows and crept, snake fashion, under the door. On the side of the room nearest the fire the plaster began to crack, and the paper shrivelled on the wall. It was difficult to breathe—David Linton's panting gasps seemed to choke him. He knew he could do no more. He added to the heap on the table cloth the portrait that always stood upon his desk—Jim and Norah's mother, sweet and young, smiling from her silver frame. Then he gathered all into a bundle and groped his way to the window.

Every available hose was already at work. The hiss of the water, falling on the flames, sounded like snakes angry at being disturbed. Beneath the office window, flames were licking at the wall; the woodwork at one side was blazing and crackling. David Linton hesitated, one hand on the sill—it was hot, and his load made him awkward.

From the garden came Jim's shout.

"Half a minute, Dad! Don't try to get out yet!"

The stream of water from his hose played suddenly upon the burning woodwork, splashing on the sill, and sprinkling the man who stood waiting. Above him the flames died out sullenly. Jim played on the hot bricks of the wall for a moment, in fear less already the fire in the house should be finding its way into the office—then he shouted again, deflecting the stream, and Mr. Linton climbed out, bringing his bundle carefully after him. He carried it across the garden, nodding at his son.

Behind the house, Murty O'Toole and Brownie had organized a bucket brigade.

"I can't carry buckets up to much," Brownie observed, "but I can pump a treat!" She worked the force-pump manfully, never ceasing, though the heat from the burning house made the metal portions of the pump too hot to touch, and her plump old face was crimson, and her breathing pitifully distressed. Sarah and Mary were in the line, passing the brimming buckets to the men with the easy swing of young bush-trained muscles. Mr. Linton, arriving at a run, shook his head.

"There's not a hope of saving this part," he cried. "We'd better concentrate on the front. Brownie, you're not to work like that—go over to the pepper trees and look after Norah. No—I'd rather you did——" as Brownie hesitated, unwillingly. "It would really be a relief to me to know you were with her—she said she had no burns, but I don't see how she can have escaped without any." Even at that moment a twinkle came to his eye, for at the hint Brownie uttered a dismayed exclamation, and fled away across the yard to her nursling. With Norah needing her, the house might burn, indeed!

"We'll save what we can from the front rooms, Murty," the squatter went on, leading the way with rapid strides. "Some of you get to work with the buckets—there are four of them hosing. It's a mercy the water pressure's good."

They flung open the French windows in the front of the house. Already every room was filled with smoke; the men dashed in and out, holding their breath—bringing out silver and pictures and books first—the things that no insurance money could replace. Jim, from his post near the tap, smiled a trifle to see his father's first load—his own silver cups, trophies of his years at school. Stopping at the edge of the lawn, Mr. Linton bowled them down the sloping grass, and hastened back for more.

From the window of the drawing-room came Dave Boone and Black Billy, staggering under the piano. At the edge of the verandah Billy's end slipped and jarred heavily upon the kerb, the strings setting up a demoniacal jangle. Billy uttered a yell of terror, and bolted down the lawn, being recalled with great difficulty by Mr. Boone, who expressed a harassed wish to "break his useless black neck." But the dusky one firmly refused to touch the piano again.

"That pfeller debbil-debbil!" he said. "Baal me hump him any more." He rescued the drawing-room fire-irons with heroic determination, while Mr. Linton came to the assistance of the bereft Mr. Boone, whose wrath was tending towards apoplexy.

Lee Wing held the nozzle of one hose firmly directed upon a dangerous point. He was a peculiar spectacle. The prudence characteristic of the gentle Chinaman had induced him to put on as many clothes as possible before leaving his hut, and he was attired in at least three suits. They were uncomfortable, but he had the consolation of knowing where they were; and a spark might send his hut up in smoke at any moment. Upon his bullet head were four hats, each pulled down firmly. His pockets bulged with miscellaneous possessions, his pigtail floated behind him. If the worst should come to the worst, Lee Wing was clearly prepared to start back to China.

His hereditary enemy, Hogg, worked not far off. As a rule the feud between the gardeners did not slumber, but just now they were as brothers. Hogg's mind was too full of woe over the destruction of his garden to be troubled by what he was wont to call contemptuously the Yaller Peril, and Lee Wing, his trim expanse of vegetables well out of harm's way, felt something resembling pity for his competitor, whose flower beds were mere highways for trampling feet. Even as they looked, Billy dashed out of the house carrying a heavy carved box—Jim's handiwork—and dropped it upon a delicate rose bush with a loud, satisfied grunt. At the spectacle of slaughter Hogg gave a heavy groan and a sudden involuntary movement of the hand that held the nozzle of his hose. It turned the stream of water from its course—a matter of which Hogg, gazing open-mouthed at the destruction of his hopes, was quite unconscious, until a wrathful shout brought him back to earth with a start.

Then he realized that he was hosing Jim vigorously, deaf to his very justifiable remarks.

"What on earth are you up to?" sang out the dripping Jim. He burst out laughing at the Scotchman's dismayed face. "I'm not sorry for the bath, Hogg, but the house needs it more!"

"Losh!" gasped Hogg, gazing at his handiwork—paralysed past any possibility of apologizing. He swung the stream of water again to the fire, muttering horrified ejaculations in broad Scotch.

The stable had almost burned itself out. A dull, red glow came from the smoking bed of coals that smouldered angrily between the broken and blackened brick walls. One of these had fallen, with a crash that echoed round the hills; the others still stood, black holes gaping in them where windows had been, like staring eyes that watched the ruin of the pride of Billabong—for there had been no such stables in the district. Harvey's little plan had hit even harder than that ingenious gentleman had anticipated.

Beyond the fences the cattle stood in interested groups, fascinated by the fire; further off were the horses, thrilled with more fear than the stolid bullocks, but unable to tear themselves from the mysterious glow. But Monarch and Garryowen and Bosun were away at the farthest corner of the homestead paddock, quivering and starting yet, their hearts still pounding at the memory of the terrible moments in the burning stable; and on Garryowen's quarter were round, burnt patches, while half of his tail was singed off. Yet pain was not so dreadful to the big thoroughbred as Fear—fear that he could not understand, that had come to him in the darkness, and was yet knocking at his heart.

At the house the fire was slackening. Billabong was built of solid brick, so that there was not a great deal of inflammable material for the flames to fasten upon; and they had been discovered soon—not allowed, as in the stables, to obtain a firm hold. The defence had been prompt and thorough. David Linton blessed the forethought, coupled with the love of his garden, that had made him equip the homestead with water laid on from the river as well as with many tanks. They had needed it all.

He was at the hose now, having relieved Jim, to whom the business of standing still and holding a nozzle had been no light penance, despite the necessity of the proceeding. One of the men had taken Wally's place, and the boys had dashed off on a tour of the homestead, to look for any possibility of a further outbreak. David Linton looked at what remained of his house, his mouth stern—going back in memory to the time of its building, and the old, perfect companionship that had been by his side. Now the rooms that he and his wife had planned were black, smoking ruins, and the roses she had planted were shrivelled masses on the wall. There was no part of the house that did not have its memories of her, so vivid that often it seemed to him that he saw her yet, flitting about its wide corridors and the rooms that even until now had borne the magic of her touch.

All the years the home had helped him to fight his loneliness and his longing. Now——. He stared at it with eyes suddenly grown old.

Then across the grass came a little odd figure—Norah, still grimy with smoke, and very shaky, with Brownie's arm near her to help, and Jean not far off. Norah, her coat open over her blue pyjamas, and her hair, in her own phrase, "all anyhow," about her, and her grey eyes swimming as she looked from the house to her father's face. David Linton put down the hose and held out his hand to her silently, and Norah clung to him.

"Oh, Daddy, poor old Daddy!" she whispered.

Jim came round the corner with long strides; even odder than Norah, for he had not waited to put any overcoat over his pyjamas, and he had been drenched and dried, and blackened and torn, until he resembled a scarecrow in an advanced stage of disrepair. He gripped his father's free hand.

"It's not so bad, Dad!" he said, cheerily. "Lots of the old place left. We'll all build it up again, Dad!"

David Linton smiled at his children, suddenly.

"Right, mates!" he said. "We'll build it up again!"

CHAPTER XII
BURNT OUT
And the creek of life goes wandering on,

> Wandering by;

And bears for ever its course upon

> A song and a sigh.

—Henry Lawson.

ADROVER on the road with store cattle miles away saw the glow in the sky that night, and reported it next morning to a farmer driving in to Cunjee; and before noon half the township seemed to be out at the station.

Little Dr. Anderson, in his motor, was the first to appear. He found the Billabong inhabitants straying about the ruins to see what remained to them. The overseer's cottage and the men's hut had given them shelter for the remnant of the night after the fire had been finally extinguished, except Mr. Linton and Jim, who remained on guard until morning.

Within, the devastation was only partial. Most of the rooms in front were practically untouched, though all had been damaged by water. The back of the house had suffered most; little but the walls were left. Jim brought a long ladder for further explorations, for the stairs were unsafe, being burnt through in two places. He found that the rooms belonging to his father, Norah and himself bore traces of flood rather than of fire. The walls were cracked with heat, but otherwise they were intact. But the water had done its worst, and he groaned over the spectacle of Norah's pretty room, its red carpet a vision of discoloured slush, and the white furniture stained and blistered. All its little adornments were lying in confused heaps, swept down by the water. It was a gruesome sight.

Within the wardrobe and chest of drawers, however, clothes were unhurt. Jim took up a rope and lowered bundles down to his father, so that when Norah and Jean awoke, very late in the morning, it was to find clean raiment laid out for them by Brownie, and breakfast waiting for them in Mrs. Evans's neat little kitchen.

"Isn't it a mercy?" Jean confided to Norah. "Last night it didn't seem to matter at all running round before all Billabong in a nighty and a coat, but I went to sleep wondering how they'd look in the daytime!"

Brownie and the maids were the most to be pitied, for they had lost everything but a few cherished possessions, snatched up as they ran out of the house. Mary and Sarah were not hard to clothe—but Mrs. Brown was a different proposition. The united wardrobes of Mrs. Evans and Mrs. Willis, the men's cook, contrived something in the nature of a rig-out by dint of ripping out gathers and tucks and using innumerable safety pins. "I'm covered, if not clothed!" said Brownie, "an' thankful to be anything!"

Mr. Linton had resolutely put away his trouble, and was inspecting the remains with a keen, businesslike face.

"It's a matter of restoring rather than rebuilding," he told Dr. Anderson, who was spluttering with indignation still, more than an hour after his arrival. "The insurance should cover the damage, I fancy; and the back of the house can be built after more modern notions, which won't be a disadvantage. The stables? No—they will go up again precisely as they were. And the place will look the same, in the main; we don't want it altered. It will look abominably new, of course; our old mantle of ivy and virginia creeper is destroyed, and the walls will be bare for a long while. Poor old Hogg is mourning over his dead roses and the general havoc in his garden.

"Well, you take it calmly!" said the little doctor, explosively.

David Linton shrugged his shoulders.

"No good doing anything else," he answered. "And, after all, I have such immense cause for thankfulness in getting Norah out of that confounded place unhurt, that nothing else really matters. It's a nuisance, of course, and what I'm to do with the youngsters' holidays I don't know; it's pretty rough on them. But—good Lord, Anderson! I want to go and feel the child whenever I look at her, to make sure that she's really all right! It seems incredible—I never saw so hideously close a shave!"

"Norah's absolutely matter of fact over it," the doctor said. "I rebuked her in my best professional manner for doing such a mad thing, and she looked at me in mild surprise, and remarked, 'Why, if I hadn't, Jim would have gone!' It seemed to finish the argument as far as she was concerned. Wonder if your fellows have got Harvey?"

"Oh, they're bound to get him," the squatter answered. "And I wouldn't care to be Harvey when they do."

Murty O'Toole had commenced detective operations with break of day. He had not ceased to abuse himself for failing to be at the stables in time to help.

"A set of useless images," said he, in profound scorn. "Slapin' an' snorin' like so manny fat pigs—an' Miss Norah an' Masther Jim on the shpot! Bad luck to the heat an' the races!—ivery man jack of us was aslape almost before we was in bed, 'twas that tired we was. But that's no excuse!" Murty refused to be comforted, and only derived faint solace from the determination to find out the cause of the fire.

It did not require sleuth-hound abilities. The little paddock had burned in patches, for here and there were green expanses of clover that had checked the fire, and the hawthorn hedge had helped to stop it at the boundary; but the west wind had taken it straight across to the stables, and in the morning light the brown, burnt ground led Murty quickly to the clump of lemon gums. Behind them a kerosene tin stood, inverted, and the burn began there. When the stockman picked it up the blackened square of charred grass beneath it showed out sharply.

"That ain't the kind of thing that happens wid an accident," said Murty between his teeth. He looked further.

Behind the burnt ground, the place where a man had lain was easily visible in the long grass. There were cigarette butts in plenty, and a little further away an empty cigarette box. Murty pounced upon it in triumph.

"Humph!" he said. "Harvey smokes that brand—an' no wan else on Billabong."

Then the whisky bottle, half hidden in the hedge, caught his eye, and he picked it up. He was sure now. The smell of fresh spirit was still in it; and he had seen the bottle in Harvey's room two days before. And, with that, black rage came over Murty's honest heart, and for five minutes his remarks about the absent Harvey might have withered that individual's soul, had he indeed possessed such a thing. Then Murty replaced his evidence, and went for Mr. Linton.

He led the men away from the homestead an hour later, each as keen and as enraged as himself.

"Mind, boys, you've promised not to hurt him," David Linton said, "He'll get all that's coming to him—but I won't have the station take the law into its hands. We can't be absolutely certain." The men were certain: but they had promised, unwillingly enough. They went down the paddock at a hand-gallop, with set, angry faces.

Wally had ridden into Cunjee, to send telegrams and letters, and with an amazing list to be telephoned to Melbourne shops, since the township could not rise to great heights in the way of personal effects, saddlery, or even groceries. Billabong was, in patches, blankly destitute. Not a decent saddle was left, save those belonging to the men: buggies, harness, tools, horse feed—all had gone in the destruction of the stables. Norah and Jean were completely hatless, their head gear having been downstairs; and as Jim was wont to keep most of his every-day possessions in a downstairs bathroom where he shaved and dressed, he had nothing left but his best clothes, and a Panama sternly reserved, as a rule, for trips to Melbourne

"Nice sort of a Johnny you look, to be wandering round ther—ruined ancestral hall!" Wally told him derisively. "You might be a bright young man on the stage. It's hardly decent and filial for you to think so much of personal adornment at a time like this!" Further eloquence was checked by sudden action on the part of his friend, who was too unhappy over his own grandeur to bear meekly any jibes on its account. He had headed the telephone list with urgent messages for riding breeches and leggings, and a felt hat of the kind his soul desired. There was something little short of appalling to Jim in finding himself suddenly without any old clothes!

Following Dr. Anderson came riders from other stations, policemen from two or three scattered townships, and many other people anxious to help, so that the fences near the homestead were soon thickly occupied with horses "hung up" in every patch of shade. There was, of course, nothing to do. Nor could Billabong even maintain its reputation for hospitality, since it had been left almost without provisions. The storeroom containing the main quantities of groceries, as well as the meat house, had been amongst the first parts of the house to catch. Bags of flour could be seen, burst open, in the ruins, and thick masses of what looked like very badly-burned toffee, and had been sugar. The men's hut had fed the exiles, and further supplies would be brought out from Cunjee by Evans in his buggy—the only vehicle, except the station carts and drays, left on Billabong.

"It's really rather like being cast on a desert island," said Jean.

Norah laughed.

"I guess it's like that to all the people who have come out," she said. "Just fancy, Jean, we can't even give them a cup of tea. There's milk, and that's all there is. Isn't it awful?"

But the visitors had not come to be fed. They condoled, and looked round the ruins, and made strong and unavailing comments, and then, in the Australian fashion, offered all they had, from their houses to their buggies, to fill in any deficiencies. Invitations to find shelter at neighbouring places poured in upon Mr. Linton and his family. The squatter would not leave the homestead, but he considered the question of sending Jean and Norah to spend a week in Mrs. Anderson's friendly care, finally referring the matter to the girls themselves, and finding them so horrified at the idea that he promptly withdrew it.

"I don't want to crowd Evans's cottage out altogether," he said, half apologetically.

"Well, Mrs. Evans has a spare room, and she lets us wash up, and I'm going to bath the baby to-night!" said Norah. "And she wants us to stay—and Jim and Wally and you are going to sleep in the tents, anyhow. Oh, Daddy, don't send us away. I would hate it so!"

"All right, all right, you needn't go!" rejoined her father, laughing. "But it will be very dull for Jean: you can't ride or drive, and the cottage isn't as comfortable in this heat as Billabong."

But Jean reassured him, hastily. She had no desire to migrate to a world of strangers.

"It is hot, though, Daddy, that's a fact," said Norah. "I was thinking——" She broke off, watching him a little doubtfully.

"When you think in that tone, I have generally no chance of escape," said he. "What is it this time?"

"Well, there's another little tent." Norah hesitated, half laughing. "Jim would put it up and fix up bunks for us. Couldn't we come and join your camp down there?" She pointed towards the lagoon, where Jim had already taken two small tents and was hunting about for ridge poles. The bank looked cool and shady, fringed with groves of wattles and big box trees. "We could keep our things up at Mrs. Evans's cottage, and dress there: but it would be lovely to sleep in a tent. That little room is certainly hot."

Mr. Linton pondered. The lagoon was only a hundred yards from the cottage. Certainly, there was no great objection to the plan. And Norah was still bearing traces of the previous night, in white cheeks and heavy eyes: it was hard to refuse her anything in reason.

"Well, you may," he said, "if you can arrange matters with Jim."

"Oh, can we, Daddy? You are the blessedest——!" said Norah. Suddenly he was alone. Two strenuous figures in blue frocks descended upon the hapless Jim.

"Whatever's the matter?" Jim asked, looking up as they raced down upon him. "Not another fire? And aren't you two hot enough without doing Sheffield handicaps across here?" He had borrowed a pair of blue dungaree trousers from the wardrobe of Mr. Evans, and was, in consequence, much happier.

"Want you to put us up a tent," Norah said, cheerfully. "You don't mind, do you, Jimmy?"

Jim whistled. "What does Dad say?"

"Says we can if you'll fix it. You will, Jimmy, won't you? We'll help you ever so. It would be so lovelier than sleeping in a hot little room!"

"Oh, all right," said her easy-going brother. "You'll have to make yourselves scarce in the mornings, you know—this is our bathing place."

"Yes, we know. We'll do whatever you say," said Norah, with amazing meekness. "You're a brick, Jimmy. Shall we carry down the tent? I know where it is."

"No, you won't," said Jim, severely. "You can't try to commit suicide overnight and then make yourself a beast of burden in the morning. Wal. and I can bring it when he comes out; he ought to be back soon. Just you sit down in the shade and think of your sins."

"That won't keep me busy," Norah retorted. But she did as she was told, and they sat peacefully under a big weeping willow until Mrs. Evans summoned them to dinner.

After lunch there was nothing to be done at the homestead. Mr. Linton had gone to Cunjee in Dr. Anderson's motor to transact much business and talk on the telephone to Melbourne insurance people and building contractors. Wally appeared about three o'clock, hot and dusty, and reported the condition of the township.

"Every one's talking fire," he said. "The police and half the men are out after Harvey. I've never seen Cunjee so excited—it seems quite appropriate that they've still got the Christmas decorations in the streets! They're considerably withered, of course, but it seems to indicate that something's in the air. I guess Harvey will have a lively time when they catch him."

"Wish I could be in at the death," said Jim, grimly. His father's wish had kept him from joining the pursuit, but he had stayed unwillingly.

"Yes, it wouldn't be bad fun, would it? Wonder is they haven't got him already. He must be pretty well planted," Wally said. "He's certainly the man you've got to thank: if he'd a clear conscience he'd be in Cunjee now, instead of nobody knows where. Whew—w, it is hot! Come and have a swim, Jim."

"No swim for you yet awhile," Jim told him, grimly. "You've got to come and fix camp."

"Me?" asked Wally, blankly. "Of all the unsympathetic, slave-driving wretches——"

"Yes, that's so," grinned his chum. "All the same, you've got to come."

"I felt there was something in the wind," said Wally, lugubriously. "I left you as beautiful as a tailor's block, and looking very like one, only woodener, in your best suit; and I find you in dungarees and a shirt, and hideously happy. It isn't fair, and me so hot. Isn't he a brute, Norah?"

"Not this time," laughed Norah. "You see, it's our tent you've got to fix. Go on, and we'll get a billy from Mrs. Evans and brew afternoon tea for you down by the lagoon."

So they spent the hot hours in the shade, while the boys made the little camp ship-shape, their tent and that of Mr. Linton close together near the bank, and the girls' a little way off in a clump of young wattles. Jim fixed up bunks in bushman fashion, with saplings run through bags endways, and supported on crossed sticks.

"You won't want any mattresses on those," he said: "they're fit for anyone. What about blankets, Norah?"

"Brownie's been drying the ones you amateur firemen soaked last night," said his sister, unkindly. "They're all water-marked, of course, but they're quite good enough for camping."

"First rate," Jim agreed. "We'll get 'em. Come along, Wally."

"More toil!" groaned that gentleman, who had been working with the cheerful keenness he put into all his doings. "Why did I come here?"

"Poor dear, then!" said a cheerful, fat voice. The creaking of a wheelbarrow accompanied it, and preceded Mrs. Brown, who came into view wheeling a load of bedclothes.

"Brownie, you shouldn't, you bad young thing!" exclaimed Wally. He dashed to take the barrow, and was routed ignominiously.

"Never you mind—I can manage me own little lot," said Brownie, cheerfully. She pulled up, panting a little. "Lucky for me it was all down hill; I don't know as I could have managed to get it up a rise."

"You oughtn't to have wheeled that load at all," Jim said, with an excellent attempt at sternness. It appeared to afford Brownie great amusement, and she chuckled audibly.

"Bless you, it pulled me here!" she answered. "I come down at no end of a pace. Now haven't you got it all just as nice as it can be. Makes me nearly envious!"

"We'll fix up a tent for you, if you like," Jim told her. "Just say the word."

"Not for me, thank you," said Brownie, hastily. "This open-air sleeping notion is all very well for them as likes it—but I'm used to four walls an' a winder. I like something you can lock—an' where can you lock a tent, Master Jim?—tell me that!" She propounded this unanswerable query with an air of triumph. "Besides, it wouldn't be fair to any bunk to put me into it, bunks not bein' built on my lines. I'd hate to come down in the night, like that there Philistine idol in the Bible."

"Why, you wouldn't have far to fall!" said Jim, laughing.

"Thank you, but any distance is far enough when you're my weight," Brownie responded, with dignity. "Now, Miss Norah an' Miss Jean, seein' as how I've got my breath again, I think we'd better start bedmaking."

"Don't you bother, Brownie; we can fix up our own," Jim said, politely—and greatly hoping that his politeness would have no effect. It had none.

"Humph!" said Mrs. Brown. "Handy you may be with tools an' horses, Master Jim, but I never yet did see the man or boy that was handy with bedmaking. I've noticed that bedclothes seem to paralyse a man's common sense when he starts to make a bed; he don't seem to be able to realize what relation they have to the mattress. Generally he fights with them quite desperate, and gets them nearly tied in knots before the job's done. So just you two lie there peaceful, an' me an' the young ladies will do it in two twos."

The boys' bedmaking ambition was of no soaring nature, and they were very content to "lie peaceful," watching the sun dip behind the trees that fringed the lagoon. Then came Mr. Linton, who nodded approval of the workmanlike camp.

"First rate!" he said, warmly. "For destitute and burnt-out people, we shan't fare too badly."

"Rather not!" Jim answered. "How did you get on, Dad?"

"Oh, all right. Telephone was as indistinct as usual, but I managed to say a good deal of what I wanted through it. There will be an insurance man down to-morrow." Mr. Linton smiled at the bedmakers, who came out of the last tent and settled down under the trees thankfully. "They've found Harvey," he concluded.

"Found the brute, have they?" Jim exclaimed. "What did he have to say, Dad? Did they hurt him?"

"Harvey had had luck," said Mr. Linton, slowly. "He'd hurt himself first."

"How? Tell us, Dad."

"Well, they hunted most of the day before they got him. They had every road searched before noon, the police were in communication with all the townships in the district, and there was no sign of him. Then the men left the roads and went across country, hunting up the river and along any creek, and through scrub. But I don't think Mr. Harvey would have trusted himself in scrub without a horse."

"Not he!" Jim agreed.

"Murty found him. He was riding across the Duncans' big plain, and thought he heard a coo-ee; but there was no cover anywhere, and he couldn't see a man wherever he looked. But he rode about, and found him at last in a little bit of a hollow. Murty said you might have ridden past it a hundred times and never have seen anyone. Harvey had shouted once, but when he saw that it was Murty he was afraid to call again, and tried to lie low."

"Couldn't he walk?"

"He broke his leg last night," Mr. Linton answered. "The poor wretch has had a pretty bad time. He was jumping over a log, he says, and came down with one leg in a crab-hole, and it twisted, and threw him down. He didn't know it was broken at first, but he found he couldn't use it. So he crawled away from the log, being afraid of snakes, and got a couple of hundred yards into the paddock. Since then he's kept still."

"What—out in the open?" Jim asked.

"Yes; not a scrap of cover. And think of the day it's been—it was 112° in the shade in Cunjee—and Harvey wasn't in the shade. He told Murty he was badly thirsty before he got hurt, and had been looking for water. His leg is in a bad state, and he must have had a terrible day. Murty came in for the doctor, and we went for him in the car—of course, Murty could do nothing on horseback. Harvey was a bit delirious by the time we got to him. Anderson says he'll be three months in hospital."

"Whew-w!" whistled Wally. "Three months!"

"Then he'll have three munce to reflect on the error of his ways!" said Brownie, implacably. "Oh, I know me feelings aren't Christian, an' I don't set a good example to the young; but what did he want to go and do it for?"

"Break his leg? But did he want to?" Jim grinned.

"You know very well I don't mean his wretched little leg," Brownie said, testily. "He never had no call to burn us all out. Now he's broke his leg, an' you'll think he's an object of sympathy an' compassion, an' nex' thing Miss Norah'll be visitin' him in the 'Ospital an' holdin' his hand an' givin' him jelly!"

"By gad, she won't!" uttered Norah's father, with satisfying emphasis. "There are limits, Brownie. But it's all very well for you to talk—if you'd seen the poor little weed you'd have been sorry for him."

"Not me!" Brownie answered, truculently. "I only got to think of Miss Norah in that horrid stable, an' every soft feelin' leaves me, like a moulting hen." Brownie's similes were apt to be mixed, and nobody marked them. "Does he say why he did it? He's got nerve enough to stick out that he never lit it at all!"

"Oh, no, he hasn't—not now," said Mr. Linton. "He admitted it to Murty meekly enough, and Murty says he was awfully taken aback at hearing the amount of the damage; he said he only thought of burning the grass. Whether his concern is for my loss or the possible results to himself, I'm not clear. I don't regard him as exactly a philanthropist."

Brownie snorted wrathfully as they rose to go up to the cottage. The sun had set, and Mrs. Evans was calling from the hill.

"I don't give him credit for no decent motives at all," she said. "He's bad right through—an' don't you ask me to be sorry for him—he'll have three munce takin' it easy in 'Ospital, livin' on the fat of the land an' doin' no work—an' that'll just suit Harvey! I got no patience with that sort of worm in sheep's clothing!" She subsided, muttering darkly, and Wally offered her his arm up the hill, while Jim wheeled the barrow.

Brownie dropped her voice as they neared the cottage.

"Ah, well," she said—and paused. "I don't suppose them gaol 'Ospitals is exackly dens of luxury. If you an' Master Jim, Master Wally, think as how a little strong soup or meat jelly might go in to that poor, wicked, depraved little wretch——?"

"Fattening him for the slaughter, eh, Brownie?" asked Wally, gravely.

"Yes, that's it," said the fierce Mrs. Brown, accepting the suggestion with ardour. "P'raps he mightn't get what he deserves if he looked pale an' thin at his trile!" She mused over the matter. "Wonder if they feed 'em on skilly when they're in 'Ospital," she pondered. "An' a leg like that. Well, well, we're all 'uman, after all, an' likely his mother never did much by him—he looks as if he had growed up casual! You find out about that soup, Master Wally." And Wally nodded, his eyes kindly as he smiled at the broad, motherly face.

"Makes you feel a bit small, though," he confided to Jim later on. "Because I'm not in the least sorry for Harvey. I think he deserved all he got, and more, and these beggars don't mind gaol. Suppose I'm a hard-hearted brute!"

"Well, I'm another," Jim responded. "When I think of young Norah—and the horses! I guess my poor old Garryowen had about as bad a time as Harvey. Says he never thought of the house! Well, he lit the grass three hundred yards from it, with a west wind blowing—that's all! When I can work up any sorrow for Harvey I'll let you know!" And the stern and unmoved pair sought the lagoon for a final swim before "turning in."

" 'Brownie, you shouldn't, you bad young thing!' "

CHAPTER XIII
BEN ATHOL
There are stars of gold on the Wallaby Track,

And silver the moonbeams glisten,

The great Bush sings to us, out and back.

And we lie in her arms and listen.

—W. H. Ogilvie.

A WEEK went by—a week of blinding heat, ending in a cool change, accompanied by a gale of wind that almost blew the tents and their occupants into the lagoon. Then the weather settled to glorious conditions, neither hot nor cold—long days of sunshine, and nights chilly enough to make the campers enjoy a fire by the water's edge while they fished for their breakfast.

But, on the whole, it was dull. The new saddles had not arrived from Melbourne, so that riding was out of the question. In any case it was deemed wiser not to ride Monarch and Garryowen and Bosun too soon. Norah and Jim had them yarded each day, and they caught and handled them, dressing Garryowen's burns, and petting all three—talking to them and leading them about while they hunted for the milk-thistles horses love. Gradually the quivering nerves steadied down, and the memory of their terror faded. But Garryowen would never face fire again; a tiny blaze was too much for him, and even smoke sent him into a panic. Even kindness could not make him forget the moments when he had been a rat in a burning trap.

They fished and walked—moderately; walking was not a Billabong characteristic; and helped Mrs. Evans and Brownie, and worshipped the Evans baby—that is to say, Jean and Norah did, and Jim and Wally pretended not to; and they watched Hogg glowering as he worked in his ruined garden, and wished business did not detain Mr. Linton during nearly every hour of the day. It was hard to settle to anything. Possibly they were feeling a natural reaction after the strain of the night of the fire. But as none of the four would have known what reaction meant, no one suggested it.

They were all in the boat one exquisite evening, floating lazily among the water lilies on the lagoon, and pretending to fish—a transparent pretence, since frequent snagging on the lily stems had made every angler disgusted, and had brought all the lines out of the water. Then Mr. Linton appeared on the bank and they pulled in and took him on board, giving him the place of honour in the stern.

"This is the most peaceful thing I've done since we became a burnt-offering," he said, as they drifted away from the shore. He lit his pipe and leaned back contentedly. "Well—business is done!"

"Thank goodness!" from Norah.

"I quite agree with you," said her father. "To be burnt out is bad enough, but it's an added penance to be forced to put in time as I've been doing. I'm sick of the sight of insurance people, and policemen, and architects, and contractors!"

"Have you made all arrangements, Dad?" Jim asked.

"So far as I can. But the men I want to employ can't begin rebuilding for three weeks at least, possibly a month; and then the job will be a long one."

"Then I won't see it before I go back to school!" came from Norah, disgustedly. "Oh, I'm so sorry!"

"No; and I'm sorry, too," said her father. "But it can't be helped. The fire has done unpleasant things to your holidays, my girl."

"Just you wait until I begin growling!" Norah said, laughing. "I'm having lovely holidays, truly, only I'm disappointed that I can't see the house."

"Well, I've a plan," said David Linton, slowly.

Norah sat up so briskly that the boat rocked violently.

"Have a little sense, Nor.!" came from Jim. "Sit still, or you'll be smacked and turned out!"

"Get out yourself!" said his sister, inelegantly. "When Dad has a plan in that voice it is time to sit up! Tell us, Dad."

Mr. Linton laughed.

"How about Ben Athol?" he asked.

"Ben Athol!" Jim whistled. "By Jove, Dad, that's an idea!"

"Oh!" said Norah. "Didn't I tell you it was time to sit up!"

Ben Athol towered from the low ranges to the north of Billabong, beyond the stations and out to the wild country that was No Man's Land because of its steepness and inaccessibility. "Old hands" told stories of well grassed valleys in the ranges, where stock might be pastured; of a mountain river, flowing clear as crystal all the year round, in a way very unlike the usual habit of Australian rivers. But comparatively few white men knew anything about the country between the hills. Blacks were reputed to camp there—some miserable, scattered families, who came into the townships as winter approached to beg for food and blankets, sometimes to hang about all through the cold months, a thievish, filthy pest.

Snow lay for the winter months upon the brow of Ben Athol. In spring, when the warm sun melted the great white cap, it slid away gradually, and the big peak stood out, dark blue among the lesser hills. Always it seemed to Norah like a friend.

For two years they had talked of climbing it. But the expedition required some organizing, for it was three days' ride even to the last township that nestled at the foot of the hills. Then came a day's stiff climbing for horses, after which it was only possible to proceed on foot, if one wanted to reach the peak. Few were adventurous enough to want to do so.

"Well, I think we may as well go," said Mr. Linton, when his excited family calmed down. "I have been turning over various plans in my mind for the last few days, for we can't stop here; it's too dismal to look at the old place. We're all in good form, fit for such a ride. I don't quite know about Jean."

"Oh, please," said Jean, in a small shriek. "I can, quite easily. Truly, Mr. Linton."

"I'm sure she's all right, Dad," Norah put in. "She wasn't a bit stiff after that long day we had in the Far Plain."

"Well, that was a pretty fair test," Mr. Linton remarked. "Anyhow, we can't start for a few days, so you had better ride a good deal, to get into form. The saddles will be out to-day. But we shan't use them for the trip—new saddles aren't advisable for a journey like that—we'd probably have the horses with sore backs."

"Rather," Jim said. "I'm never really friends with a saddle until it has been re-stuffed."

"Oh, they are like new boots—they must get accustomed to a horse," Mr. Linton answered. "We'll have to exchange with the men. Murty will see that the new ones are looked after. We'll use the old ones from to-day, so that you girls can find out which are the most comfortable for you."

"All right," nodded Norah. "When do you think we'll start, Dad?"

"This is Thursday—we'll get away on Monday morning," her father replied. "We'll take Billy, to lead a packhorse and make himself generally useful. It will not be necessary to carry a great amount of provisions, because we can lay in a stock of food at the various townships as we go. Atholton is the last one, at the foot of the ranges, and I've sent a note to the storekeeper there, telling him to have various things ready for us. Until then we need only have a day's rations. We'll take a tent for you girls——"

"Oh, need you, Dad? Can't we put up a wurley?" Norah begged.

"No," said Mr. Linton, firmly. "We don't know if we'll always be in timber to make wurleys, and it's as well to be prepared for bad weather. That little tent is no trouble to take, and, as it's waterproof, it will make an excellent covering for the pack. We'll take some fishing tackle. They say the fishing in that mountain stream is very good. For the rest, Norah, you and I will have a heart-to-heart talk with Brownie. I believe it will make the old soul quite happy to have to cook for an expedition again."

The time until Monday seemed all a cheerful bustle of preparation. Jean and Norah rode each day, generally with Wally in attendance, since Jim and his father had much to do together. There were jobs of moving cattle from one paddock to another; of riding round the Queensland bullocks, now settling down contentedly in the Bush Paddock, and only becoming excited when the three riders tried to count them; of inspecting the fences, with sharp eyes alert for a broken panel or a sagging wire. No one at Billabong need ever ride aimlessly; there was always work of this kind—work that the three regarded as the best possible fun. And always they talked of next week's expedition, and made quite a hundred thousand plans in connection with it. Jean had never been camping out in her life, and, considering how calm a person she was ordinarily, it became almost alarming to behold her state of simmering excitement.

Mr. Linton sternly hunted his flock to bed early on Sunday evening, and dawn, had scarcely broken next morning when they were astir, Norah and Jean running hurriedly to the Cottage to dress, while Murty dismantled their little tent, and had it, with the bags that formed their bunks, neatly packed and made ready for transport.

Breakfast was despatched hastily by all but Mr. Linton, who declined altogether to bestir himself unduly, and demanded of his excited charges if they had visions of catching a train? Finally, they were all in the saddle, the horses fidgeting and dancing with excitement—save the packhorse, who looked upon the world with an embittered gaze, and Black Billy's scrawny piebald, old Bung Eye, who was supposed to be proof against any kind of excitement whatever.

"Now do come back safe an' sound, all of you!" Brownie begged. "Me nerves have had enough to bear lately; I don't want any broken heads or cracked legs. An' if you find a gold mine out there, then I'll give notice, if you please, sir, an' take out a miner's right, an' go off makin' me fortune!"

"Anybody in this party finding a gold mine is hereby ejected summarily!" said Mr. Linton, promptly. "The penalty would be too heavy to make the find worth while."

"We'll live and die poor, but we'll keep you, Brownie!" Jim told her.

"Me own prospects don't seem to matter much to you, do they?" retorted Brownie, enjoying herself hugely. Occasionally it gave her immense delight to toy with the fiction of leaving Billabong—knowing very well indeed, as did they all, that a team of bullocks would scarcely have been strong enough to tear her away. "Often I says to meself that I might end me days as a prospector—there's no knowin' how much gold is lyin' about in them ranges for the pickin' up."

"If it's there, Brownie, I will bring you a necklace of nuggets with my own fair hands," said Wally. "Steady, you brute!"

Brownie beamed over the portion of the speech addressed to her.

"Thank you—an' take care of that horse, dearie, for I know he ain't safe," she said anxiously—to the great delight of Jim, and Wally's no small embarrassment. The men grinned widely.

"The halters is in the pack, sir, an' likewise the hobbles," said Murty. "If y' don't be watchin' that black image of a haythen on Bung Eye, he'll put the wrong hobbles on Bosun—there's a small, little pair I made special for the pony. He'll get his feet out of nearly anny other hobbles on the place."

"Thank you, Murty!" from Norah. Murty beamed.

"A good ride to ye all," he said, "an' don't be afther breakin' your neck on thim ridges, Miss Norah. 'Tis the only neck like it on Billabong, an' we can't spare it, at all."

"We'll take care of her, Murty," said her father.

"Bedad," said Murty, "I have not forgotten that wan time 'twas y'rsilf did not take care of y'rsilf in that very same place! How am I to be thinkin' anny of ye safe afther that misfortunate time?"

David Linton laughed.

"Ah, Monarch and I have learned sense now," he said. "He won't get rid of me in the same way again."

"Divil a wan of me knows!" said Murty, darkly. "Well—that ye may come home wid whole bones, annyhow! Is it gettin' up a search party we'll be if ye're not back this day week, sir?"

"Certainly not!" said the squatter. "If we find Brownie's gold mine, there's no prophesying when I shall get my party away from it!"

"Then ye'll find hersilf an' me joggin' out in the old dray to meet ye," Murty averred. He took his hand from Bosun's bridle, and stepped back. Good-byes floated to the little group by the cottage as the riders cantered down the track.

CHAPTER XIV
ON THE TRACK
A homely-looking folk they are, these people of my kin—

Their hands are hard as horse shoes, but their hearts come through the skin.

—V. J. Daley.

THEY camped that night half a mile off the road, in a paddock belonging to a station Mr. Linton knew well.

"Henderson would give me leave if I asked him—so I won't," he said. "It's a short stage, but that's advisable, seeing that it's our first day out, and that it has been uncommonly warm. And we're sure of good water in the creek over yonder."

So they found some slip-rails and rode into the paddock and across the long grass to the creek, a fairly large stream for that time of the year, fringed with a thick dark green belt of wattles. The horses were short-hobbled and allowed to graze, and the camp was pitched quickly.

The tent for the girls was put up in a little grove of trees, near which the bank of the creek sloped down to an excellent place for bathing—a deep hole with a little stretch of clean grass growing over a sunken log at the water's edge—a place, as Norah said, simply planned to stand on while you were drying. Most Australian creeks are unkind in this respect—either the bank is inaccessibly steep, or the few available places are so muddy that the difficulty after a bathe is to keep clean.

"We'll fish there before you bathe," Jim told Norah, regarding the hole hopefully. "If there aren't blackfish there I'm very much mistaken."

"It wouldn't be the first time," Norah told him, unkindly. "Don't leave any fish-hooks in our pool, that's all."

"You'll get no fish for tea if you don't practise civility!" Jim grinned. "I'm worn to a shred putting up your blessed tent, and there's really no reason why I should allow you to be impolite. Why don't you take pattern by Jean? Her manners are lovely!"

"I wish my family heard you say so!" said the lady referred to, longingly.

"Don't they appreciate you? I'm like that!" Wally said. "I often think I'll die without any one finding out my true worth."

"Jolly good job for you if they don't, old man!" quoth Jim, retreating hastily, and cannoning with violence into his father as he dodged round a gum tree. Explanations ensued, and the party settled down to fish, soon catching enough to make tea a memorable meal. Then they lay about on the grass and talked until it was bedtime—a period which came early, though no one would admit any sense of fatigue.

It was a still, hot night—so hot that the girls slept with the tent flap tied back, and were openly envious of the men of the party, who disdained to erect a "wurley," and slept bushman fashion out in the open, with their blankets spread in a soft spot, and their saddles for pillows. Black Billy disappeared along the creek, camping in some select nook after his blackfellow heart. Then silence fell upon the camp, and all that could be heard was a mopoke, steadily calling in a dead tree, throughout the night.

Norah was the first to awaken. It was daylight, but only faintly; looking through the opening of the tent she could see the sun coming slowly over the edge of the horizon, flushing all the eastern sky with gleams of pink and gold. A little breeze blew gently. She slipped quietly from her bunk, put on a light overcoat and went out barefooted into the sweetness of the morning.

There was an old moss-grown log near the tent, and she sat down upon it. Just beyond the belt of trees that marked the creek, the yellow paddock stretched away, unbroken by any fence, so far as her eye could reach. She could see grazing cattle here and there, and a few half-grown steers were standing in a little knot and staring towards the camp with curious, half-frightened eyes. From further down the bank came the chink of hobbles, and the chime of the bell on old Bung Eye's neck. Near the tent her father lay sleeping; a few yards away were Jim and Wally, far off in the land of dreams. The clean bush scent lay over everything; the scent of tree and leaf and rich black earth, where the night-dew still lingers. Just below her the creek rippled softly, and the splash of a leaping fish sent a swirl across the wide pool.

Norah sighed from very joy of the place, and the beauty of the morning, and the certainty of a happy day ahead.

Then she became aware that some one was awake—in the curious way in which we become conscious that the thoughts of another have entered into our solitary places. She looked round, and beheld one intent eye regarding her from the end of the roll of blankets that represented Wally. For a moment the eye and Norah continued to watch each other; at which point Norah suddenly realized that it was faintly possible that Wally might feel a shade of embarrassment, and modestly withdrew her gaze. She did Mr. Meadows great injustice. He yawned widely, sat up, and wriggled out of his blankets. Then, discovering that Jim's mouth was slightly open, he proceeded to place within it three dandelions, which accomplished, he fled while his unconscious victim was waking up and spluttering. Wally sat down on the log beside Norah, with a face like an unusually lean cherub.

"You're a horrid boy!" said that damsel, laughing. "Dandelions taste abominably—at least that milky stuff in them does."

"Never tried it," said Wally. "What funny things you seem to have lived on!"

"Poor old Jimmy!" said Norah, disregarding this insinuation, and bending a glance of pity on Jim, who was coughing violently, and evidently prepared for battle. Mr. Linton had wakened, and was regarding his son with curiosity.

"It's a pneumonia cough, I should say, sir," explained Wally, considerately, from the log. "Nasty lungy sound, hasn't it. Shall I get you some water, my poor dear?" At this point the outraged Jim arose and hurled himself upon his tormentor, who dodged him round a bush until Jim managed to pick up a thorn with his foot, when he retired to a log for purposes of investigation.

"Wait till I get you in the creek, young Wally!" he growled.

"Not too many larks," commanded Mr. Linton, who had also cast off his blankets. "We've got to get away as early as we can, so as to have a long spell in the hottest part of the day." He shook himself vigorously. "I think I'm too old for sleeping without a mattress."

"So am I," said Wally, who was sitting cross-legged on Norah's log. "That bit of ground looked the softest I could see, but it found out every bone I have before I'd been there an hour. It would be a tremendous advantage to be fat! I was afraid at last that my hip bone would come right through, so I got up and scraped a little hole for it. Then I was much more comfortable, except when I wriggled in my sleep and failed to hit the hole."

"Well, I've had a lovely night!" Norah averred.

"I should think so—sleeping in the lap of gilded luxury—at least in a beautiful sacking bunk!" said Wally, indignantly. "Then you get up at your elegant leisure and jeer at those whose lodging was on the cold, cold ground! Women were ever thus!" He choked, dramatically, and rose. "James, if you've finished operating, are you ready to come and bathe?"

"I must wake Jean," said Norah, disappearing within the tent. Then they scattered up and down the creek for their swim—not a matter to be dawdled over, for even in the summer morning the water was very cold. Jim returned, fresh and glowing, before the girls were ready to vacate the tent, and proceeded to loosen its fastenings in a way that caused them great anguish of mind, since it threatened to collapse bodily upon them. The last stages of their toilet were performed hastily, and without dignity.

"Can't be helped," said Jim, imperturbably, as they emerged, wrathful. "Got to strike camp, and this is my job." He brought the tent to earth with a quick movement. "Help me to fold this up, Nor."

"Where's Wally?" Norah asked, complying.

"I left him diving for the soap," Jim grinned. "He was pretty cold, and didn't seem exactly happy; but I couldn't wait. Here he comes. Did you get it, Wal.?"

"I did—no thanks to you!" said Wally, whose teeth were still inclined to chatter, while his complexion was a fine shade of blue. "He's just the champion mean exhibit of the party, Jean. I was nearly dry, out on the bank, and threw the soap at him in pure friendliness; and the brute actually dodged! Dodged! And then he wouldn't dive for it: fact is, I believe he's forgotten how to dive. So I had to go in again after it!"

"Any mud at the bottom?" asked Jim, grinning.

"About a foot of soft slush. I loathe you!" said Wally. He proceeded to roll up blankets vigorously, still slightly azure of hue.

Billy had the horses already saddled, and when breakfast was over the pack was quickly adjusted and a start made. They travelled through country that became rapidly wilder and more rugged. A wire fence bounded each side of the road, which was a track scarcely fit for wheeled traffic. The paddocks on both sides were part of big station properties, on which the homesteads were far back; so that they scarcely saw a house throughout the day, except when now and then they passed through sleepy little townships, where dogs barked furiously at them and children ran out to stare at the riders. They were typical bush children, who scarcely ever saw a stranger—lean, sun-dried youngsters, as wild and shy as hares, and quite incapable of giving an answer when addressed. They paused in one township to buy stores, and Norah dashed to the post office to send a postcard to Brownie, assuring her that so far they were safe.

The post office was a quaint erection, especially when considered in the light of a Government building. Had it not been for this mark of distinction, it would probably have been termed a shed. It was a little, ramshackle lean-to, against the side of a shop that was equally falling to decay. There was no door—only a slit barely two feet wide, through which Norah entered, wondering, as she did so, if the township contained any inhabitants as fat as Brownie, and if so, how they contrived to transact their postal business. It was very certain that Brownie could not have entered through the slit unless hydraulic pressure had been applied to her.

Within was emptiness. The sole furnishing of the office was a small shelf against the wall; above it, a trap-door. This artistic simplicity was complicated by the appearance of a head in the trap-doorway, after Norah had tapped vigorously five or six times.

"I clean forgot the office," said the owner of the head—a tall, freckled damsel, with innumerable curling pins bristling in her "fringe." She favoured Norah with a wide and cheerful smile. "Fact is, I was out in the garden lookin' at your lot. Ain't your horses just corkin'!"

"They're . . . not bad." Norah hesitated. "I want a postcard, please."

"Not bad!" said the Government official, disregarding her request. She propped her elbows on the ledge within, evidently ready for conversation, and put her face as far through the trap-doorway as nature or its designer would permit. "Well, I reckon they're fair ringers! That big black 'ud take a lot of beatin', I'll bet. Is it your Pa ridin' him?"

"Yes," Norah answered. "Can I——"

"Goin' far?" asked the postmistress. "You all look pretty workmanlike, don't y' now? Where d' y' come from, if it's a fair question?"

"From this side of Cunjee. And we're going up Ben Athol. I want——"

"Up Ben Athol! You're never!"

"Well, we're going to try. Can I have——"

"I never heard of any one but drovers an' blackfellers goin' up there," said the postmistress, gaping. "You two kids'll never do it, will y', do y' think? I wonder at your Pa lettin' you. Rummy, ain't it, what people 'll do for fun!"

"They'll be calling me in a moment," said poor Norah. "Let me have a postcard, please." She held out her penny firmly.

"Oh, all right," said the postmistress, unwillingly. Without removing her face from the little window she fished in an unseen receptacle and extracted a card, which she poked through to Norah.

"There's no pen here," said that harassed person investigating. "Can I have one—and some ink?"

"Right-oh!" said, the official. "This chap's a bit scratchy, but the office is clean out of nibs. There is another—but it's worse. This one'll write all right when you get used to it. I say, is them divided skirts comf'table to ride in?"

Norah assented, stretching out her hand for the ink.

"I read in the paper that ladies was riding astride," said the postmistress, apparently soul-hungry for companionship. "But me father won't let me get a pattron an' try an' make one. Yours don't seem to mind."

"He won't let me ride any other way," said Norah, writing busily.

"Go on! Well, ain't men different!" said the postmistress. "Never know where you have them, do you? Is those long fellers your brothers?"

Norah nodded, feeling at the moment, unequal to detailed explanation.

"Thought so. An' you're re'ly goin' to try old Ben Athol! Wonder if you'll ever get there," the postmistress pondered. Her freckled face suddenly widened to a smile. "Look at that blackfeller, now! Well, if he ain't a trick!"

Billy was jogging up the street on old Bung Eye, smoking vigorously. Behind him, taking the fullest advantage of a long halter, the packhorse led, very bored by Life. The township children shouted and ran, but nothing affected Billy's serenity. He passed out of sight, and the Postmistress, oblivious of further possible wishes on the part of her customer, quitted her little office and rushed outside to gaze after him. In this pleasurable occupation she was not alone, since three parts of the township was hanging over its front fence, gazing likewise.

From the street came Jim's whistle, for the third time—this time with something peremptory in its note.

"Coming!" Norah called. She dropped her card into the slit marked "Letters," and ran out, receiving voluble farewells from the postmistress as she fled.

"Good-bye!" Norah called. She swung herself upon Bosun's back, and trotted down the street with Jim. Already the others were some distance ahead.

The postmistress came in, regretfully, as the dust of their going died away.

"Wonder who they were?" she pondered. "Well, at least, there's the postcard!" She opened the letter box, and drew out the documentary evidence, receiving not much information from Norah's hastily-scrawled lines. She turned the card over.

"Well, I'm blessed!" she gasped. Keen disappointment was in her voice. She pondered for a moment and then hurried out, locking the office door firmly, and affixing to it a battered notice, which read: "Closed for dinner." The fact that she had already dined did not trouble the free and independent soul of the postmistress.

Half an hour later the sound of galloping hoofs on the road behind them made the Billabong party look round. A cloud of dust resolved itself into the vision of the postmistress, mounted on a raking chestnut, and somewhat bulky in appearance, by reason of the fact that she had slipped on a habit skirt over her other apparel.

"She's waving," said Norah, much puzzled. "Let's pull up."

They waited. The postmistress arrived with a wide and friendly smile.

"Thought I'd never catch you up!" she panted. "Blessed if you didn't forget to put any address on that postcard you wrote!" She produced the card, a good deal crumpled by the vicissitudes of travel.

"Well, I am a duffer!" ejaculated Norah. "But how awfully good of you to come after us!"

"It was indeed," said Mr. Linton, warmly. He produced a pencil, and Norah scribbled the address and handed the card back. "Uncommonly kind and thoughtful. We're very much obliged to you. I hope it didn't give you very much trouble?"

"Not a bit!" said the postmistress, genially. She read the address with care, and tucked the card into her bodice. "Fact is," she said, "I was just dead keen to know it meself! Well, I must be gettin' back—me office is shut up, an' the coach is nearly due. So long!" She wheeled the chestnut, galloping back to the township.

CHAPTER XV
THE HOUSE BY ATHOLTON
The little feet that run to me,

   The little hands that strive

To touch me at the heart, and find

   The heart in me alive.

O God! if hands and feet should fail!

   If Death his mist should fling

Between my heart and the touch of

The little living thing!

—R. Crawford.

IT was late in the afternoon of the third day, and in a cloud of thick dust the riders were hurrying along the road towards Atholton. Ahead they could see the scattered roofs of the little township, showing white among the trees; but everything was obscured by the dust that swirled and eddied, now tearing away before them in a cloud sixty feet high, or seeming to stand still all around them, blinding any vision for more than a few yards. Behind a leaden sky glowered through the dust clouds, or was revealed, darkly purple, when they rose for an instant to swirl and scurry, and grow dense again, as the shrieking wind came in a fresh gust.

Three days of gradually mounting heat had worked up to a tempestuous change. All day, riding had been anything but pleasant. Even in early morning the air had been still and heavy, after a night of breathless heat. They had left camp not long after sunrise, intending to rest during the middle of the day; but the weather had tried the horses; they had travelled badly, sweating before they had gone a mile, so that progress was slow. Mr. Linton had cut the noon "spell" ruthlessly short.

"We'll have to hurry," he said, glancing uneasily at the sullen sky. "This means a big storm, and it's very doubtful if we can escape it, even now. As far as I remember there's no shelter at all between here and Atholton, and there is too much big timber along the track to be safe in a storm. Billy, you travel the slowest—cut along!"

Billy proceeded to "cut," not unwillingly. He hated storms, even as a cat, and firmly believed that thunder was the noise of innumerable "debbil-debbils," let loose dangerously near the inhabitants of earth, and at any moment likely to fall on the just and the unjust. He mounted Bung Eye and jogged off along the track, the packhorse toiling in the rear. Ten minutes later saw the rest of the party in pursuit.

From the first it was evident that the ride would be a race with the storm. Mr. Linton made all the haste that was possible for the horses; but the way was long and the heat so breathless that it seemed cruel to urge the poor brutes along. A purple cloud came up out of the west, and spread up and up; then a murky haze obscured the sun, yet brought no lessening of heat. Finally came a low sighing of faraway wind, and long before it struck them they could see distant tree-tops swaying and bending before the fury of the blast. They came to a sharp turn in the road, facing eastwards.

"Thank goodness, there's Atholton!" uttered Mr. Linton, pointing at the roofs far ahead. "We may get off with dry skins if we gallop."

They shook up the horses. Even as they did so, the beginning of the storm was upon them in a furious gust of wind that gathered up the loose summer dust of the road and carried it high into the air. It was impossible to see more than a few yards ahead except between the gusts. They rode blindly, trusting to their horses, and fairly sure that on such an afternoon there would be no other obstacles of traffic on the lonely bush track. On either side the thick timber creaked and groaned in the wind, and occasionally a sharp crack told of a limb or a treetop breaking under the strain. Then the horses bounded as a sharp crackle of thunder came out of the west and ran round the sky in a heavy, echoing roll, followed by a vivid flash of lightning. Heavy drops began to fall, splashing into the thick dust underfoot.

"Gad! There's a house!" said Mr. Linton thankfully. "Make for the gate, Jim."

A hundred yards ahead a white cottage stood near the track, in the midst of a pleasant orchard. As they clattered up to the road gate, a woman came out upon the verandah and waved to them energetically, beckoning them in. Garryowen propped at the gate, and Jim swung it open. The sky seemed to split with another thunderclap as they rode through, and then came rain, like a curtain, blotting out everything behind them.

The woman rushed down to the little garden gate as they raced to it.

"Let the young ladies come in here—quick! There's a shed over there for the horses."

"Off you get, girls!" Mr. Linton said. Jean and Norah slipped to the ground, yielding their bridles into ready hands, and ran up the garden path behind their hostess. The rain was pelting upon the iron roof of the little cottage with a noise like musketry.

"I don't think you're very wet," panted the woman. She darted into the house, returning with towels, and rubbed them down as they stood on the verandah, despite their protests.

"We're truly all right," Norah told her. "Thank you ever so much. But what luck! Five minutes later and we'd have been soaked to the skin but for your house. And it isn't a joke to get everything wet through when you're camping, as we are, and travelling as light as possible."

"I should think not," said their hostess—a tall woman, whitefaced and delicate in appearance, with tired grey eyes, that had black half circles beneath them. "Fact is, I've been looking out for you—the storekeeper in the township was telling me Mr. Linton's party was to come through Atholton this evening. I've been thinking about you all the afternoon, wondering if the storm would catch you."

"You were very good," Jean told her, shyly.

"Oh, I don't know. There isn't so much to think about in these places—one's glad of any excitement. I'd have been more excited if I'd known it wasn't only men riding. It's a big ride for you two girls."

"We're used to it," said Norah. "It's been lovely, until to-day; that has certainly been a bit hot. It's hot still, isn't it?"

"Close as ever it can be," said the woman. "But the rain'll cool it." She peeped round the corner of the verandah, putting her head into the rain. "They're all right in the shed, horses and all. Will you go into the house and sit down and rest?"

"I think it's nice out here," Norah said, hesitatingly.

"Well, it is better than inside—the house is heated right through," said the woman. "Wooden houses cool quickly, but they heat like an oven, don't they? I'll bring out chairs." She disappeared—her movements were curiously quick—and came out laden. They sat on the verandah, with the pelting rain beating all round them, and a sense of wet coolness gradually coming over the hot atmosphere.

She was anxious to talk—this gaunt, hungry-eyed woman of the Bush. She went from one subject to another almost feverishly, asking them a hundred questions—of home, of school, of the life that was so busy hundreds of miles away from her lonely home in the timber. And always her eyes wandered restlessly, as if she were seeking. Once she failed to answer a question, staring before her with a strained look that was half expectancy and half despair. Then she came back to attention with a start, and begged their pardon.

"I—I was listening," she said. "I didn't quite hear what you were saying."

The storm began to wear itself out after a while, and she took them into the house, saying that they would be glad of a wash and brush up while she made some tea. She showed them into a neat little bedroom, and brought a brimming can of hot water.

"Just you make yourselves quite at home," she said. "Don't hurry; I'll call you when I got tea made." She went out, closing the door.

It was a bright little room, with a cheap blue paper on the walls, and crisp, fresh curtains at the window. Everything was poor, but spotlessly clean.

"Isn't it nice?" Jean said. "It smells of lavender and things!"

"And as if the window were always open," said Norah, approvingly. "I like it—and I like her, too. Don't you, Jean?"

"Yes—I do," Jean said, slowly. "She—she's a bit queer though, isn't she?"

"She's got a scared sort of look," Norah said, trying to find words. "Perhaps she's had a lot of trouble. Ever so many women in the Bush do, I think. But I like her eyes, though they're so tired."

"They're mother-y sort of eyes," said Jean, her thoughts suddenly flying to her own mother, in far-off New Zealand. "I wonder if that's her little girl?"

A photograph smiled at them from a cheap frame on the wall—a little laughing child, taken in the stiff, conventional manner of the country photographer, yet dimpling into merriment as if at some suddenly happy thought.

"Oh!" said Norah. "What a dear little youngster! Isn't she a darling!" She faced round as the door opened, and their hostess came in, bringing clean towels. "We're just in love with this," she said, indicating the photograph. "Is she your little girl?"

The woman put down the towels in silence. Her face was working, and before the misery in her eyes Jean and Norah shrank back aghast. There was a moment's dreadful silence. Then she spoke in a strained, unnatural voice.

"She was—once," she said. "But she's dead. We lost her. She's dead. Dead!" Suddenly she was gone, the door slamming behind her.

The girls looked at each other dumbly, horror-stricken.

"Oh, I say!" said Jean, presently. "Oh, weren't we idiots! I'm so sorry we asked her."

"Poor thing!" Norah said, her voice a shade unsteady. "Oh, poor thing! Did you see how terrible her eyes were?"

Jean nodded. "There couldn't be anything more awful than to have a kiddie like that, and then for it to die," she said. "No wonder she looks so—so hungry. I wish we hadn't asked her."

"So do I," Norah said. "It must have hurt her dreadfully—and she's been very kind to us. But how could we guess?"

"I don't half like going out," said Jean. "I wish we could slip away."

"We couldn't do that," Norah said, shaking her head. "Come on. We'd better hurry, because Dad and the boys will be over. The rain has nearly stopped."

They found the rest of their party in the kitchen, when they made their way out presently, considerably refreshed. Their hostess was bustling about, setting out cups and saucers. She met their half-nervous glances quite cheerfully.

"Perhaps you two would butter some scones for me," she said. She smiled at them—a kindly look that told them they had nothing to worry about. And Norah and Jean took the task thankfully.

"Now what are you going to do?"

Their hostess asked the question of Mr. Linton across the empty teapot. It was a large teapot, but it had been filled and emptied twice. Now every one was feeling better.

"You can't go camping to-night," she went on. "The ground will be soaking and you'd get your death of cold. Besides, it may rain again; I don't believe it's all over yet."

"Oh, camping is out of the question," Mr. Linton answered. "We'll have to find shelter in the township, that's all. I suppose there's an hotel?"

"If you call it one," said the woman, sniffing. "Sort of bush shanty, I should call it—and not too good a specimen at that. Very rough style, and not too clean—and that's putting a pretty fine point upon it. You couldn't possibly take these children there." She nodded in a friendly way at Jean and Norah.

"H'm—that's awkward," said the squatter. "Are there any farms about that would take us in?"

"I don't know of any. Most of the people about here have small houses and they're pretty crowded." She hesitated. "If you gentlemen could manage at the hotel, I'd be very glad to have the girls here."

"That's very good of you," Mr. Linton said, hesitating in his turn. She read the shade of doubt in his eyes.

"You know my husband, I think," she said; "he's Jack Archdale, that used to be boundary rider at the Darrells' station."

"Why, of course!" said Mr. Linton. "And you—weren't you teaching in the State school at Mulgoa? I seem to remember hearing of Archdale's wedding."

"Yes, Mr. Darrell gave us a great wedding," said Mrs. Archdale, smiling. "Five years ago, nearly; we came up here soon after." Her face clouded momentarily, as if remembering. "Jack's doing contract work; he'll be in after a while. So, will you trust your belongings to me, Mr. Linton?"

"Only too gladly," said the squatter, in a voice of relief. "It's exceptionally lucky for us, Mrs. Archdale. One has to take risks of finding rowdy bush inns when one goes for wild expeditions, but I confess I'm glad not to have to take the girls there. I'm greatly obliged to you."

"Oh, it's a real treat to me," she said. "It's lonely here; I don't seem to make great friends with the township people, and Jack's away all day; and you can't be always scrubbing and cleaning a house of this size, to keep yourself occupied. You don't know how glad I've been of a talk with them already—and they took pity on my questions!" She flashed a smile across at Norah that suddenly made her tired face quite like that of the little laughing child in the photograph. "You won't mind staying with me?" she asked, a little wistfully.

"We'll be awfully glad to," Norah said. As a rule, she was a little shy of strangers, but there was something about this woman that made her feel more like a friend; and Norah was desperately sorry for the brave heart behind the haggard eyes.

It was a little hard to say good-bye to Mr. Linton and the boys, seeing them ride off to the township in the clean, rainwashed dusk. But they found plenty to do in helping their hostess, although she would have had them sit still and do nothing. And there was an odd fascination about her—about her quick voice and quick movements, and quaint, unexpected streaks of merriment, that set them laughing very often. Archdale was a big, silent fellow, who evidently worshipped his wife's very shadow. His eyes scarcely left her as she flitted about the kitchen preparing the evening meal. The photograph that they had seen was in every room—a big enlargement of it in Mrs. Archdale's bedroom. It even smiled from over the polished tins upon the kitchen mantelpiece, and sometimes Norah saw the father's eyes wander to it sadly.

After tea they talked on the front verandah, having made a joint business of the washing up. Jack Archdale went to bed soon. He had had a long day's work in the heat. But his wife kept Jean and Norah up a little longer, always talking. A strong restlessness never left her. It was evidently hard for her to sit still, and to keep silent a harder thing yet. Still, she made them so merry when she talked that they forgot that they were tired, and were sorry when at last she packed them off to the fragrant little bedroom with the blue walls.

"I do like her," Jean said. They were tucked into bed together, the moonlight coming in through the open window, and making a white ray across the sheet.

"She's just a dear," Norah agreed. "But, oh! hasn't she sorry eyes! Don't you wish one could make her forget?"

"My word!" said Jean, with emphasis. "But no mother ever could forget losing a little kiddie, I expect. And she hasn't got any others."

There came a tap at the half-open door, and Mrs. Archdale came in. She sat down on Norah's side of the bed, which was nearest the door. The moonlight fell on her face, showing it quite colourless.

"You're quite comfortable?" she asked. "That's right. I thought I'd like to see. I like some one to tuck up. I thought I'd come and—and tuck you up."

Something in her voice kept them silent. But Norah put out a half-nervous hand, and Mrs. Archdale took it and held it.

"And—and tell you about her," she said.

Then she was silent again. Outside in the paddocks a curlew was calling wearily across the timber.

"I'm sure I must have frightened you this afternoon," she said at last. "I was dreadfully ashamed of myself."

"Please, don't!" Norah whispered. "We shouldn't have asked you."

"Why not? If I can't stand being asked, I have no business to keep the pictures about. Only—you see it was on just such a day as this that we lost her—fearfully hot, and ending in a big thunderstorm. Just like to-day—and whenever one comes, I go nearly mad. I can't keep still, and all the time I'm listening and looking. I know it's terribly foolish, but I can't help it. Jack knows; he always understands, and he doesn't go away from me these days unless he can't get out of it."

She stopped, and they felt her shivering.

"You see, we lost her in the scrub," she said, dully.

"What!"

"She slipped away into the timber. She was only just three, and no little child has much chance in the Bush. How would they have? It's so big and lonely, and cruel—oh, how I hate it! We hunted—we were hunting so soon! and all the district turned out, and we got the black trackers. But it was so hot—and then the big storm came up, and when it was over there were no tracks."

She ceased, looking out of the window—so long silent that it seemed that she had forgotten them.

"So we never found her," she said at length, quite calmly. "The Bush just took her and swallowed her up. We looked for weeks; long and long after all the other people had given it up—and they didn't give up soon—Jack and I were hunting. All day long, and often all night too; calling and calling, as long as we thought that she could answer. And after that we hunted, only we did not call. And then, like a fool, I got brain fever, and while I was ill the big Bush fires came and burnt all that part of the scrub. It's fifteen months ago, now."

Jean was sobbing softly. But Norah could only cling to the hard, work-worn hand she held, very tightly.

"I often think how lucky mothers are who see their kiddies die," the tired voice went on. "They know they helped them as much as was possible, and they have their graves to look after. I haven't got anything—no grave, and no memories. Then I think of her lost and wandering in that horrible green prison—tired and frightened, and calling me; and I don't know how much she suffered. Why, it scares men to get lost in the Bush—and my little Babs was only three. If I knew—if I knew that she died easily. It isn't fair on a mother not to know, when she was such a baby thing. It isn't fair."

She had quite forgotten them now. It was as if she was talking to herself.

"Jack wants to go away from here," she said. "But I can't go. I can't go. I always keep thinking that some day when I am walking through the scrub I might find—something. And then at least I would have the little grave. It would be easier than having just nothing. Jack doesn't like me to go looking, now. But I have to keep on. When you've put your baby to bed every night for three years—kissed her and played with her—how she used to laugh!—and heard her say her little prayers, and tucked her in, you can't settle down to leaving her alone at night out in the timber. You just can't do it."

Again the voice ceased, and she sat staring out of the open window. After a long while she got up, still holding Norah's hand.

"Good-night," she said. "Perhaps I oughtn't to have told you. But I had to, somehow. If it hadn't been this kind of a day I could have told you lots of funny little things she used to do." And with that dreadful little speech on her lips she went away.

CHAPTER XVI
BEYOND THE PLAINS
The little feet have left the house,

> The little voice is still;

Without, the wan, wind-weary boughs;

> Within, the will

To go and hear the wee feet tread

Within the garden of the dead.

> —R. Crawford.

THERE were no traces of storm when the girls awoke next morning. Mrs. Archdale came in with tea as soon as she heard their voices. Her face was quite smiling and happy.

"Very likely that dear old 'Brownie' of yours would say I shouldn't give you early tea," she observed. "And I'm sure she'd be right. But I do love it myself, and I've only got you for one morning, so I had to bring it! Jack says I'll ruin my system with tea, and all I can say is, it's a beautiful ending for a system!"

No one quarrelled with the tea or with the wafers of buttered toast that accompanied it. Mrs. Archdale talked briskly while the girls ate.

"It's just a perfect morning," she said. "Blue sky and a little breeze, and everything so clean and beautiful! You will have a lovely ride into the ranges. I've often threatened to make Jack take me up Ben Athol, but he regards me as quite insane when I mention it. But I should love to go."

"Come with us," Norah cried.

She shook her head.

"Oh, I couldn't leave my old man," she said. "We never go very far away from each other now. Some day I will persuade him to go, and perhaps we'll find the remains of your camp. But the blacks won't have left much of it."

"Are there many blacks?" Jean asked, wide-eyed.

"No, very few. Two or three families, I believe. They used to be in one of the aboriginal settlements, and sometimes they go back there in the cold weather; but they won't stay there when the spring comes, and they say two or three camp in the hills all the year round. Sometimes they come down to Atholton and hang about the township for a week or two begging for food and old clothes; but they are a perfect nuisance, and they'd steal your very clothes-lines! So everybody hunts them, and after a while they clear out."

"Do they come out here?"

"It's a bit far from the township for them to come much," Mrs. Archdale answered. "One young darkey, who calls himself Braggan Dudley, visits us occasionally, and tries to sell us very badly-made boomerangs; and his old mother makes rush baskets rather well. I buy the baskets, and scorn the boomerangs. But last time Mr. Braggan came he helped himself to one of Jack's hats. Unfortunately for him, Jack happened along at the moment, and made things lively for him with his stock-whip; so I don't fancy we shall see much of the gentleman in future. Not that you can tell—they have cheek enough for anything."

"I hope we'll run across some of them," Jean said. "I haven't seen any Australian blacks."

"Don't get excited over the prospect," Mrs. Archdale told her. "They may have been worth seeing when they dressed in paint—not that they often wore so much as that!—and roamed the forest before the white people came; but in their present state of half civilization they are as miserable a set as you could imagine. I haven't met any that are not whining, thieving, pitiful creatures—filthy beyond imagination, too, most of them. There used to be a woman in the ranges of a rather better type—she had been employed as a housemaid on one of the stations, and had learned some decent ways, though, of course, she ran off and married a blackfellow.

But she must have gone back to one of the settlements, I fancy; at any rate I haven't heard anything of her for two years or more. I'd like to know what became of Black Lucy; she wasn't at all a bad sort."

Mr. Linton, arriving with the boys at an early hour, had more to say on the subject of the blacks.

"Green—the storekeeper—tells me it won't be safe to leave our camp unprotected," he said. "Those wandering natives are a perfect nuisance—there's nothing they won't steal. That ends Master Billy's chance of getting to the top of the peak. He'll have to stay and mind camp, poor chap. Still, he'll think himself terribly important, and if any of his dusky brethren should come along he'll quite enjoy hunting them off; so he's not altogether to be pitied.

"Was the hotel bad?" Norah inquired.

"Don't allude to the hotel!" Wally said. "We've had a busy night, and we're all soured—and sore!"

"Oh, you poor souls!" Norah said. "Did they feed you decently?" At which Jim and Wally gave vent to a simultaneous groan, charged with bitter recollection.

"It was pretty dreadful," said Mr. Linton, laughing. "I think we're fairly certain to want an early lunch!"

They said good-bye to Mrs. Archdale reluctantly, with many thanks and promises to see her on the return journey. She held Norah's hand a little, looking at her wistfully. The others had ridden on down the hill.

"Would you mind if I gave you a kiss?" she asked, hesitating over each word. "I haven't kissed any one but Jack since—since . . ." Her voice trailed off into silence.

Norah bent down from the saddle quickly, and the poor woman flushed at the touch of the fresh young lips. She stood looking down the track long after the riders had vanished into the timber.

Atholton was not an exciting city. It consisted of a few scattered houses, most of them bark-roofed, since the cartage of roofing iron to this remote district was an expensive matter. No railway was within sixty miles, and communication with the outer world was by means of a coach, which ran twice a week. The Peak Hotel was the high-sounding appellation of the inn, where Mr. Linton and the boys had suffered many things. The Atholton inhabitants referred to it briefly as The Pub. There was a store, combining various matters; within its small compass could be found groceries, drapery, bread, meat, saddlery, and the post office; while at a pinch the storekeeper would undertake a commission for a plough, a tombstone or a piano. The only other business establishment was a blacksmith's shop, where just now the smith was busy in shrinking a tyre for the wheel of a bullock dray. The bullocks, a fine team of ten polled Angus, were drooping their black heads wearily outside, the heavy yokes falling forward on their necks. Their driver propped his long form against the doorpost, and exchanged district news with the smith.

At the store Black Billy might be seen adjusting to the pack-saddle a bundle done up in sacking, and containing provisions. The storekeeper came out as the party rode up; after the manner of Bush storekeepers, all agog to talk.

" 'Mornin', Miss Linton," he said, addressing Jean and Norah impartially. "Lovely day you've got for your ride, now—haven't you? All the same, I wouldn't mind bettin' you'll be pretty tired before you get up to the peak of old Ben Athol."

"Oh, I don't know," Norah said. "We don't mind getting a bit tired."

"In a good cause?" finished the storekeeper, chuckling at his own lightsome play of words. "Well, some have one idea of a lark, and some have another; I can't see much meself in climbing up that stony old hill, but it's all a matter of taste. And how did you get on at Mrs. Archdale's?"

"She was very kind to us," Norah answered, warmly.

"Not a kinder woman in the districk," said the storekeeper, producing a fragment of black and ancient tobacco, and proceeding to cut up some. "Pity she's gone a bit queer. I was tellin' your Pa last night how rummy she's got since their youngster died, an' I believe I fair worried him about you. But, of course, Mrs. Archdale's all right—she's only a bit queer on that point."

"I don't call her queer," Jean burst out, indignantly. "She can't help thinking about her little girl, of course."

"But she's just awfully nice!" Norah seconded. "And she was as good to us as ever she could be."

"There, now, I told your Pa she would be," said the storekeeper, quite unmoved. "Keeps that little home of hers like a new pin, too, don't she? Of course, Mrs. Archdale's a cut above the ordinary—had a bit of education, and all that. And, as you say, no one could blame her for frettin' about that poor little kid. Such a jolly little youngster she was—always had a laugh for you. I can tell you the whole districk was cut up over that youngster's loss—an' it wasn't for want of huntin' that the poor little body was never found. Of course, that's what's on her mother's nerves."

"One can't wonder at that," said Mr. Linton.

"No, of course you can't. Bad enough for a child to die; but not to be able to give it decent burial makes it mighty rough—especially on a woman. Not the first, by a long way, that has never been found in these ranges, they're that thick an' full of gullies; but the wonder was we didn't get little Babs Archdale. All the district was out. There wasn't a yard of scrub unbeaten for ten mile, I don't think."

"Poor little baby!" said Norah, very low.

"Ay. An' the mother—my word, I don't reckon any of us as were huntin' 'll ever forget Mrs. Archdale's face. She's not the kind as shows her feelin's very ready; an' that made it all the worse. Poor soul! Poor soul! An' after we'd had to give up, and the black trackers had gone back, an' every one knew it was hopeless, she an' Jack kept on looking, night an' day I dunno at last what old Jack was most afraid of—not findin' her or findin' her. Twas a relief to every one when we heard the mother had gone down with fever. She was ravin' for weeks."

The storekeeper dropped his voice, looking round.

"An' there's a yarn," he said. "I dunno if it's true. Some people say it is. Half her time Mrs. Archdale's off in the scrub alone; an' the yarn is that she's got a little cross stuck up in the ground in some gully, an' 'Babs' carved on it; an' she keeps flowers there, like as if it was really her little kiddie's grave. An' they say she goes down there an' just sits still an' looks at it. I dunno. Old Jack can't know anything about it, or he'd never leave her; but it ain't the kind of thing you like to think of a woman doin'—not a woman you like. An' all this district thinks the world of Mrs. Archdale."

Norah rode beside her father, and they were silent long after they had bidden the storekeeper good-bye and left the roofs of Atholton low among the timber as they mounted into the hills. She looked up at him at last.

"Oh, Dad," she said; "if only any one could help her!"

"Ay," said David Linton. "But that's beyond human power, my little girl."

"I think she liked having us, Dad," Norah said, half shyly. "That's nothing, of course, unless it kept her from thinking. Can we go back there for another night on our way home?"

"If you like, dear," he said. "But you'd rather camp, wouldn't you?"

"I don't think so—not if she'd like us. She asked me if she could kiss me, Dad."

"Did she?" Mr. Linton said. "Poor lonely soul! It would really be better if Archdale took her out of the district altogether—if she'd go. But that would be the difficulty, I expect. I could give him a good billet on Billabong if he'd take it. I'll be looking for a storekeeper next month."

"Oh, I wish he would," Norah exclaimed. "But I don't think Mrs. Archdale would ever leave here She feels she's a bit nearer that poor dead baby, perhaps."

Above them they could catch glimpses of the track as it rose spirally into the hills. Atholton nestled back into the very foot of the ranges. Scarcely half a mile from its last house the flat country ended, and the hills, tier on tier, rose ahead. Indeed, only for a little while was there any real track. A few isolated mountain farms were perched on tiny flats among the ridges, but as soon as the last of these was passed the wheel track, rough as it was, ended abruptly, and there was only a rough Bush path. Sheep had made it originally, and it had been widened by drovers bringing down stock; but at best it was narrow and uneven, and often the scrub grew so closely on either side, that it was only possible for two to ride abreast.

It was too exquisite a day to be sad. Later the sun would be hot, but now the jewels of last night's rain still hung, trembling, on leaf and bough, and caught the sunlight in liquid flashes. As they rode brushing the dewy branches, they seemed to shake loose the hundred scents of the Bush, and the sharp fragrance was like a refreshing draught. There were not many wild flowers left, but there was no sameness in the scrub, that showed varying shades of colour—tender green of young branches; grey-green and blue-grey of the gum trees, shading to bronze in the distance; on the topmost boughs of young saplings translucent leaves that showed against the sunlight, yellow and red, and glowing crimson. Overhead a sky of perfect blue, deep and pure, wherein sailed piled masses of white cloud, flushed with pink where the rays fell. And all about them birds that sang and chirped and whistled, flitting busily in the green recesses of the scrub; such tame birds that it was evident that few humans came this way to break into the peace and safety of their hills.

"I guess we've had our last canter for a day or two," Jim said. "Nothing but climbing now. How's the pack standing it Billy?"

"Plenty!" said the sable retainer, vaguely. "Baal that pfeller slip—Boss packed him on." His grin suddenly was a streak of light in the darkness of his countenance.

But for the deep whisperings of the Bush it was a land of silence. They had mounted above the last of the hill farms; no longer the faint bleating of sheep came to their ears, or a cattle call sounding through the timber. Here and there they caught glimpses of a steer, poking through the scrub in search of the sparse native grass; but presently there were no more fences, and they had climbed into the country that was No Man's Land.

No one would have had it. Even the easily pleased rabbit would have found scant pickings on the stony soil. The scrub became scanty and gnarled—the winds that blew across the face of the ranges in winter twisted the saplings into queer, bent shapes, and whirled the very earth from their roots. The horses, unused to such unkind ground, slipped and stumbled on the sandstone outcropping here and there. Sometimes there were gullies where the growth was dense—often the site of some old landslip, or a deep cleft between two hills; and sometimes the sound of falling water carried their eyes to where a spring, concealed in some rocky hollow, sent a miniature fall drip-dripping down a steep slope—its margin daintily green, with little plants striving for a hold among the stones.

They camped for lunch early, seizing a patch of deep shade, where a great blue gum grew out of a gully—the only big tree visible among the sparse scrub. A huge boulder had sheltered it as a sapling, protecting it until it had won strength sufficient to outgrow the kindly refuge, and fling its great head towards the sky. The boulder lay at its feet now, and the riders camped in its shadow. Near at hand a spring trickled softly into a rainwashed hole, which brimmed over, sending a silver thread of water down among the stones below. There was little or no grass for the horses; but for this halt they had carried a small ration of hard feed for each horse, and the sweating steeds welcomed it eagerly. The night camp was to be made on a flat further up, where, the storekeeper had told Mr. Linton, they would find grass.

Through the afternoon they climbed steadily. Soon it was easier to walk than to ride, since riding was no quicker—and to lean forward grasping a handful of your horse's mane to ease the strain on his back, and prevent yourself slipping over his tail, is not an especially fascinating pastime, when pursued for any lengthy period. So they led the horses, stumbling over the rocky pathway—though stumbling was a somewhat exciting matter, as, if you fell, your steed would probably walk upon you, since you would be apt to roll back under his fore feet. It was a tiring day, even though the fresh mountain air helped them to forget the sun, beating down hotly upon their shoulders. They enjoyed it all—the English race, all the world over, has a way of taking its pleasure strenuously. No one thought of wanting the way made easier.

Then, just as Mr. Linton was casting somewhat uneasy glances at the weary horses, and wondering how much more acrobatic ability would be demanded of them, they came to a belt of deeper scrub, where moisture was suddenly perceptible in the soil that for hours had been arid and dry. For a few moments they climbed through it, in single file, and then a turn in the narrow track led them out upon a little plateau lying in a nook among the hills. Not more than fifty yards square, it showed green against the rugged slopes beyond. Water, unseen, trickled musically, and a few trees were dotted about.

"Whew-w!" whistled Jim. "What a ripping place to camp!"

"Couldn't be better," his father said, with relief.

"I'm going to stay here for a week!" Wally declared, casting his hat upon the ground.

"Then you'll be living on gum leaves most of the time!" retorted Jim. "Perhaps you might get a monkey-bear if you were lucky."

"I could stand devilled bear very well indeed, just now," responded his friend. "Never met such hungry air in my life—in the words of the poet, there's nothing in the world I couldn't chew!"

"Well, that may be the poet's opinion, but you're not going to chew anything here until camp is fixed," said Mr. Linton, laughing. "Jean has us all beaten—her saddle is the first off."

"Jean will get beastly unpopular if she's not careful," said Wally, favouring the energetic Jean with as much of a scowl as his cheerful countenance would permit. "These horribly-good people nearly always come to a bad end, and nobody loves them!" A tirade that left Jean quite unmoved, as she inquired of Mr. Linton if Nan were to be hobbled?

Besides the tent, there was a "wurley" to be put up to-night. The boys were inclined to scorn this at first, but found later on that they were glad of its shelter, for the keen mountain air was very different to the milder temperature of the plains, and their stock of blankets was not large. They built it of interlaced boughs, thick with leaves, and when finished it looked most inviting. By that time Jean and Norah had tea ready, and the camp fire was glowing redly in a rocky corner.

They sat about it afterwards, singing every chorus they could remember, to a spirited accompaniment by Wally on the penny whistle. The whistle was pitched in a higher key than Nature had rendered possible for most of the singers—a circumstance which did not at all impair the cheerfulness of the quartet, though Mr. Linton threatened to flee into the fastnesses of the bush if the "obbligato" were not discontinued. Black Billy, washing cups at the spring, and gathering kindling wood for the morning fire, grinned all the time in sympathy with the freshness and merriment of the young voices. They rang out cheerily, their echoes dying away on the lonely slopes. Never had such sounds disturbed the brooding silence of old Ben Athol.

To David Linton, lying awake in his "wurley" in the moonlight, gazing dreamily out at a star that trembled in the west, it seemed that the last chorus still lingered on the night air:—

"Wrap me up in my stock-whip and blanket,

And say a poor buffer lies low—lies low,

Where the dingoes and crows can't molest me,

On the plains where the coolibars grow."

CHAPTER XVII
THE PEAK OF BEN ATHOL
By rolling plain and rocky shelf,

With stock-whip in his hand,

He reached at last, oh, lucky elf,

The Town of Come-and-help-yourself,

In Rough-and-ready Land.

—A. B. Paterson.

OH!" said Jean, despairingly. "I wish to goodness I hadn't been born fat!"

"Very possibly you were not," Jim's voice said. "Don't lay all the blame on your parents; it seems to me more an acquired habit on your part." His cheerful face came over the edge of a boulder, and peeped down upon her.

" 'Tisn't my fault at all!" said Jean, indignantly. "You know very well I hardly ever eat butter or potatoes, and I love them both. We're all fat; and Dad and Mother are the fattest!"

"It must be the New Zealand air," said Jim, regarding her with interest. "Perhaps, if we turned you out into a poor paddock for a while, you'd come down in condition. Not that I'd advise it, because we like you as you are—but I hate to see you worried."

"Oh, don't be an ass!" responded the harassed Jean. "This isn't a time for polite conversation—I want to get over that horrid old rock. And I'm so hot!"

"Well, didn't I hear your bleat of woe, and come back to help you, though I was making for the peak like the gentleman in 'Excelsior,' you ungrateful woman?" asked Jim. He swung his long legs over the boulder, and came scrambling down to where she stood. "Poor old thing! It's pretty steep, isn't it?"

"I'm not a poor old thing, and I won't be pitied," retorted Jean with indignation. "I haven't got long legs like all of you, but I can climb hills, for all that. I only want a leg-up over this boulder."

"Of course you do," said Jim, in his best soothing manner—which was wont to have anything but a soothing effect. "Lend me your foot, Miss Yorke, and be prepared to put some spring into your portly frame. One, two, three—up you go!" He hoisted her deftly, and with a quick movement Jean had scrambled to the top of the rock.

It was one of a hundred similar sandstone boulders scattered over the side of the hill. Sometimes, by dodging through crevices and under jutting points of rock, it was possible to avoid them; but often they lay so thickly that to skirt them was impossible except by a detour too long to be practicable. There was not much vegetation to be seen. Grass was practically non-existent, but tough young gums grew here and there among the rocks, with twisted stems, finding a foothold in some mysterious manner by thrusting deep twining roots into the crevices. There leafage was too sparse and stunted to give any real shade, and the sun beat down with blinding force; though it was not yet noon, the rocks were hot under the touch.

Ahead, straggling forms could be seen pushing their way upward. Wally and Norah were in the lead, by virtue of long legs and tough muscles; then came Mr. Linton, with whom Jim had been climbing until he heard Jean's small "bleat" of distress, and turned back to help her. The camp was far below: for a long time they had lost even the faint curl of the smoke of their fire, where Billy had been left disgustedly washing up the breakfast things, and with strict orders to remain on guard throughout the day.

Mr. Linton and the boys carried valises strapped across their shoulders, containing food and water. Already it had been found necessary to husband the latter, since climbing on such a day was thirsty work, and the supply of water bottles was not large. To brew tea at the Peak was considered out of the question; that was a luxury to be anticipated on getting back to the camp. Even now, Jean looked longingly at Wally's diminishing burden, and solaced herself indifferently by chewing an exceedingly dry gum leaf, which tasted very strongly of eucalyptus, and made her, if anything, thirstier than before.

There were scarcely any small birds in this high region—cover was too scarce, and food supply correspondingly low. Once they caught sight of an eagle-hawk, sailing leisurely across a path of blue sky, visible between two hills; and, even as they looked, his wings ceased to beat, he hovered, motionless, for a moment, and then fell like a stone, swooping on some prey descried in a distant gully. Occasionally there were holes that looked like rabbit-burrows, and sometimes an opening that marked the entrance to a wombat hole: but of wild life they saw nothing, save here and there a lizard sunning itself on a patch of warm rock, and sliding off with incredible rapidity at the unfamiliar sound of voices.

"As for the blacks," said Jean, resentfully, "I believe it was only a yarn about them—or they're all gone. We haven't seen even a trace of a camp."

"Well, there's a good deal of room for a camp or so to exist without our coming across them," Jim answered, wisely. "But I think it's quite likely there are none left—why on earth should they stay in country like this when they can be fed and housed decently at one of the settlements? Of course, the gentle black is a peculiar sort of chap, and hates to be shut up within four walls. Still, I think this sort of thing would scare even a native back to civilization."

"Well, I'm sorry," Jean made answer. "I did want to see some."

"There's old King Billy at the Darrells' station," Jim told her, kindly. "He lives there, and reckons he owns it. If you like, we'll get him trotted out for your inspection. He's our Billy's father, and I've no doubt he'd be glad to call on his loving son, especially if he thought his screw had just been paid." Which handsome offer did very little to appease Jean's longings, even when Jim supplemented it with a further proposal to make the monarch appear in war-paint and utter horrifying tribal yells. After having been acquainted with William, junior, it was difficult to expect any romantic attributes in his royal father.

Ben Athol was a deceptive mountain. Often the summit seemed quite near, as if but a few yards more would land them at their destination. This was cheering, and led them to climb with great ardour, each striving to be first over the toppling edge that appeared to be the margin of the crest. But when it was surmounted, it was found to be only a shoulder, and the actual Peak loomed high above them yet. This occurred so often that it moved Wally to wrath and eloquence.

"I never saw anything rummier than the anatomy of this blessed hill," he said. "It's got as many shoulders as an octopus ought to have, only they're all on the same side! I think we'll be climbing it like this till the end of time, and never getting any forarder. Do you think it would pay to cut round and try to climb up its chest instead?"

Jim said, "Don't be personal!" and patted him on the shoulder with such friendly force that the orator, who chanced to be sitting on the extreme edge of a boulder, slid off, and continued sliding until he found Mother Earth—which happened with some force. This led to reprisals, and by the time that the combatants, somewhat dusty, had adjusted their differences, the remainder of the expedition was some distance up the Peak.

It was the Peak itself, and the last pull was a steep one. All the ground was heaped with stones, great and small. To dodge them was out of the question, and every foot of the way had to be climbed. There were no trees here, though on the very summit a few clung amid the rocks. It was hot work, crawling, climbing, slipping—the rough sandstone grazing the hands that clung to it and the knees as they scrambled across. But it was the top. Jean and Norah raced for the last few yards—a contest abruptly ended by the latter's catching her foot in a crevice and falling headlong. Jean arrived at the Peak by herself, and looked round in some astonishment, to behold her chum rising from the earth and ruefully surveying a hole in her skirt.

"Oh—I'm sorry!" said the victor, laughing and flushed. "Are you hurt, old girl?"

"Only my feelings—and my skirt!" laughed Norah, inspecting a grazed hand as a matter of lesser moment. "It's a good thing we packed needles and cotton." She came up beside Jean, and caught her breath in quick ecstasy. "Jeanie! what a view!"

The ranges lay beneath them, rolling east and west. Darkly green, their clothing of timber hid all ruggedness and inequalities, and only that waving expanse of foliage rippled softly from their feet. Here and there a peak, higher than its fellows, reared its crest, or a giant tree flung a proud head skywards; but there was little to break the softly-rounded masses of green. But out beyond the hills, the plains lay extended, mile on mile, spreading away illimitably. Dark lines winding sinuously over their bosoms showed the timber bordering the courses of creeks and rivers. Once a sun ray caught a glint of blue where a lake rippled thousands of feet below. On one lonely plain a belt of pines made a dark mass, easily distinguishable, even at so great a distance. On all was silence—so profound that it was easy to imagine that the green country lying below was as desolate and uninhabited as the rugged Peak where they stood.

David Linton, coming up silently, looked out long over the country he loved, one hand on Norah's shoulder. Then he sat down on a boulder and lit his pipe, still watching and silent, as the blue smoke trailed away.

The boys arrived hastily, flushed and panting.

"Beat you!" gasped Wally.

"Dead heat, you old fraud!" Jim retorted.

"Be quiet, you duffers," said Norah, affectionately. "Come here and look across the world!"

So they looked—and were impressed even into silence for three minutes, which is a remarkable tribute to be exacted by any landscape from any boy. Then Nature reasserted itself.

"I could drink in that view for hours," said Wally, with fervour, "if I weren't so thirsty!" He undid his bundle in haste, and looked longingly at the water bottle. "May we all moisten our lips just once, Mr. Linton—one little moist?"

"We'd better take stock," responded that gentleman, coming out of his reverie, and proceeding to unstrap his load. "Jim, how much have you got left?"

They inspected the supply, which was found to be barely sufficient to assist in washing down luncheon. This once settled, they threw care to the winds, and demolished all, since going down hill would be a quicker matter, and the heat less than on the journey up. "Horses travel well when there's water ahead, so perhaps I may expect the same from you!" remarked Mr. Linton, to the just indignation of his party, who averred that his willingness to allow the water to be finished proceeded solely from anxiety to have no load to carry down.

It was still hot when they left the summit. Resting there was scarcely a comfortable business; there was little shade, and the rocks were uneasy places for repose. "Better to have another spell on the way down, when we strike a good place," said the leader; and the others chorussed their agreement. So they went down, slipping and sliding on the boulders—digging their heels into a patch of earth whenever one was discovered soft enough to act as foothold. It was not without risk, for the Peak was steep, and a false step among the stones would probably have resulted unpleasantly. David Linton was free from minor anxieties concerning his irresponsible clan, holding the happy-go-lucky Australian belief that worrying does not pay; still, he breathed more freely when the descent of the Peak itself was accomplished, and a slightly easier slope lay before them. Broken legs are at all times awkward—but to carry a broken leg down a mountain side is not a performance to be lightly contemplated.

He pulled up an hour later.

"Well, I have no idea as to the views of the clan," he remarked. "But I am going to have a spell. It is borne in upon me that I am getting old, and that I have not had a smoke for a long time."

"You're not old, at all, but we'll all have a spell," Norah responded. They had halted in a shady spot, where native grass tried to grow, and there were stones of a convenient shape to serve as seats. The Peak loomed far above them, grim and remote, although they were yet on its side. They had climbed down so far that the view all round was blotted out, since now they were below the level of the timber-crowned hills that clustered round Ben Athol. Already the fierceness of the sun had gone, and there was even a breath of chill in the shady stillness where they rested.

They lay on the ground or found stony seats, and for half an hour talked lazily or did not talk at all, as the spirit moved them. Jim and his father were deep in a discussion of bullocks. Suddenly Norah, who had been industriously biting the tough grass stems, as an aid to thought, scrambled to her feet.

"I want to go and explore," she said. "Who will come?"

"Me," said Jean and Wally, simultaneously, and with painful disregard of the King's English.

"Not I, I think," said her father. "I want to finish my pipe."

"Then I'll keep you company," Jim said. "Don't get lost, you kids!"

"Kid yourself!" remarked Wally. "Then we'll meet back at the camp, sir?"

"Yes, I suppose so. Don't get far off the track, Wally," said Mr. Linton; "and take care of my daughters!" He smiled at Jean.

"I'll keep 'em well in order, sir," said Wally. "Observe, children, Papa has put you under my charge!" Whereat Norah tilted her nose disdainfully, and they scrambled off among the rocks.

The prohibition against getting far from the path made exploration limited—not that there was much to be gained by exploring, since one part of the hill seemed precisely the same as another. Very rarely, a lean mountain sheep appeared, to scurry off among the timber in bleating affright at the strange apparitions; but in general the scrub and the rocks were monotonously alike, and travelling, once off the sheep track, was considerably more difficult. So they made their way back to it, resolving that exploration was a mistaken ideal, and journeyed down hill cheerfully.

Wally paused when they were beginning to think that the camp must be close at hand.

"Cease your foolish persiflage!" said he, severely. "I've an idea."

"Never!" said Jean, with open incredulity. "Where?"

"It's this," said Wally. "Somewhere in my bones it is borne in upon me that young Billy is asleep. Let's see if we can't take him by surprise."

"All right," Norah said, twinkling. "But why you should think poor old Billy is snoring at the post of Duty is more than I can say, unless you're thinking that in similar circumstances you'd be sleeping yourself!"

"There may be something in that," said Wally, regarding the supposition with due consideration. "If Billy has kept awake all day he's a hero and a martyr, and I should like to crown him with a chaplet of 'prickly Moses,' laurel leaves being unobtainable. Anyhow, let us creep upon him, and make him think he's attacked by sable warriors, clad principally in ferocity."

They went on softly, in single file. The path was easier, as the slope became less acute; an hour earlier, quiet walking would have been impossible, owing to shifting stones that had a way of rattling down hill at a touch; but now they could prowl, soft-footed, through the scanty undergrowth. It was, perhaps, five minutes later when the first glimpse of the green plateau came into view, and at a signal from Wally they stole forward noiselessly, halting in the shadow of the scrub that fringed its edge.

It was immediately evident that Wally's instinct had been entirely correct. Black Billy had succumbed to the heat, or the soporific effect of the eucalyptus scents, or his own loneliness—or, very possibly, to a combination of all three. He lay on his back under a little tree, his battered old felt hat pulled over his eyes, and his skinny limbs flung carelessly in the abandonment of sleep. His mouth was wide-open, and snores proceeded from him steadily.

"Sweet child," said Wally admiringly. "Nothing lovelier than a sleeping cherub, is there? What did I tell you, young Norah Linton? Grovel."

"I grovel," whispered Norah, laughing. "Poor old Billy, he must have been horribly dull."

"Not he, lazy young nigger. Plenty to eat and nothing to do is a blackfellow's heaven," responded Wally, in an energetic whisper. "Hold on until I collect my breath for a yell."

Norah caught his arm.

"Wally! Look there."

From behind the tent suddenly emerged a figure, looking round cautiously. As she straightened up they could see her face plainly—a black woman, shapeless and bent as in the manner of all black "gins," when their first youth is passed. Her broad face, hideous in its dark ugliness, shone with the peculiar polish of black skins. She was dressed in rags, principally of sacking, amidst which could be seen the remnant of an old print frock that had once been red; a man's felt hat covered her matted hair ineffectually, since here and there stray locks stuck out of holes in the crown.

"Great Scott," Wally whistled. "And that young beggar, Billy, snoring. Well, Jean, there's your noble savage, anyhow, and I hope you like her."

"Why, she got a picaninny," Norah whispered eagerly.

As the woman moved they could see a tiny form clinging to her skirts on the other side. She faced round presently, and they saw the small aboriginal—a queer mite, in rags of sacking also, and a piece of the same elegant material tied over its head.

No one could have said off-hand that it was boy or girl—it was merely picaninny. Elfish eyes looked out from a tangle of black hair under the sacking. One little dark hand clung to the black gin's skirts; the other grasped a tiny boomerang that was evidently a toy. There was something uncanny in its perfect silence and caution of the little thing.

"Rum little beggar!" Wally whispered. "Fine Australian native in the making! Jean, are you impressed?"

"The woman's awful," Jean murmured back. "But the baby's a jolly little chap. I wonder if he's a boy or girl"—a confusion of genders which sent Wally off into a fit of silent laughter that was almost alarming, since it made him apoplectic in appearance.

"Do be quiet!" Norah whispered. "She's certain to hear you."

But the black gin was quite unsuspicious of the watching eyes. She poked about the camp, here and there picking up some trifle and concealing it somewhere about her rags. Billy's recumbent form she avoided carefully, and her eyes never left him for more than a moment. She wandered softly about the tent, longing, yet fearing, to untie the flap and make more detailed investigations. And always at her side trotted the picaninny, clinging to her skirt and entirely unconcerned by the adventure, except in its silence and stealthy movements.

Presently, however, it stopped suddenly, released its hold, and sat down on the ground with a comically knitted brow. The gin looked down, an impatient frown on her heavy features. The little creature was evidently concerned with a thorn or splinter its bare black foot had picked up; it was searching for it, twisting itself to try to get a view of its case-hardened sole. The gin cautioned it with uplifted finger, and leaving it on the ground, stole off on a further tour of exploration.

The black baby was evidently very cross. It frowned and twisted over its foot, and seemed to be telling the splinter, under its breath, its unbiassed opinion of it. Meanwhile, the lubra was lying flat on her face beside the tent, groping under the canvas with one hand, and her soul apparently charged with hope. Norah and Jean watched her, choking with laughter, since, so far as they knew, she could only encounter a bunk.

"You'll have to take steps if she tries another spot, Wally," Norah whispered.

"Right-oh!" was the noiseless response, given somewhat absently. Wally was watching the picaninny. He turned to Norah in a moment.

"That's a rum little blackfellow," he said. "See its foot; I've never seen a darky with a foot like that, and we used to live amongst 'em in Queensland. They're all just as flat-footed as a—a platypus. But look at the instep that rum little black coon has got; it's as high an instep as I've ever seen, and the foot's quite pretty."

Norah looked as desired. The dusky baby was still contorting on the grass, fishing vigorously in its foot for the offending splinter. Its face was turned towards them, but bent so intently over its task that they could scarcely see it. There was no doubt that the small foot was pretty—a slender foot, with arched instep, incongruous enough, sticking out of the sacking rags.

Then, as they watched, success rewarded the picaninny's efforts. The hard little fingers, with talonlike nails, found the head of the splinter, and drew it carefully out. The child looked up triumphantly, a smile breaking out suddenly and illuminating all its dark face. And at sight of the smile Norah gave a great start, and cried out aloud:

"Wally—did you see! It isn't a picaninny at all! It's Mrs. Archdale's baby!"

"The little creature was evidently concerned with a thorn or splinter its bare black foot had picked up."

CHAPTER XVIII
THE WURLEY IN THE ROCKS
And yet there is no refuge

   To shield me from distress.

Except the realm of slumber

   And great forgetfulness.

         —Henry Kendall.

QUICK as they were, the black woman was quicker.

She was lying full length on her face when Norah's startled voice rang out across the camp. Almost with the first word she was on her feet, twisting to an erect position with a quick movement curious in one so ungainly. Like a flash, also, the child was running to her, screaming with sudden terror. The gin caught her up with a swift clutch, and in three strides had gained the shelter of the scrub.

"Oh, Wally, run!" Norah cried.

But Wally was running. His long legs took him across the grass so swiftly that he seemed to gain the scrub almost at the same instant as the lubra. Behind him came Jean and Norah, scarlet with excitement. They pulled up sharply.

There was no sign of any one. The spring that had its source near the plateau trickled out at the side, and the scrub grew more densely than anywhere else. It seemed to have swallowed up their quarry. Not even a broken or trembling branch or a mark in the bushes told where she had gone. They listened, their hearts thumping heavily.

Then, from the left, came the sound of a breaking twig, and Wally turned in its direction, and went crashing through the undergrowth, the girls at his heels. For a moment he feared that he was on the wrong track; then, with a great throb of relief, he caught a glimpse of a faded red print skirt, and ran wildly on.

Once he looked back with a quick call.

"Don't get bushed if we miss each other. I'll coo-ee!"

"Right!" Norah had no breath for more.

They ran madly through the scrub, dodging, twisting, scrambling among the saplings and bushes. The stones were the worst; they cropped out of the ground, often with a coating of dry lichen or dead leaves disguising their outlines, and it was almost impossible to dodge them, running at top speed, in the gloom of the trees. A dozen times the pursuers tripped and went sprawling over the unseen and unyielding obstacles, only to pick themselves up, bruised and shaken, to run harder than ever, to make up for lost time.

The black gin always kept before them. Sometimes they caught a glimpse of her red skirt, and once Wally saw her across a little cleared space, fleeing silently, with the child clasped to her breast; but generally she was out of sight, and they could only follow her by sound. She ran with all the stealthy cunning of her race, her bare feet making little noise when contrasted with the crashing of her pursuers, who shouted to her loudly and unavailingly to stop. Nor did she ever run in a straight line—like a hare she twisted and doubled, though always as if she had some definite end in view, for, despite her tortuous course, she always kept to the same direction. The child uttered no sound; the woman ran as though she had no burden.

Norah fell behind presently; not only was the pace too much for her, but she feared to leave Jean, who was lagging far in the rear. She waited for her to catch up, and they jogged on together, listening anxiously for Wally's voice.

Wally had set his teeth, suddenly indignant at being outpaced for so long by a woman—"a black one at that!" he uttered, forgetting that no woman, save a black one, would have had the slightest chance of keeping ahead. The pride of the schoolboy, to whom none of his mates had been able to show the way on the football field, surged up in him, and he flung himself forward, shouting. He knew he had lost sight of Norah and Jean—and they must not be left to run the danger of getting "bushed." The chase must end.

He was gaining yard by yard—the pad of flying bare feet came closer and closer. Then he heard a heavy fall, and a loud, piteous cry—a child's cry—that sent the honest blood surging to his heart. He was almost upon the black woman as she picked herself up, clinging to the child—and then she doubled suddenly, twisting herself through a gap between two great boulders. Not quite quickly enough; had the boy been a dozen yards further off he might never have seen where she disappeared. But he was on her heels, following. Then he knew that the chase was over.

They were in a tiny triangular space, nearly filled by a "wurley" formed by roofing in the stones with boughs, and leaving a few upright ones as a doorway. The boulders hemmed it in. The place was hardly larger than a dog kennel at Billabong—searchers might have passed it a hundred times, never guessing that there was any space left among the masses of rock. It had evidently been inhabited a long while, for the ground was beaten hard, and it reeked with the "blackfellow" odour that is worse than the majority of smells. The black gin dived into the tiny hut, and faced about; Wally could see her fierce eyes gleaming—could hear her breath, loud, panting gasps. He was panting himself; the "Coo-ee!" he uttered, turning towards the direction where he had last seen the girls, quavered a little. He sent it echoing through the bush twice before an answer came. Then the boy's heart gave a throb of relief as Jean and Norah came into view.

"Got 'em!" he said, indicating the "wurley" with a jerk of his hand. "Moses! can't that lady run! I'd like to enter her for the Oaks! Are you girls all right?"

They nodded.

"Is it—is the kiddie——?"

"Blest if I know!" said Wally, laughing. "You said so, and so I ran. If it isn't some one else's youngster, then the lady in here has a mighty uneasy conscience on some other score, that's all. But if you've given me that little jog-trot for nothing, young Norah——!" He broke off, endeavouring to look threatening.

"Why, I saw it laugh!" said Norah. "And it was the face of that photograph and Mrs. Archdale's face rolled into one!"

"Never saw Mrs. Archdale with a face as black as that," Wally rejoined. "You aren't complimentary, Nor. Let's have a look at them, anyway."

But the black gin cowered back in her den, and refused to move. Persuasion and threats alike were unavailing. Finally Wally shrugged his shoulders.

"Awfully sorry to pull your house about your ears, ma'am," he said. "But if you won't come out, it'll have to be. Look out, you girls—I shall stir up awful smells!"

He fulfilled his prediction as he pulled away the interlacing boughs—hygienic principles are not in vogue in an aboriginal "wurley." It was pitifully scanty—a moment's work sufficed to reveal the lubra and the child she grasped firmly. She tried to hold its face against her—but the baby wriggled free at the strange voices, facing the grave young faces.

Now that they were so close only a glance was needed to show that this was no black picaninny. A dark stain covered the child's face and its legs and arms: but through it the features were those of the baby who had laughed to them from the blue wall of the little room at Mrs. Archdale's. And there was no fear in the wide, dark eyes that met theirs—but rather an unspoken greeting, as though instinct told her that she was once more among her own kind. Norah held out her hand to her; but the black gin cowered back, holding the little body yet more closely.

"Mine," she said; "that pfeller picaninny mine!"

"Qui s'excuse s'accuse," said Wally, in his best French. "We never said she wasn't, old lady—'twas your own guilty mind. That feller Mrs. Archdale's picaninny, Black Mary."

"Mine," she said, sullenly, fear glowing in her eyes. "Baal you take her?"

"Baal I'll leave her?" retorted Wally. "You give it me that picaninny, one time, quick!" He swung round at a step behind him. "Thank goodness, here's Billy! I don't think I'm much good at international complications."

Billy grasped the situation in a few words. Then he addressed a flood of guttural remarks to the black gin, who shrank visibly from him, and answered him, trembling. He turned to Wally.

"That pfeller, Lucy," he said, briefly. "She bin marry mine cousin, Dan. S'pos'n' she have picaninny, it tumble-down (died) one-three time. So Dan he gone marry Eva." He told the small tragedy of Black Lucy, unconcernedly, and the lubra listened, nodding.

"So that pfeller Lucy plenty lonely," went on Billy. "Then, s'pos'n him meet li'l white picaninny down along a scrub, him collar that pfeller. That all. Every pfeller lubra want picaninny," finished Billy in a bored voice, as if marvelling at the ways of womenkind.

There was a long pause. At last Wally spoke, hurriedly.

"Well—she knows we've got to take the kiddie, anyhow, doesn't she?"

"Mine bin tell her that," said Billy. "She bin say not."

The black woman broke in, in a high, shrill voice.

"Not take her. That li'l pfeller, picaninny belongin' to me."

"Picaninny's mother's wanting her," Norah said her voice pitying.

"Mine!" said the black woman, uncertainly—"mine!" She held the child closer, rocking her to and fro; and the children stared at her, not knowing how to solve the problem.

Billy had no illusions. He grasped the gin's arm, and jerked her to her feet.

"Baal you be a fool?" he said, roughly. "S'pos'n' p'liceman come, you bin find yourself in lock-up, plenty quick! P'lice bin lookin' for you this long time 'cause you bin steal picaninny."

She winced and shivered, looking at him with great stupid eyes, like an injured animal's.

"You come and see my father," said Norah, gently, putting one hand on her arm; and somewhat to their surprise, the gin came, making no further outcry, but holding the child to her. So they went back through the scrub. Billy led them swiftly, making but a short distance, in a straight line, of the long and tortuous race that the fugitive had led them. It seemed a very few minutes before they saw the canvas of the tent shining white through the trees, and heard voices beyond.

Quite suddenly, the black gin stopped. For a moment she held the child to her so savagely that the little thing cried out in pain. She muttered over her.

"My li'l pfeller picaninny!" she said. "Mine!" She turned to Norah.

"Mine bin good to her," she said, thickly. "Baal mine ever beat that one!" Just for an instant she stood looking at them in dumb agony. Then she put the child down with a swift gentleness, and, turning, fled into the gloom of the Bush.

CHAPTER XIX
THE LAST NIGHT
The gray gums by the lonely creek,

   The star-crowned heights,

The wind-swept plain, the dim blue peak,

   The cold white light,

The solitude spread near and far

Around the camp-fire's tiny star,

The horse bells' melody remote,

The curlew's melancholy note

    Across the night.

—G. Essex Evans.

WELL, she's a queer little atom," said David Linton, surveying the treasure trove. "Strong and healthy, too, I should say, if one could see anything for stains and dirt. She's inconceivably dirty. Has she made any remarks on the situation?"

"She seems to approve of you, at any rate, Nor.," said Jim. "What on earth are you going to do with her?"

"Bath her," said Norah promptly. "Thank goodness, Mrs. Archdale isn't going to see her looking like that!"

"I don't fancy the poor soul would worry over that point of view," said her father. "But bath her, by all means—you'll certainly require to do so, as she'll have to be in your tent all night."

"A mercy we've got the washing-up tin," remarked Norah, looking with approval at a half kerosene tin which had formed a somewhat disputed part of their pack; "and ammonia—I'd never get her clean without it. Brownie put in a bottle in case of insect stings."

"You'll need it all," Jim said, grimly. "Will she speak, Nor.?"

"She won't say a word so far," Norah answered. "I wonder if she has forgotten how? A baby like that would forget nearly everything in a year and a quarter, wouldn't she?"

The child stood in the midst of the group, one hand clinging tightly to Norah's finger. She had said nothing since she had been suddenly left among the strangers. As the black woman rushed away from her she had made an instinctive movement to follow her, but Billy had been too quick, his hand falling on her tiny shoulder before she had taken two steps. At his touch the little thing had given a terrified start, and then, moved by some hidden instinct, had fled to Norah, whose hands were held out to her. Since then she had not relinquished her grip on Norah's finger. She gazed from one to the other with great, unwinking eyes.

"Perhaps she hasn't forgotten her name," Jean suggested. "Try her."

So Norah knelt down before the ragged little figure.

"Babs!" she said softly. "Babs!"

The baby looked at her. Something like a gleam of recognition came into her eyes. But beyond that she would give no sign, and at last Norah gave up the attempt.

"I'd better bath her now," she said; "her hair must be quite dry before she goes to sleep. Billy, you boil the billy quick as you can."

"What on earth are you going to dress her in?" Jim asked. "You can't put those rags on her again."

"I should think not!" his sister answered, eyeing the malodorous tatters disgustedly. "Jean and I will fix up something."

"You had better fix it up out of a blanket, then," her father observed. "I don't suppose she has encountered water for fifteen months—and we don't want her to take a chill."

"All right," said Jean, nodding wisely. "I've got an idea, and we have needles and thread."

"Then we can leave it to you two," said Mr. Linton, with relief.

"You can," said Norah. "Only keep the supply of hot water going!"

They needed all they could get, and the soap was at a low ebb and the ammonia bottle empty before they made little Babs Archdale clean. At first she objected strenuously to the process, and her screams rent the air, and she struggled furiously, so that it took both attendants of the bath to hold her, and much soap went in her eyes. But once her hair was washed and tucked up out of her way, she suddenly became good, and submitted happily to their ministrations, revelling in the warm soapy water.

They stripped her rags off with gingerly movements, and Jean carried them on a stick into the scrub. All the child's skin was stained with some dark juice and grimed with the dirt of long months; but it yielded to the scrubbing, and Babs emerged from the final rinsing water a very different being from the grubby picaninny who had gone in—the white skin of her shining little body a startling contrast to the deep sun-brown of her face and arms and legs. Norah rolled her in a towel and tossed her upon a bunk in the tent, rubbing and patting her gently, in sheer happiness over the slender, sweet-smelling little form. Out of the final towelling, Babs sat up, glowing and dimpling. She broke into sudden, happy laughter.

"Oh, you darling!" Norah said, catching her up. "Jean, isn't she just lovely? Babs! Oh, I do want your mother to see you!"

Babs looked at her, opened her mouth, and then closed it.

"Muvver!" she said, quite clearly. "Muvver!" At which Norah and Jean, unable to contain their emotions, hugged each other very heartily—to the great delight of Babs, who sat upon the bed like a piebald Cupid and dimpled into laughter again at this strange pair.

Over the tangled curls both girls worked despairingly, while Babs submitted with a stoicism that said much for her sojourn as an aboriginal.

Norah stopped at last, and put down the comb.

"I think we're a pair of duffers," she said. "We might work all night at that mop, and it wouldn't be right—indeed, I believe most of it will have to be cut off. But can't you imagine how Mrs. Archdale will just love doing it!"

"Well, it's clean, at any rate," said Jean philosophically. "And that's the main thing."

It was a quaint little figure that they led out for inspection; and the boys roared with laughter, to the great disgust of the object of their mirth, who tucked her damp head into Norah's neck and refused to face the audience for some time. Finally she condescended to sit on David Linton's knee and inspect his watch—and brought down rounds of delighted applause by suddenly bending forward and "blowing" in the time-honoured fashion for the case to be opened.

"Jean, may I employ you as a tailor?" Wally asked, solemnly.

The small person was attired in a fearful and wonderful garment contrived by Jean out of a soft blanket—coming high round her neck, and ending in brief trouser legs, from which the bare, brown knees emerged. Over it she wore a linen coat of Norah's—the sleeves turned back almost to the shoulders, and a world too wide for the tiny arms that seemed to be lost within them. But there was no doubt that Babs was happy and comfortable, albeit not clad according to the dictates of fashion.

"It's peculiar, isn't it?" said Jean, surveying her handiwork. "Most of it is sewn together on her, and she'll have to be unpicked for her next bath. Don't you think I was clever to manage to get the pink stripes right down the front?"

"You're a genius!" Wally said, greatly impressed. "There is, however, a sterner side to it. Do I not recognize my blanket?"

"You do," said Jean. "It happened to be the softest. Anyway, you've got another, and it's going to be a hot night."

"A fair exchange isn't any robbery," said Norah, with striking originality. "The other part of Babs' attire is in the scrub, if you'd care for it!"

"I scorn you both," said Wally. "It's an abominable thing to be made a philanthropist against one's will!" He fell to tickling Babs' brown toes with a stem of grass, to the great delight of the mite.

She was quite friendly with them all by the time tea was ready, when she displayed an appetite that would, Wally averred, have shamed a hippopotamus, and ate until she bulged visibly, and Norah had fearful visions of her exploding. Nothing, apparently, came amiss to her, and her cheerful desire to eat anything whatever led to harrowing conjectures as to what could have been her principal diet during her life in the scrub.

"Kangaroo rat and wallaby, most likely," Jim remarked; "varied with fish, in various stages of preservation, and nice succulent tree-grubs!"

"Be quiet, you disgusting creature!" said Wally, in extreme horror. "You spoil my appetite." He helped himself to a mammoth slice of cake.

"Looks like it!" Jim grinned. "Well, Babs can't furnish you with details of her late guardian's menu, I suppose; but I wouldn't mind betting it didn't vary much from my ideas."

"Bless her!" said Norah, fatuously. "We'll give her everything we've got that's nice now to make up." She tempted Babs with a chocolate, and Babs swiftly fell before the temptation.

"I think you'd better call a halt," observed Mr. Linton. "That child has eaten as much as any two of the party—and she'll be asleep in about a minute. You ought to put her to bed, Norah—we shall want to make an early start for Atholton."

Babs was nearly asleep by the time Norah had tucked her into her bunk. She clung to her finger still, and drowsily put her face up to be kissed—a forgotten instinct, coming back as consciousness slipped away. And all through the night she nestled to her closely, one little hand clinging to her sleeve. Norah did not sleep much. She did not want to; it seemed to her that she dare not cease protecting the tiny dreaming mite for this last night—to keep her safe for the morrow, that meant such bewilderment of joy for the forlorn hearts in the little cottage by Atholton. At the thought she thrilled with an eagerness that left her almost trembling. Even the short few hours seemed long to wait—thinking of Babs Archdale's mother.

"But it's only one more night!" she whispered. "You'll know soon." She smiled in the moonlight, raising herself a trifle to watch the little face nestling near her.

David Linton slept across the tent doorway this night.

"Just as well," he said. "I wouldn't risk to-morrow for the Archdales for all Billabong!"

And out in the gloom of the scrub, where the moonlight scarcely filtered through the tracery of boughs to the boulder-strewn ground, a woman crouched, lonely, in her ruined wurley among the rocks. Sometimes she muttered angrily; sometimes her wild eyes, fiercely stupid, closed in sleep, and then her hands moved restlessly, seeking for a little body that no longer lay against her breast. She was outcast, loathsome, a pariah; every man's hand would be against her, and only the wild hills left to her for refuge. But perhaps the calm stars, that see so many lonely mothers, looked down pityingly upon this black mother, who had been lonely, too.

CHAPTER XX
DOWN THE MOUNTAIN
Oh, little body, nestled on my heart!

—M. Forrest.

THEY fixed a saddle-pad for Babs in front of Norah, and she rode proudly into Atholton. The horses did not make her afraid at all; indeed, she welcomed them with shouts of glee, appearing a little doubtful as to whether they were pets or things to eat—but in either case greatly to be desired. And when she was mounted before Norah, with one hand clutching a lock of old Warder's mane and the other holding Norah's finger, she had nothing left to wish for. She chuckled at frequent intervals; any object along the track, from a kookaburra to a lizard, moved her to little shouts of laughter, though it was painfully certain that she wished to devour the lizard. "I never saw such a merry baby," said Jean.

Gradually words came back to her. At first they caught fragments of native dialect, chiefly unintelligible; but, with the talk about her, and the kind voices that spoke to her, English words returned brokenly to the baby tongue. She answered quite soon to her own name, looking up whenever she heard "Babs" with a quaint, elfish half smile; and before breakfast was over she had made a hesitating attempt at "Norah"—finding the "r" altogether too hard a stumbling block. Her vocabulary was not large, but she made the most of it. And all the time as they rode down Ben Athol, Norah taught her one word—leaning forward, holding her closely, one arm round the quicksilver little body. One word, over and over again—Mother, Mother, Mother.

Norah never could have told much about the way down. It was steep, she knew, and stony; she was glad old Warder was surefooted, since to him was left most of the responsibility of the track. There were birds singing everywhere, in the Bush and in her own heart; there was blue sky overhead, and a little breeze that just redeemed the day from heat. It could not have been otherwise than a perfect day. But for Norah there was no view beyond the mat of black curls against her breast; no thought beyond the one that surged and sang within her. An old verse beat in her happy brain—"For this thy brother was dead and is alive again; and was lost and is found."

"Contented, my girl?" David Linton asked, riding beside her.

"I'm happy," Norah answered, and smiled up at the tall man on the great black horse. "I'm not quite contented yet. But I will be, soon." Then Babs developed a determination to ride Monarch, and lurched forward so suddenly that she only saved her by a spasmodic grip that included some of Babs, as well as her clothing—to the no small indignation of Babs.

"Don't be ambitious quite so early, my lass," said Jim, gravely, regarding the scarlet and wrathful picaninny with a judicial air. "Time enough to hitch your waggon to a star when you're a bit older." Hearing which profound reflection, and understanding no syllable of it, but deciding that she liked the voice in which it was proffered, Babs promptly transferred her affections to Garryowen, and was with difficulty restrained from transferring herself as well. Norah evaded both difficulties by seizing advantage of a tiny stretch of flat ground and, cantering across it, thereby so entrancing her passenger that she was never again satisfied with anything so ordinary as a walking pace—which was unfortunate, as to canter down Ben Athol demanded four-footed agility usually withheld from all but circus horses. There was no lack of excitement in riding with Babs Archdale.

They lunched on the lower slopes of the mountain—cutting the spell short, since Norah's restlessness to be gone made it impossible for her to sit still. Then, still in the early afternoon, they saw the roofs of Atholton below them, half hidden in the timber.

On the flat, just where the hills ended, they shook up their horses and cantered quickly over the half-mile that lay between them and the village. Scarcely any one was in sight; Atholton slumbered peacefully, oblivious of intruders. The storekeeper, shirt-sleeved and with pipe in mouth, lounged on his verandah, and greeted them jovially as they came up, Jim and his father in the lead.

"Got back, have you?" he said. "And had a good trip, by the looks of you!" His eye travelled back to Norah. "Didn't knock you up, Miss Linton——" His voice stopped abruptly on a note of amazement. Staring, he was silent, and his pipe clattered from his mouth to the ground. "Why!" he gasped. "Good Lord—you've got little Babs Archdale!"

"Let us have a frock of some kind for her—quick as you can, Green," said David Linton. "Anything will do."

"I'll take her in," said Norah, slipping from the saddle, and carrying into the shop the extraordinary vision in the suit and blanket. They emerged in a few moments, the blanket hidden by a brief dress of blue print; and Babs reluctantly consented to allow the strange man to lift her up to Norah again. Mr. Green found his tongue, with some difficulty.

"I never heard of such a thing in all me born days!" he said. "Gad! to think of Mrs. Archdale——" He stared after them, open-mouthed, as they clattered off, swinging round the bend of the track. The sound of the cantering hoofs echoed in the still afternoon air as Mr. Green, leaving his store to its own devices, hurried off to tell the township.

Near the cottage David Linton pulled up.

"There are too many of us," he said. "You three youngsters found her—go and give her back!" Jim and he moved into the shade of a big messmate tree, and the others rode on.

The little white cottage was fresh and inviting, the garden gay with flowers. The front door stood open; at any moment they looked to see Mrs. Archdale's tall figure come out upon the verandah. Suddenly Norah found she was trembling, and that the cottage wavered mistily before her.

At the garden gate they got down, and Wally tied up the horses. There was no sign of any one. But Babs gave them no time to wonder. The gate was ajar, and she flung herself at it, uttering shrill little squeals of joy, and raced up the path.

"I say—catch her!" Wally said. "The shock may be too much for Mrs. Archdale."

Babs was battering at the steps of the high verandah as Norah caught her. She wriggled fiercely in her arms.

"Down!" she said. "Want down!"

"Wait a minute, darling!" Norah begged her. "Wally, you go on—find her. I—I'm going to howl!" She sat down on the step, desperately ashamed of the sobs that shook her; and Jean, in no better case, patted her back very hard.

Perhaps Wally was not very sure of himself either. He cleared his throat as he stood at the door, after knocking, not sorry that no answering step came at once. Presently he came back to the girls.

"There's no one about," he said. "I've been round to the kitchen. Wonder where they are?"

"Let's come and look," Norah answered, doubtfully sure of herself once more. Wally picked up Babs, who wriggled and squeaked on his shoulder, a quicksilver embodiment of excitement that she could not voice in words, since words were all too slow. So they went through the silent house.

There was no sign of any one. In the little blue room the bed was dainty and fresh, with crisp linen, and roses smiled a welcome from the table; and the fire burned low in the kitchen stove, where a kettle bubbled busily. But the house was empty. They looked into Mrs. Archdale's room, half afraid to find her ill; but she was not there; and Babs went into a fresh ecstasy of excitement at the vision of her own picture, which laughed down at her from the wall.

"Babs!" she cried, and pointed a brown forefinger; "Babs!"

"You blessed kid," said Wally, in perplexity, "I wish you could tell us where to look for your mother."

"Muvver!" said the lady addressed. She wriggled ecstatically, and grasped a handful of Wally's hair, to his extreme agony. A fresh effort of memory came to her. "Dad," she said, half inquiringly, and drummed her heels upon her bearer's chest.

At the back of the house the little kitchen garden stretched to the brush fence. Beyond came a narrow, timbered paddock, and then the deep green of the scrub—the unbroken curtain that had fallen behind the baby on Wally's shoulder more than a year ago. They came out of the back door and stood looking towards it doubtfully.

Then from the scrub they saw Mrs. Archdale coming slowly. No one might say what dreadful pilgrimage had led her into its silent heart. She stumbled as she walked, bent as though her body had given way under the stress of agony of mind too great to be borne. Even across the shining grass it was plain that she did not know where she walked—that all that her eyes could see was the dark maze of the Bush, where a little child had wandered, and called to her. A fallen log lay across her path, and she sat down upon it, burying her face in her hands.

"Oh, Wally, go and tell her," Norah said. "I'm such an idiot—I'm going to howl again. Let me have Babs—I'll bring her." She followed Wally slowly down the path, with Babs patting her tear-stained cheek gently, saying, "Poor, poor," in a little crooning voice.

Mrs. Archdale raised her head as the swift steps came to her across the grass, and looked at the tall lad for a moment without recognition. Then she collected herself with an effort that was pitiful in its violence, and smiled at him.

"Why, you've got back!"

Wally nodded, seeking desperately for words. His brown face was flushed and eager.

"I——" he said, and stopped. "We——. Mrs. Archdale." Words fled from him altogether, and he pushed his hat back with a despairing gesture. "I've got something to tell you; and I'm such a fool at telling it."

"Nothing wrong?" she asked him swiftly. "Not little Norah?"

"No—nothing wrong. Everything's all right; everything's perfect!" he told her. He put out a lean, boyish hand, and gripped hers strongly. "We saw you—coming away from the scrub."

"Don't!" She flushed, miserably.

"I didn't mean to hurt you," said poor Wally, his task almost beyond him. "I only want to say you needn't ever go there again. She—she isn't there, Mrs. Archdale!"

"Are you mad?" The colour died out of her face, and for a moment the agony of her eyes robbed the boy of speech.

"I mean it," he said, faltering. "If it was all—all wrong, Mrs. Archdale? If your little kiddie had never died?" Something choked his voice; he could only look at her with honest, pitying eyes. But the mother's eyes were keen.

"You know something!" she said; "there is something!" Her voice rose to a wailing cry. "Tell me, for God's sake!"

Across the grass came a voice that rang shrilly sweet.

"Muvver!"

Babs came running with swift bare feet; behind her, Norah, half afraid, yet wholly unable to restrain her once the remembered voice had raised its mother cry. At the sight of the baby form, with outstretched arms, the mother uttered a low, incredulous sob—a sound so piteous that Wally turned away sharply, lest he should see her face. Her feet would not carry her to meet her baby. She fell on her knees on the grass, and Babs flung herself bodily upon her, soft and sweet, and quivering with love.

There came a clatter of hoofs. Jack Archdale, riding home, had pulled up to speak to Mr. Linton and Jim; and suddenly he broke from them like a madman, and, not waiting for gates, put his horse at the log fence of his paddock, cleared it, and raced to the house. He flung the bridle over a post, and ran wildly to them—past Jean and Norah, sitting together on a stump, not able to speak, and speechless himself, to where his wife crouched over their child; Babs, who stroked her mother's cheek gently, crooning in her funny little voice: "Poor—poor!"

Norah felt Wally's hand upon her shoulder.

"Come on," he said. "I guess we'd better get back to the horses."

CHAPTER XXI
BACK TO BILLABONG
And thro' the night came all old memories flocking,

White memories like the snowflakes round me whirled;

"All's well!" I said. "The mothers still sit rocking

The cradles of the world!"

—W. H. Ogilvie.

"SO you'll come?" David Linton asked.

"Yes, and glad to." Jack Archdale pulled at his pipe, which would not draw. He took it out of his mouth, shook it, and put it back again with a shrug. It needed a grass stalk to clean the stem; but that is a performance that demands two hands, and one hand was given over to Babs, who sat on her mother's knee on the next step of the verandah, imprisoning her father's big finger in her moist little grasp. So the pipe went out, its owner deriving what comfort he might from holding it in his mouth.

"I never want to see the place again," Archdale went on. "I'd have left it long ago but for the one thing. Now I'd go to-morrow if I could. Wouldn't we, Mary?"

Mrs. Archdale nodded. Babs had one forefinger tucked into her neck, and nothing else mattered very much just then.

"Do you see, Jack?" she asked, smiling at him. "It's her old trick; she always put her little finger into my collar. She hasn't forgotten anything." They bent together over the baby form, and forgot the world.

"I'll have to sell off here," Archdale said, straightening up, presently. "That won't take very long, though. Then whenever you're ready for me, sir——?"

"Any time next month," the squatter answered. "The storekeeper goes on the first, and I suppose Mrs. Brown will want a few days to have the cottage put in order for you. She has violent ideas on disinfecting; not that I'm quite sure what she wants to disinfect, but it seems to make her happy."

"But come soon," Norah said eagerly. "I want to see Babs again before I go back to school."

"I guess," said Jack Archdale,—"I guess what you and Mr. Wally want about Babs is likely to happen, if ever I can manage it. You've got a sort of mortgage on her now, haven't they, Mary?" To which Wally, who was lying full length on the grass with Jim, near the verandah, was understood to mutter, "Bosh!"

"Maybe it's bosh; I don't know," Archdale said, drawing hard at his cold pipe. "But that's the way we look at it. I—we . . . Well, it's no darned good tryin' to say anything."

"It was only a bit of luck," Wally mumbled, greatly embarrassed.

"Any one would have found her," said Norah, incoherently. "We just happened to."

"I don't know," Mrs. Archdale said, her cheek against Bab's black curls. "I suppose I may be foolish—but it seems to me it was a bit because you cared so much. It—it seemed to hurt you, just like it did Jack and me."

"And lots of people would never have noticed that the kid wasn't really a picaninny," Archdale put in. He put his great hand down and took Bab's little bare foot in it, looking at it with eyes half misty, half proud. "Well, thank the Lord, you wasn't born flat-footed, my kid!" he said—and Babs chuckled greatly.

She climbed down from her mother's knee presently, and after falling over Jim and Wally, and treating each with impartial affection, toddled off round the corner of the house, on a voyage of discovery. It was curious to see how little she had forgotten, and what joy she found in the old familiar places. Archdale watched her go, and with the last flutter of the scanty blue frock heaved his long form up from the step, and followed slowly.

"It don't seem safe to let her get out of one's sight," he said as he went. "I wouldn't trust that black gin not to be hanging round in the timber."

Mrs. Archdale followed them both with her eyes.

"Jack swears he'll tell the police if old Black Lucy shows up," she said. "But I don't want him to. It wouldn't do any good—and I'm too happy now to care. She had lost all her kiddies, poor thing—and, after all, she took care of my baby."

"You would have been sorry for her if you'd seen her," Norah said. "I know you would."

"Well, after all, you can't judge them by our standards," said the squatter. "They are only overgrown children, and we haven't left them so much that we can blame them altogether for seizing at a chance of happiness. Probably old Black Lucy's family owned Billabong, and can't quite see why I should hold it now; and certainly she would find it hard to understand why her babies should all die while other women keep their children."

"To be broken-hearted with loneliness—and then to find a little child wandering alone in the scrub—oh, I don't know that I blame her," said Bab's mother, wistfully. "You—you'd really think it was sent to you. I only lost one, and I thought my trouble was greater than I could bear. And she had lost three!"

"Yes—but you can't quite look at it that way," Mr. Linton said. "The blacks don't regard a child's life quite as we do."

"Don't they?" Mary Archdale asked, doubtfully. "Perhaps not." She pondered over it, and shook her head, at last. "Oh, I don't believe your colour makes much difference to you when you've lost your baby!" Her voice broke—just for a moment she was back in the wilderness of pain, where she had wandered for so many weary months.

Then, round the corner, came her husband, with Babs perched high on his shoulder—triumphant in her elevation, yet with her tangled black head nodding sleepily, and the sandman's dust making her eyelids droop.

"Some one's sleepy," Archdale said, smiling at his wife. "Coming, mother?"

"I'll put her to bed," she said, rising and stretching her arms to the little daughter. Archdale put Babs tenderly upon the grass.

"I guess there's two of us in that contract," he said. "Say good-night, Babs."

They watched her with quick curiosity to see if the command would be intelligible. It was long since Babs had said "good-night." But some far-off echo was awake in the childish brain, and she obeyed mechanically; moving from one to the other with drowsy, soft kisses and drowsier "Dood nights"—until the last was said, and she turned to her father again and held up little brown arms to him. He picked her up, with infinite gentleness in his strength. One arm went round his wife's shoulders as they disappeared into the silent welcome of the lighted house.

* * * * *

Outside the slow moon climbed into a starry sky, and for a while no one spoke. Far off, a bittern boomed in some unseen marsh—the eerie note that makes loneliness more lonely, and warm companionship the more comforting, by contrast. Then two mopokes began to call to each other across a belt of scrub, and a fox barked sharply. The fragrant peace of the summer night lay gently upon the blossoming garden.

Norah leaned back against her father's knee, with Jean close at hand. It was to Jean that Mr. Linton spoke presently. There were many times when, between him and Norah, speech was not necessary.

"Well, you're not having anything resembling the holidays I planned for you, Jean," he said. "All the same, they have not been without incident!"

"It's lovely!" Jean breathed. "Thank goodness, they're not over yet!"

For to-night they were to sleep in Mrs. Archdale's little blue room. The men of the party, scorning the excitements of the hotel, were to camp near the scrub; already preparations were made, and the white tent glimmered faintly in the moonlight. To-morrow would begin the ride back to Billabong.

"I heard from Town to-day," the squatter observed. A sheaf of letters had awaited him at Atholton. "They will be able to begin work on the house next week, so the rebuilding won't be so long drawn-out an affair as I feared."

"That's a mercy, anyhow," Jim said, fervently. "I'll be jolly glad not to see those blackened walls. Seems to hurt you, somehow. But how does that affect your plans, Dad?"

"What plans?" Norah asked.

"Well, Jim and I, as the only level-headed members of this irresponsible party, have been planning," said her father. "Billabong being unfit for habitation, and two young ladies, to say nothing of one Queensland gentleman, on our hands, justly expecting an agreeable vacation——"

"Dad, how beautifully you talk!" said Norah.

"Such wealth of language!" breathed Jim.

"Diogenes revivified! Or was it Demosthenes?" said Wally, uncertainly.

"Diogenes inhabited a tub, if I remember rightly," said Mr. Linton, laughing. "As far as I can see, I am likely to be driven to somewhat similar expedients, until I have a house again. However—not that any of you deserve my kind explanations, except Jean, who probably wouldn't deserve them either but that she's too shy to voice her thoughts in the way you do."

Jean giggled assentingly.

"H'm," said Mr. Linton, gazing at her severely "I thought so. If ever there was an unfortunate brow-beaten, burnt-out man, he sits here! Well, to come to the point—if you'll all let me—Jim and I came to the conclusion that we must migrate somewhere for the remainder of the holidays. We thought of the seaside—Queenscliff or Point Lonsdale, or possibly the Gippsland Lakes. That was to be a matter for general consideration. There's no reason why we shouldn't adhere, in the main, to the plan. But since the workmen will be at the station, we'll have to choose a spot not far away, as I must be most of my time at home. I can go backwards and forwards, and Brownie can go with you to keep a watchful eye on your pranks."

"H'm!" said Jim thoughtfully. "That's pretty rotten for you, isn't it?"

Nobody spoke for a few minutes. Then Wally said.

"What's the matter with Billabong?"

Jean conquered her shyness with a tremendous effort, sitting up abruptly.

"If you're going away for me, Mr. Linton," she said, speaking very fast, and plucking grass with great determination of purpose, "please don't. I don't want to be taken anywhere."

"But, my dear child," David Linton said, "I can't have you all in tents. And there isn't any house. You didn't come for your holidays to rough it."

"There isn't any roughing it," said Norah, quickly. "If Jean and Wally don't mind——"

"Mind!" said Wally. "Why, I'll feel like a motherless foal if you take me away, and go about bleating!"

"Well, there you are!" said Norah, inelegantly, but very earnestly. "Oh, Dad—let us all stay! We don't want to go away. You don't want us to go, do you?"

"Why, no; I don't," said her father, in perplexity. "As a matter of fact, I'd far rather be at home; indeed, I couldn't be away for more than a very few days at a time. But the whole place will be upset, and I can't see much fun for you youngsters in being there. It doesn't seem quite fair to you."

Jim began to laugh.

"It's uncommonly difficult to plan for people who don't want to be planned for, isn't it, Dad?" he said. "Such a waste of noble effort! I believe we may as well give it up—they don't seem to hanker after fleshpots!"

"Well, are you any better?" asked his father, laughing. "This was to be your holiday, too. You know you've put in a year of fairly hard work on the place, and I think you're about due for a spell."

"Me?" said Jim, in blank amazement. "Why, I haven't killed myself with work—at least, I didn't think so!" He grinned widely. "But I'm glad to know my valiant efforts impressed you. Anyhow, you needn't make plans so far as I'm concerned; the old place is good enough for me, and if the other chaps don't want to go away, I'm certain I don't!"

"You see, Dad," said Norah, earnestly, "we've got the tents—and perhaps we might put up a bigger one, in case of bad weather, and make a really ship-shape camp down by the lagoon, and just have our meals at the cottage. And everything will be so interesting at the house—and we'd have the horses!"

"It's really all your own fault, sir," Wally told him. "You've given us the taste for tent life, and you can't blame us for becoming nomads. There's already something of the Arab sheikh about Jean, and any one would mistake Jim for a dervish! Fancy shaking down to a boarding house at Queenscliff after this!" He waved a brown hand towards the dim outline of scrub, seen faint against the starlit velvet of the sky.

"It would be awful!" said Jean, with such fervour that every one laughed.

"And we can't leave you, Dad," Norah said. "It would spoil everything. I don't believe you'd enjoy it, and certainly I wouldn't call it really holidays unless we were with you. It seems all wrong to go away—not a bit like being mates. And we're always mates."

David Linton found her hand looking for his in the dusk, and gripped it tightly.

"Very good mates, I think," he said. "Well—if you've all agreed, I'm not likely to want to hunt you into exile. Only remember, it will not be quite like home—tents are a poor substitute."

"But—it's Billabong!" said Norah, happily.

THE END

CPSIA information can be obtained
at www.ICGtesting.com
Printed in the USA
LVHW031106250821
696066LV00009B/1426